One
of
These
Mornings

Betty Bernard

CREATIVE ARTS BOOK COMPANY
Berkeley • California 2000

One of These Mornings is published by Donald S. Ellis
and distributed by Creative Arts Book Company

For Information contact:
Creative Arts Book Company
833 Bancroft Way
Berkeley, California 94710
(800) 848-7789

ISBN 0-88739-275-X
Library of Congress Catalog Number 98-88648

Printed in the United States of America

*Dedicated to the memory
of my brother Bill;
and for Peter, of course*

I would like to acknowledge quotes from the following songs and books:

"Black Crow Blues." Bob Dylan. 1965. Warner Brothers, Inc.

"It's Alright Ma (I'm Only Bleeding)." Bob Dylan. 1965. Warner Brothers, Inc.

"It's Raining." Peter, Paul, and Mary. New York: Pepmar Corporation.

Lines from "Cuttings (later)." Theodore Roethke. *The Lost Son and Other Poems*. 1948.

Lines from "The Fourth Elegy." Rainer Maria Rilke. *Duino Elegies*. (Translated by Stephen Spender and J. B. Leishman.) 1939. New York:W. W. Norton.

"Loving Her Was Easier (Than Anything I'll Ever Do Again)." Kris Kristofferson, *The Silver-Tongued Devil and I*. 1970. Combine Music Corporation.

"Summertime." 1935. Lyrics by DuBose Heyward, music by George Gershwin. Gershwin Publishing Corporation.

"The End." The Doors. *Strange Days*. 1968. Electra Records.

"Today." Traditional folk song.

"Tomorrow Is a Long Time." Bob Dylan. 1963. Warner Brothers, Inc.

Acknowledgements

I would like to acknowledge the following people for their help during the process of writing this book: Peter Bernard, for his early reading and patient criticism of this manuscript; my children, Jennifer, Alex, and Rebecca, for their understanding when I would shut myself in the study for lengthy periods; my UC Berkeley faculty wives' writing group–especially Maxine Zalkin, Katherine Caldwell, Susan Fadley, and Joan Mastronarde for their support, invaluable criticism, and encouragement of this novel and my work in general; Suzan Hall at Two Rivers Editing, for her careful reading, her honest appraisal, and insightful suggestions; and my Maryland writing friends—Sharon Beck, Beverly Glover-Wood, and Frederica and Conrad Berger for their constant faith and support.

For their assistance I would like to thank Donald Ellis and Richard Silver of Creative Arts Books for their original enthusiasm about the work, Courtney Chittock for her careful edit and exquisitely handled cover design, John De Fabbio for his photographic help, and Jennifer Malnick for her editorial assistance throughout.

One of These Mornings

"One of these mornin's
You goin' to rise up singin'
Then you'ss spread yo' wings
An' you'll take to the sky..."

DuBose Heyward/George Gershwin
Summertime

Part One

"Sometimes I'm thinkin' I'm
Too high to fall.
Sometimes I'm thinkin' I'm
Too high to fall.
Other times I'm thinkin' I'm
so low I don't know
if I can come up at all."

Bob Dylan
"Black Crow Blues"

# One

It was how he had played the night she met him: the raga-like melody built to a frenzied peak and as gradually dissipated. Melanie was certain that his fingers would fly from his guitar and bounce around the room. Between long runs, as if for relief, he played songs: *"It's All Right, Don't Think Twice"* and *"Gentle on My Mind,"* switching hastily from his six-string guitar to a tinny twelve-string.

He was from California, the place she had dreamed of visiting since she was fifteen. This information alone had impressed Melanie's two roommates; on that basis, they had invited this stranger, Ray, back to the apartment they shared on West Ninety-Seventh Street and Broadway. In 1970, California was synonymous with adventure and potential romance, although as seemingly remote as Kenya or Bali. Along with Boston, Chicago, and New York City, perhaps superseding them, the West Coast was the place to be.

That night he slept on the living-room couch, and the following day he approached her. As they stood talking in the hallway, their bodies half in shadow, half in dim afternoon light, Melanie felt keenly aware of Ray's attraction for her, but while she found it flattering, it also made her nervous. She had just said goodbye to Steve, who had been on spring break from school somewhere in the middle of the continent. They had gone sailing near his parents' house on Long Island, had taken walks, watched films at the Thalia, sharing deli afterwards sitting on her bed. Although it had been an enjoyable week, Melanie couldn't remember what university he attended or where she put the address he had so carefully written down for her.

Because she was going anyway, Melanie asked Ray if he wanted to walk with her in Central Park. He talked a mile a minute—or a blue streak as her grandmother would say—more frenetic than any New Yorker, while striding so animatedly that she kept being pushed toward the curb. Ray advanced upon a person, asked embarrassing questions, emphatically nailed down points, virtually nipped at one's heels. His short, compact body and scraggly brown hair intensified this impression, as did his dark brown eyes, which stared relentlessly and challengingly at a person. She turned away, slightly irritated. At five feet three inches and weighing barely one hundred pounds, Melanie was usually overlooked in a crowd. Her large emerald green eyes and thick waist-length hair lent her some height and presence, but even she saw herself as a slip of a girl. The kind of girl that men in former eras would hasten to lift across a large puddle and set down gently on the opposite side.

They crossed Amsterdam Avenue and walked past the Spanish restaurant where she frequently ate huevos rancheros and drank Cuban coffee, past apartment buildings similar to her own, past the dry cleaner's. When they reached the park, they wandered down one path after another. As if in anticipation of summer, couples already leaned against trees, kissing passionately or stretched out on blankets on the grass. Melanie heard the rhythmic pounding of steel drums and bongos in the distance. Children darted by on roller skates. It was a perfect, late-April afternoon.

Along one of the more secluded paths, Ray stopped and, turning her toward him, kissed her. After a few minutes, she pulled away and stood looking at the ground, hands thrust in the pockets of her jeans.

"Are you mad, Melanie?" He cupped his hands gently around her cheeks. "I couldn't help myself. You looked so cute, frowning like that. I've never met anyone with such a serious expression!"

"I'm not angry. It's just . . . well . . . I just said goodbye to somebody else. I'm not sure I'm ready to get involved again so soon." Her mouth involuntarily quivered, still feeling the pressure of his kiss. "Look, can we just talk? I mean, it's nothing to do with you. It's my problem . . ." Her problem! But it was him. He was not her type, really; there was something coarse about him that offended her. It was more than not being ready. She didn't even understand why she was out walking with him. Was it whatever wind came along?

However, starting from the night of that walk—after he insisted on treating her to dinner at the Spanish restaurant, although she realized he probably had less money than she—they returned to her room and, after sitting on her bed a while, talking, spent the night together.

"Let me just hold you," he said, "just lie next to you. I promise I won't touch you if you don't want me to. Let's just lie quietly and listen to each other's breathing. I love to look at your face, Melanie; it's so wide open. I just want to feel you in my arms. Please."

And even though she felt unsure, she let him. Eventually she relaxed in his embrace as his thin arms pressed comfortingly around her own, listened to his heart thudding in his chest, amazed at its rapidity. And as she breathed in the scent of his chest, his underarms, male, salty, deep, her body on its own pressed closer to his. He stroked the planes of her back, and they instinctively moved toward each other, their mutual breath shallow, insistent.

She usually found sex painful. But as Ray first parted her thighs and moved slowly inside her, moved almost as if he were building momentum on the guitar, she found herself opening up, meeting his thrusts easily. Then, what had never happened before happened: Melanie felt herself breaking apart, spilling open. Ray squeezed her forearms in delight, whispering, "We came together, didn't we? The first time, didn't we?" All she could do was nod, as he clasped her even more tightly against him, while tears slid down her cheeks.

After that night, Ray stayed with her, though Melanie was still not certain, even after months of living together, if she truly knew him, if she altogether liked him. They did get along comfortably. When he suggested that they hitchhike to California because he was fed up with New York and its hustle, fed up with trying to make it there as a musician, she went along readily with his plans. Since graduating from high school two years earlier, she had drifted from low-paying job to low-paying job, intent only on making enough money to support herself, leaving the rest of her time free to read and write poetry. But she was already bored with her cashier's job of selling golden-age tickets to senior citizens during the matinee shift. There was nothing holding her to Manhattan except familiarity and a few friends; her family had never played a significant part in her plans. She was free; she might as well burn her bridges behind her and set out for where she had always longed to go. Or as she put it to Ray, in Bob Dylan's words: "When you got nothing, you got nothing to lose."

"I'll help you find something," he assured her. "We'll find something new together." At the end of June they headed west.

Shortly after arriving in Berkeley, needing a place to live, they chose the Rosaline Apartments. Ray's mother, in the last throes of alcoholism, had lived there a few months before her death the previous year. The studio was inexpensive and came completely furnished. The exterior of the building was attractive. A wrought-iron sign hung from an archway shaped like a strip of ribbon candy; foundation hedges and vines bearing clusters of tiny white flowers partially camouflaged the stucco structure. A sand-colored path wound between ponds of polished red stones, confirming Melanie's concept that California was more beautiful than any other place she had known.

The furnishings were more ratty, consisting of a speckled Formica kitchen table with four mismatched plastic-covered chairs, a double bed that pulled out from a wall in the main living area, an overstuffed rocker, and a dilapidated plaid love-seat convertible. The pots, pans, and dishes were bent, chipped, or blackened from use. But Melanie grew excited when she saw a bay window with an attached window seat and French doors that reminded her of those in the Riverside Drive apartment, where she had spent her childhood.

* * * * *

They had been at the Rosaline Apartments for several weeks. Ray was playing as he had played the evening they had met. But now—accustomed to its frenetic quality—Melanie found it comforting. She sat staring at the shadows created by the erratic candle flame that provided the only light in the room, her feet tucked beneath her in the rocker she had already claimed as her own. Across from her, comfortably arranged on the love-seat, sat Marie and Pete, friends of Ray's from Oakland.

That afternoon, Ray had told her, "Marie went to Berkeley, I think. She writes poetry, too, so you've probably got stuff in common. Pete was in the Navy, but now he works in a cage at Wells Fargo Bank."

"With wild animals?" Melanie had asked, astonished.

"No," Ray laughed, "it's a money cage. He rips up bills that are no longer in circulation. Look, they've entertained me a lot, and I'd like to return the favor. Let's make a beef stew together. I remember this recipe my mother used to make. You'll like Marie and Pete; they're really mellow people. I'll introduce you to everyone else later." Everyone else, she assumed, meant the bulk of his friends from Richmond. Several small towns north of the Rosaline Apartments was the city of Richmond, Ray's home base. So far, all she had seen of it were its oil refineries.

The beef stew had been eaten, and now they sat sipping California burgundy. After a while, Pete lit a joint, and they passed it around in a circle. California was obviously where she belonged, Melanie thought, taking a toke. The weather was great; the fruits and vegetables seemed fresher than those back East; and Marie and Pete were as truly laid back as Ray had told her they would be. When Ray introduced them, Melanie thought instantly of Tweedle Dee and Tweedle Dum because both of Ray's friends were equally rotund. Marie's gentle voice matched her pale blonde hair and Elizabethan features, while Pete's coloring was dark and his voice boomed. Melanie couldn't help thinking of the White Queen and the Red Queen. Conversation flowed easily. It began with the upcoming Renaissance Fair and moved to questions about their travels, Melanie's background, and what life was like in Berkeley and California in general.

When Melanie discovered that Marie had been an English major at UC Berkeley and that they enjoyed the same authors, she excitedly agreed to show Marie her poetry.

As they joined in with the music, banging their hands on whatever surface they could find, Ray attacked the guitar with redoubled fury, as if it were something he had to tame, like a wild bronco. He strummed hard, using his entire hand, knuckles clenched and rigid on the strings. When his fingers thumped, spent, on the body of the guitar, Pete shouted "bravo," and Marie yelled "encore." Ray mopped his forehead with the blue bandanna he always wore around his neck, like a cowboy, and grinned, saying they should probably call it a night.

"Hey, tomorrow's the big day," he said, referring to his and Melanie's first day at the business school they had enrolled in the previous week.

"Becoming part of the straight life?" Pete asked.

"It's gonna help us pay the rent."

After Marie retrieved her purse, Pete gathered the four of them in a group hug that lasted for several minutes. At the door, he handed Ray four joints. "To maintain your cool," he said with a wink.

* * * * *

Lytton Business College, which had a program subsidized by the State of California, occupied the top floor of a two-story building in El Cerrito. It was a fifteen-minute bus ride from the Rosaline Apartments. In addition to their training, the students received a small stipend twice a month. Most of the courses lasted nine months. Upon completion, the students received certificates and then were helped to find jobs in their chosen area. Ray had learned about the program before leaving for New York, so when their funds began to dwindle, he urged Melanie to go with him to the Human Resources center in Richmond, so they could apply. After testing, at the suggestion of the director, Mrs. Duran, Ray enrolled in an accounting course, while Melanie chose secretarial training, which included shorthand.

The shop below the school was a dry cleaner's, and when Melanie and Ray passed its open doorway each morning, they were met by blasts of heat and the suffocating smell of chemicals, which made them almost grateful to mount the steps to Lytton, as if they were rising from hell to heaven. In the main room of the college, there were six long tables which each held six manual typewriters. This was the practice typing room and where the "lesson of the day" was held at two o'clock. Business English, math, shorthand, and accounting were taught in four smaller classrooms. Along with twenty other students, Melanie and Ray went back and forth between these rooms all day, with five minutes allowed between periods. Melanie felt as if she had returned to high school; the only thing missing was the bell.

Seeing letters appear on the page in response to her clacking, especially when they showed up as a straight, even line, afforded her some satisfaction, which increased as she moved from f's and j's to #'s, b's, and x's. There was something relaxing about sitting next to the other students—many of whom were young women from welfare or working-class homes, such as Ray's—making similarly repetitive motions. As each woman at her Royal or Smith-Corona flung back the carriage return or slammed down the typewriter bar to hold a piece of paper still, Melanie had the sense that she was part of a larger rhythm. Some typewriters were older, or the keys were stiffer, and in the morning everyone made a rush for the easier-to-use machines. Melanie usually sat near the window, so she could gaze out at the shopping plaza across the street.

Ray sat in the last row in the room, looking incongruous among the women, as if he had wandered into the building by mistake or was there in the capacity of a typewriter repairman. The two black women, who sat on either side of him, teased him about being the only male student, but soon Ray, like an annoying but cute kid brother, was generally accepted, and most of the women took pride in helping him if he was stuck on a lesson.

* * * * *

Shortly after their dinner with Marie and Pete, Melanie stood in the doorway of the school building waiting for Ray. Although she was getting used to the routine, it had been a particularly difficult morning. They had dashed out of the house without breakfast, and she had found the ABC shorthand she was learning more slowgoing than ever. When Ray finally joined her, they walked in silence to the plaza. Panting slightly, he grabbed her arm.

"Whoa, is there a fire, Miss Racehorse? Slow down. We've got plenty of time to eat still. Sorry, I was bullshitting with Mrs. Duran." He grinned at Melanie, forcing a feeble smile in return. Lifting the cigarette she held tightly between her fingers, he took a drag and handed it back to her.

"You seem awfully pleased," she commented dryly. "What happened? Did you score with Mrs. D?"

"Ha, aren't we perceptive! I finagled an invite to dinner Saturday night. With the entire Duran clan," he said, winking at her.

"I thought we were hitching to San Gregorio."

Reaching for her Marlboro before she crushed it out, Ray said, "Shit, I forgot. Oh well, it'll be good weather at the beach for a while longer. Hey, babe, invites don't grow on trees, you know."

Melanie stepped on the cigarette Ray had dropped and then shoved her hands into her jeans pockets. "I was looking forward to seeing the Pacific Ocean. Besides, I'm not as comfortable with the Duran clan as you seem to be; they're a bit overly hearty for my taste. You really want to go?" she asked, biting her lip and glancing sideways at him. He didn't say anything. "Well, there's my question answered."

They had reached the entrance to Pat's Coffee Shop, which was at the end of a row of shops, next to a Hallmark store. She and Ray had discovered it their first week of school, and now they ate there whenever they felt too lazy to fix sandwiches. Before he opened the glass door, Ray held Melanie by the shoulders.

"Gee, Melanie, I'm sorry I didn't clear it with you first. I just thought it would be an experience. Mrs. D already treats me like I'm one of her sons."

"It's not that, Ray. It's . . . forget it. We'll go if you want to."

They walked to a booth at the back of the room. As they waited to be served, Melanie lit another cigarette, and Ray lit one from hers. She opened the greasy, plastic-coated menu the waitress handed her and then immediately shut it; she always ordered the same thing—a turkey club—although each time she told herself she should try something new. After they had given their orders to Irene, who now knew them by sight, Melanie stretched her legs out along the torn, red vinyl seat of the booth.

"I don't know if I can hack this secretarial shit." She smoothed back a clump of hair that had fallen across her eyes. "But that's not what I was going to say. I guess . . . well, I guess it bums me out that you're so extroverted, Ray. Not that there's anything wrong with that, but I don't enjoy being with people in the same way. I mean, I like Marie and Pete okay," she added. "They're as easy as you said they'd be. But I'm kind of a loner. That's why I always sit by the window at Lytton—so I can pretend that I'm not really there at all, that at least half of me is out on the street. I guess that doesn't make any sense to you," she said, twisting up her mouth. When Ray only smiled teasingly, Melanie found herself smiling in return. "Oh shit, you know what I mean. Take this dinner, for example. You're all revved up to go, and then I come along and put a damper on things." She dropped her cigarette quickly. "Fuck it, I just burned myself! This isn't my day, is it?" Ray's smile widened. "Jesus! What are you trying to do? Grin down a bear?"

"You're such a sweetie, Mel," he said affectionately. "I don't mind that you're a loner. I thought artistic people were all that way." He leaned away as she growled at him. "Are you the bear then? I think you'd make a good bear . . . soft, warm, huggable . . . as long as you don't bite me with those great big teeth, Grandma."

"Sorry, wrong fairytale," she said.

When their sandwiches and Cokes arrived, they discussed the morning. Ray was in the middle of explaining what he had been learning in accounting when, suddenly, he reached over and grabbed her hand.

"I've figured it out! It's Wednesday. You're always moody on Wednesdays," he declared. "There's a pattern. You take life too seriously . . . that's your problem, hon." He squeezed her hand.

"Gee, I'm glad you've got me all figured out."

"It's not that, but your face shows everything, Melanie. It's one of the things I most like about you."

"I hate it. I can't hide anything from anybody," she said, grimacing.

"But everybody knows where they stand with you. They know they can trust you. That's good," he said, smiling before he took a large bite out of his cheeseburger. Melanie watched as red juice from the meat soaked through the hamburger bun and dribbled onto the plate beneath. Ray ordered a different sandwich on the menu each time. To be systematically experimental, he explained.

"Glad you approve," she said, pushing away her own half-eaten sandwich and reaching for another Marlboro, "but, you know, sometimes I feel like I'm this big baby that everyone has to take care of all the time. Everybody always has to watch that they don't hurt my feelings. I'm too fucking sensitive." She tapped the cigarette on the table top before lighting it. "You're right, I suppose. It *is* difficult for me to get through an entire week feeling good. Hell, maybe the dinner will be fun. After all, with you present, I won't even have to talk."

Melanie ran her fingers through her hair while she stared at the blurry grey and white surface of the Formica table. After a few minutes, she looked up at Ray, who was leaning back, relaxed, smoking also now that he had finished his cheeseburger.

"Mrs. D's daughter-in-law, Cindy, is sexy, isn't she?" Melanie ventured.

It was partly why she didn't want to go to Mrs. Duran's for dinner. She knew that the whole family would be there, and Cindy, the wife of Mrs. Duran's son, Jim, had already flirted with Ray during a stop she had made at Lytton.

Ray covered her hand with his.

"Yeah, she's sexy all right; she certainly makes a point of showing off what she's got. Does that mean something?"

"Well . . . it could."

Ray lifted his hand from hers and, cupping her chin, forced her to look into his eyes.

"Oh, sweetie! Is that what you're worrying about? I love you; don't you know that by now?"

"I suppose." Shifting her gaze, she picked up her purse and slid the pack of Marlboros inside. "It must be time to return to the salt mines."

When they reached the parking lot, Ray draped his arm across her shoulders.

"Little Baby Blue, what am I gonna do with you?" He pulled her roughly against his side, knocking their hips together. "I wish we could go home and screw; how 'bout you, Mellie Blue?"

"Only if you can catch me," she said. Yanking free, she began running frantically down the hill. When he caught her at the bottom, Ray swung her around in circles, while she laughed hysterically. Then suddenly, holding her absolutely still and staring into her eyes, he pressed his lips hard against hers.

Two

*T*hroughout September and October, on warm, clear, weekend afternoons, Ray took his guitar up to the UC Berkeley campus to play for a few hours on Sproul Plaza as previously, when they were still in Manhattan, he had played in Central Park at the entrance to Columbus Circle. There was always a rush of people walking by, especially now that school was in session. Most people stopped to listen for a few minutes; many hung around for the afternoon. Other musicians came with instruments: guitars, flutes, violins, bongo drums, and frequently they jammed together. By the time Melanie and Ray were ready to leave, Ray's guitar case—which he always left open beside him—was filled with bills and change, along with an occasional pamphlet dropped there by one of the religious or political speakers.

Ray knew many of the regulars, having met them before setting off for New York; some of them spent the entire weekend on the plaza or nearby on Telegraph Avenue. One woman walked around blowing bubbles and distributing copies of her poems. Another girl, barely out of her teens, who originally hailed from Kansas, lived on the Avenue itself. She dragged a worn backpack and sleeping bag behind her, and when Ray was playing, she danced alongside him. Although her steps and gestures usually did not correspond with his melodies, she moved her lithe body continuously, even after he had finished playing. Invariably, when Ray took a break, he gave the girl, whose name was Francie, a few dollars to get something to eat, telling her that her dancing helped promote him. Francie always took the money in an absent-minded manner, slipping it quietly into a zippered pocket in her backpack, and then drifted away. To Melanie's knowledge, Ray had never had a real conversation with her. He had learned her history from others on the Avenue.

While she waited for Ray to finish, Melanie sat on the steps of the Student Union or on the edge of a stone fountain, not in use, on the side of the plaza. She always carried a notebook with her, hoping to see something that might inspire a poem, but often she merely listened to Ray, all the while observing the passing mix of hippies and students. Melanie realized that others probably perceived her as a hippie, too, but she emphatically denied this, saying that she had no desire to be part of any Love Generation.

Because she was unfamiliar with campus life, she was surprised at the number of card tables that lined the walkway, each promoting a different political or religious doctrine or campus club. Only a short time earlier, the campus had been a center of political activity because of People's Park and other demonstrations; but now it appeared peaceful, and it was the rare student who stood on the steps to harangue the Berkeley administration. Marie told Melanie that when she had been a student police helicopters had circled the buildings, like Tolkien's Nazgûl.

Although Ray had to play loudly at times to be heard above the din, he told her he loved being in a place where Jesus freaks and radicals had the freedom to deliver their messages. It helped him pick up new ideas, broadened his own philosophy of life, which he wanted to be ever expanding. Melanie, however, found it troubling that people seemed concerned only with what they had to say; no one seemed receptive to anyone else's message. Ray laughed and said that was the state of the universe.

Food concessions that lined the street beside Sproul Plaza sold everything from egg rolls to Orange Julius, so if she grew tired of sitting, Melanie went to get something to eat. She avoided the Ave, as Telegraph was called, because it felt potentially dangerous to her and always seemed filled with tourists trying to catch a glimpse of the hippies. To pass down that street it was necessary to wind between people and vendors' tables, sitting slapdash against each other, selling handmade jewelry, candles, and T-shirts. Melanie was used to crowds, coming from Manhattan, but on the Ave, she felt there were too many stores squeezed too close to each other. Though she told herself that it could not be true, the sidewalk seemed as if it were half the size of a normal one. Melanie seldom regretted it when it was time to return home. Once back, she usually curled up with a book, and in her more ambitious moments, she wrote.

There was no real privacy in the main living area, so she chose practically anywhere to write—the rocker, the bed, the window seat if Ray was not already occupying it. She always felt as if she were on the run anyway; she hated to be pinned down. Her purse was filled with scraps of paper—impressions, potential lines for poems scribbled on matchbooks, on the backs of grocery receipts. Melanie seldom bothered to develop most of the ideas, but it reassured her to see the pieces pile up, to know they were there; their presence made her feel strangely legitimate. In contrast to the plodding attention to detail she showed at Lytton, with her poetry Melanie acted lackadaisical. She justified this with the belief that too serious attention squelched inspiration.

One fall afternoon after school, she sat in the rocker watching sunlight make patterns on the curtain while she waited for Ray to return with Chinese food. Noting a particularly pretty design, she jumped up and took from the bookshelf the file folder that held her work. Inside were twenty poems, all in different stages of "completion."

During their trip across the country, they had misplaced the valise containing her notebooks and poetry from the previous five years. It had been left behind in someone's car, or abandoned by the side of the road when they scrambled with their belongings to catch a ride. When she realized her loss, Melanie had tried to be philosophical. Much of it had been written in her early teens. After all, she was alive; she could always write more poems. All that remained was what she had crammed into a smaller bag—her most recent pieces—along with the scraps in her purse and what she had written since arriving in California.

After quickly jotting down some images that came to her, Melanie slid out a poem she had begun the previous winter, several months before meeting Ray.

> *Sorrow sickness I done got—*
> *not up to its mug-filled edge but*
> *pouring quick already,*
> *feeling vomity all right.*
> *Climbing, rising, to my chin . . .*
> *not sure I can keep my head*
> *if it comes much further—*
> *I will drown in its pale white foam.*

It was as far as she had gotten in being able to describe the way sadness could physically swallow her, come—as it were—right to the edge of her throat. Melanie liked the rhythm and the image of the beer-filled mug but had no idea how much further she should take the poem. After adding several new lines and crossing out others, she substituted and rearranged some words. Irritated, she rubbed her pen nub back and forth across the arm of the rocker. Some poems seemed to roll out all on their own, all of a piece. Did this one just not want to happen? Maybe it would come later—next week, next year. Did it even matter in the end? Noticing Ray's jaunty figure coming down the walk, Melanie returned the poem to its folder and ran to open the door. It was time to get ready anyway, because they were spending the evening at Marie and Pete's.

* * * * *

When Pete opened the door, Melanie and Ray were met by the aromas of chocolate and cinnamon and the sound of lute music. Marie called hello from the kitchen and a few minutes later came out, wiping her fingers on a full-length apron. The apartment, a one-bedroom in North Oakland adjacent to Telegraph Avenue, was bigger than their Rosaline studio. A half wall separated the living/dining area from the kitchen, and beyond that was a genuine bedroom. A framed Chagall fantasy and a poster for a long-past San Francisco Ballet performance of Stravinsky's "Fire Bird" hung above a sofa covered with an Indian print shawl. Macramé hangings that she later learned Marie had made decorated the other walls, and Marie's crocheted doilies were draped over available chairs and tables. The largest lay beneath a wooden bowl of fruit on the dining-room table. A garish-looking, yellow glass lamp, which had come with the apartment, dangled from the ceiling on a black metal chain, and Marie and Pete both referred to it as "the thing," as if it had a life of its own.

Two large bookcases had been shoved against the wall beside the sofa, and were jammed with volumes of poetry, novels, and books whose subject matter ranged from cooking, and gardening, to bicycling, sailing, and home repairs. The focal point of the apartment, however, was the turntable. It rested on a black metal television cart set up close to the bedroom door, and beside it were stacks of LPs.

Pete returned to the sofa, where he had been lying when they rang the doorbell, while Melanie and Ray opted for the beanbag chairs facing it. On the walnut coffee table, Marie had stuck several candles in attractive ceramic holders and, after a while, she lit them, along with a stick of jasmine incense. Because it was a pleasantly cool evening in October, nearly Halloween, Melanie draped one of Marie's afghans across her lap and burrowed into its warm layers. While Pete shook marijuana from a small, suede satchel and began, methodically, to roll joints, Marie brought out a pot of Red Zinger tea and a plate of chocolate scones.

Each time she entered their apartment, Melanie felt as if she were stepping into an elven circle, where nothing harmful could touch her. If something should try, she believed that she would be instantly, magically, transported to a safe place. Although they had begun to see each other regularly—going to the movies and afterwards to McCallum's, a local ice cream parlor—only nights at Marie and Pete's apartment had this dreamlike essence, enhanced as they were by Marie's baking, the candlelight, and, above all, by the astonishing variety of music Marie and Pete played. If Ray brought his guitar, Melanie noticed, it was usually when they visited during the weekend days. Here, in their own space, Marie and Pete had dominion.

Melanie sank deeply into her cushion and closed her eyes, concentrating on the pure, clear notes of the Gregorian chant that came on after the lute music. When they finished eating, Ray lit a joint, and Pete suggested he continue reading aloud to them from Tolkien's *The Hobbit,* which they had started the week before. Soon, entranced by his deep, husky voice, Melanie was totally immersed in the story. Even as a teenager, she had enjoyed reading about elves and fairies, and if asked whether she would prefer to live in the ordinary, everyday world or the world depicted in fairytales, she would gladly have chosen the latter.

Pete read a chapter, and then Marie brewed a second pot of tea and brought out another plate of scones "for fortification." Snugly grounded in her beanbag and listening to Pete's voice rise and fall, melodiously, changing as each new character came on the scene, Melanie began to feel as if she were floating, as if she herself had become part of the air and was merely another scent, flavored with spice, incense, and the sickish-sweet odor of marijuana. She found it difficult to move—to lift her hand toward the teacup took a tremendous amount of concentration. After a long spell, Pete stopped. Rising, he bent at the waist and declared in a formal tone, "Forever at your service and your family's."

Ray extended a half-finished joint to Pete and, bowing in return, said, "And we are at yours. Here is a token of our appreciation." Pete brought the tightly wrapped joint to his lips and, after inhaling, bowed even more humbly. Melanie fleetingly thought that he would make a complete obeisance.

When she and Ray eventually stepped out into the night, Melanie felt as if she had been thrown out of the nest into the proverbial dark forest depicted in fairytales. They usually hitchhiked home or took the bus, but this night they felt like walking, although the distance between their apartments was several miles. Fog had rolled in from the Bay, and the air was cool and misty. Feeling billowy and light, they drifted down each street, the night's moisture and the marijuana they had smoked adding to the effortlessness of their movements. Everything they passed was closed and silent; shop windows were blackened, so that it was difficult to see what was inside. When they saw another person on the street they wondered, afterwards, if they had imagined it. Without knowing how much time had elapsed, eventually they found themselves walking down the long blocks of

University Avenue, toward the freeway and home. They could see the Marina in the distance, and the Bay; a few lights in San Francisco and Marin County still twinkled. When they reached the Rosaline Apartments and their own studio, they embraced sleepily and fell together, fully clothed, against the cool sheets of their bed.

Three

Melanie had met Ray's father, Norm, briefly when, a few weeks after their arrival in Berkeley, they had stopped by at the wrecking yard where he was supervisor to borrow money for their first and last month's rent. Norm and his lady friend, Kathleen, lived in a California-style bungalow in Richmond. It differed from its neighbors only by its color; from a distance the block gave the impression of an open box of pastels. The grass in the front yard was long, full of clover and crab grass; a rusty hand mower stood by the steps. The porch was cluttered with automotive tools, obliging visitors to walk around them if they wished to use that entrance. Ray automatically went to the back screened door, which led into the kitchen.

This Sunday, Ray and Melanie were coming for what Norm called his "steak special." As they walked from the bus stop to Norm's house, they passed children roller skating and playing hopscotch. Toddlers tore by on tricycles or bikes with training wheels on them. Groups of women sat on lawn chairs in their front yards smoking and drinking beer. Ray and Melanie overheard one mother yell to her son, who was wrestling on the grass with a smaller boy, that if he didn't break it up, he was going to get smacked. Several girls were playing clapping and rhyming games that reminded Melanie of the ones she had played in elementary school. It was the most sense of neighborhood that she had seen in California.

At the door, Norm claimed what he called a father's privileged hug from Melanie and afterwards, Kathleen stretched out her arms dramatically.

"What a pretty girl! Norm, will you just look at that red hair and those great big green eyes. Why, they're the size of silver dollars! Come on, give me a hug, too, darlin'." She embraced Melanie hard and then looked at Ray. "So, this is your eldest son. He's got your forehead, that's for sure, honey. Well, don't just stand there. Come in already."

Kathleen pulled out two chairs at the kitchen table, and then Norm handed Melanie and Ray each a can of Pabst Blue Ribbon. Several steaks lay on the drain board with a trail of blood beneath them. When Ray finished the cigarette he had lit before entering the house, he took down a deck of his father's cards and a cribbage board from a shelf in the living room. As they talked, he dealt hands. Instead of beer, Kathleen nursed a glass of Seagram's 7, which she kept adding to. After several rounds, she began to drop her cards and question each of Norm's decisions. At first, Norm took Kathleen's behavior in good humor, but after telling her once or twice to be a good girl and shut up already, he finally slapped her cards off the table. He slammed his hands palms down in front of Kathleen and stood glaring at her. Avoiding his gaze, she continued to sit, but tears began to slide down her cheeks. Finally, she said that perhaps she should just take herself off and leave them to it. Ray shrugged impatiently.

"Forget it, Kathleen. C'mon, simmer down, Dad. You're gonna upset my old lady here."

"It might be a good idea if the bitch did just take herself off," Norm replied, ignoring Ray's interruption. "I've had enough of her goddamned, pitiful whining. What I'd like to know is why can't we simply have a good time without you having to get all weepy? Jesus Jumping Jehosephat! You're a goddamned faucet." Norm picked up his cards, but Melanie saw that he was still angry. When he retrieved his cigarette from the ashtray, his hand shook violently. She sat chain-smoking, trying hard to concentrate on her cards because she was unfamiliar with the game. Her throat felt raw from the cigarettes she had smoked since they'd arrived, and she took frequent sips of beer to dull the pain. The coral pink, bent metal ashtray in the center of the table was filled with crushed-out and still smoldering butts. Kathleen and Norm both tended to forget they had a cigarette going and were constantly lighting new ones.

After a few more rounds, in which Kathleen sat wearing a mulish expression and refusing to participate, she finally said she had better tend to the string beans.

"I'm only fit to be his assistant anyway. Yessir, he allows me to snap off the ends of the beans and stir together the mashed potatoes. Salt of the earth, ain't he? You'd think I'd never cooked in my life before," she muttered.

"Hell, if you think I'm fool enough to let you go and ruin the meat I pay my damn good money for, you have another thing coming," Norm snapped back at her. "What I do," he explained to Melanie, "is season it with a little black pepper and Accent—none of that liquid smoke nonsense. Then I cook each piece a bare five minutes t' each side. Longer than that and you might as well not put it in your mouth. Oh, Katy, don't even sit there bitching and making a fool of yourself. I gave you plenty of chances, and you messed it up every time."

Kathleen stood without saying a word and walked to the sink, slowly, to rinse off the beans. She brought them back in a colander, setting it on the table in front of her, and snipped one bean at a time; each snapping movement was punctuated by a sob. Ray grinned at Melanie, but when he got up to get another beer, he squeezed Kathleen's shoulder. Kathleen smiled pathetically at this gesture and said it looked like the son was a whole lot nicer than the father. Melanie rose unsteadily and asked Kathleen about the parakeets she could see in a cage in the living room.

"Those two in there now are new," Kathleen answered. "The last pair—the female just up and died, and the male went right after. From lonesomeness, I guess. Norm's always bringing back new birds, but I believe those two are the sweetest ones yet."

Ray had told her beforehand that his dad's birds were always sick or dying, and Melanie wondered if this was because of all the bickering. "Maybe their little ears just can't take such awful vibes," she told Ray later. Steadying the cage with her hand, she poked her finger through the bars, chattering softly, but the parakeets only inched away together on the swing inside, cocking their heads up at her. As she called to them gently one finally began to chirp back, but after a while, she gave up and walked aimlessly around the room.

Ray and his father had shifted to the living-room couch and were discussing a used Ford that Norm had located at the yard, which he was willing to give them for $150. Ray bargained him down to $100, since it wasn't totally clear that the car could be driven or how long it would last. On a shelf above the couch stood a collection of crystal figurines of birds and other small animals, which, Norm explained, were Katy's prize possessions—be careful you don't drop one, she'll have a conniption. Melanie picked each one up and replaced it and then, returning to the kitchen, set out the loaf of white bread and tub of margarine Kathleen handed her.

Dinner went more smoothly. Everyone praised Norm on how good, truthfully, the meat tasted. Afterwards, over coffee and bakery apple pie, they played another hand of cribbage. As it was quite late by then, and they had Lytton the next day, she and Ray finally rose to go, with the promise that they would return soon. Back home, as Melanie undressed and straightened out the bed, Ray paced around the apartment.

"What the fuck does he see in that stupid bitch? She's a disgrace to my mother's name!"

Melanie came up behind him and, putting her arms around his waist, laid her face against his back.

"Kathleen was difficult to take," she murmured. "I felt sorry for her, though; she seemed such a mess. Actually, it worried me because I think I'm a little like her, or could be. You haven't seen much of that side of me, but it's part of my personality, too. You know—moody, self-pitying."

Melanie kept to herself how depressed she had been made by the visit, as well as how afraid she was that real violence would break out. In the middle of dinner, Kathleen had come from the kitchen, thrusting out a carving knife, and though Norm had taken it from her as if it were only a glass she was handing him, Melanie had seen the despair in Kathleen's face and the way she had pointed it at Norm, as if longing to stab him.

Ray turned around and took her hands in his own. "Christ, Melanie, if you were anything like Kathleen, I would have split months ago."

But Melanie continued to feel troubled, and she lay thinking about Norm and Kathleen's situation long after Ray had fallen asleep.

* * * * *

The anxiety that she resembled Kathleen only increased when, the following Saturday, Ray took her to meet his Richmond friend Helga. Melanie had been nervous about meeting Helga because she knew that Helga and Ray had once been lovers. The two-bedroom house she rented seemed a replica of Norm and Kathleen's. A red wagon handle propped against the front door held it ajar. After Ray had rapped for a few minutes and called Helga's name, she emerged, wearing cutoffs and a stained T-shirt that fit loosely over her girlish breasts. She was thinner than Melanie, and her blonde hair looked washed-out, as if it had had too many peroxide treatments.

"Well, look what the cat's dragged in." Shading her eyes from the bright sunlight, as if she were unused to it, she walked slowly around Ray, checking him over from every angle. "And this must be your new old lady. I've been hearing you was back. I see you brought your gi-tar. Where would old Ray be without his gi-tar? Hey, Jimmy," she yelled to a young mulatto boy who was running around the living room waving a truck up and down, as if he were flying it, "run down to 7–11 and get us all some sticky buns."

"What's in it for me?" he asked, continuing to run.

"I'll show you what's in it for you, you little bastard." She grabbed the corner of his shirt and shoved two dollar bills into his hand. "Keep fifty cent back, but you bring me that change now." As he ran off, she looked at Ray again, appraisingly.

"My, my. You have been traveling, son."

They entered the house and sat at the kitchen table. Helga heated some water in a saucepan and then set out a jar of instant Kava coffee, one of artificial creamer, and an open five-pound bag of sugar. Presently Jimmy returned with the sticky buns, and Helga poured three cups of coffee and distributed them on chipped saucers. After stirring sugar into her coffee, Melanie offered Helga a cigarette from their pack as she took one out for herself. Sitting pretzel-fashion in the chair at the end of the table, Helga leaned forward to take it and nodded thanks. Ray put his feet up on another of the chairs, and soon they were engrossed in catching up on each other's news.

As if the word truly had gotten out that Ray had returned, various friends and acquaintances dropped in during the afternoon; one was a deaf mute, whom Ray leaped up to greet and hug affectionately. They talked together in sign language for nearly an hour and then—to Helga's amusement, because she said Ray was always trying to learn somebody something—tried to teach Melanie the alphabet. Jeffrey, the deaf mute, took whatever was said in good humor and rose every once in a while, as if apologetic that he was monopolizing Ray's attention. Before he left, he made up a sign for Melanie to indicate that she was Ray's new girlfriend.

There were seldom fewer than six people at the table at any given moment, and most of them were men. Although Helga was on Aid to Families with Dependent Children, Melanie soon discovered that she was also an intermediary drug dealer. Many of the people who came stayed for only a few minutes, there to either pick up a dime bag of marijuana or to pay Helga money they owed her. Helga was generally pleasant, without showing particular interest in anyone, and introduced Ray to those who didn't know him as a hot-shit guitar player, who had just returned from New Yor-ick, new old lady in tow. Grinning, Helga nudged Ray's leg with her bare toes and came up behind him in his chair. She draped her arms around his neck and said he was her good buddy—always was, old Ray. Some things never changed, even if he had been away forever and a day.

"Mike's up in Vallejo for a spell," she said during a lull in the activity, "but he'll get the word from some of these folks. He's heavy into heroin now."

Ray absent-mindedly shook a cigarette from the pack of Winston's Helga had tossed on the table and frowned. Melanie knew that, besides Helga, Mike was Ray's closest Richmond friend. When Ray left to go back east, Mike was shooting methedrine, but in a letter Helga had written Ray, she told him that he'd kicked it.

Ray poked ashes around in the frog-shaped ceramic ashtray next to him. When Melanie had asked where Helga had found it—it was so cute—Helga had laughed and said that it was a stand-in for her last old man. "He couldn't stay himself, but he left his frog behind. It's half cracked, like he is, too," she muttered.

"Mike's into some deep shit," Helga continued, as if relishing the news she was imparting. "He always was a hard-assed motherfucker. He stole Lennie's girl, and now she's strung out, too. You know that Mike always has to have company for the ride. Especially female company, like somebody else I know."

"I know you wouldn't be talking about me. Does he still live over Jack's store?" Ray asked, sighing.

"Last I heard. He's been kind of ashamed to show his face around here for a while. But yeah, same place, same Mike. Except maybe more fucked up."

Helga's two older children ran in and out of the kitchen, grabbing sodas and sticky buns, while her youngest, a baby, crawled beneath her feet. Ray shook hands with Jimmy and Lee Ann, the older two, and sitting one on each of his knees, he asked them how they were doing in school. They giggled and squirmed until he released them, while Helga watched, amused.

"Everybody's getting along just fine, thank you, sir. Lee Ann's top of her class." She finally picked up the baby and, pinching his cheeks, said: "You should know better than to be underfoot; a body's liable to be trampled that way." When Ray asked about the baby's father, Fritz, Helga shrugged and said he was off traveling somewhere, same as Ray; the last she heard he was in Texas.

"Everybody splits, don't they?" Ray murmured softly.

The television blared in the living room whether anyone was watching it or not. When it sounded louder than normal, Helga leaned her head toward the open doorway and yelled for the kids to turn that shit down, unsuccessfully. After several times of this, Ray pushed back his chair and went and turned it off. He noticed a mound of dirty clothes lying near the front door and teased Helga that it looked like the pile that had been there before he left. Helga chuckled and said, "Well, maybe it is, and maybe it isn't, but now is this any occasion to be doing wash?"

During the afternoon, Helga continuously drank coffee and chain-smoked and merely picked abstractedly at her sticky bun after licking off the sugar. Ray whispered audibly to Melanie that Helga lived on sugar, caffeine, and dope. Helga only shrugged in response, which made her T-shirt slide down her shoulder, exposing bony, chalk-white skin. Its paleness made Melanie wonder if Helga ever left her house. The three of them played round after round of five hundred rummy, although no one added up the score. The spreads covered the table, but if someone new entered, the cards were swept aside as if the game didn't matter anyway. Sunlight streamed in through the back kitchen window, but otherwise the house appeared dark. The drapes in the living room were closed to cut down the glare on the television screen and hide the drug transactions. Although Lee

Ann and Jimmy finally did go to play in the yard, no one suggested sitting out back with them. Feeling almost as if she were butting in on private conversation, Melanie found herself looking around the room, staring fixedly at the same objects, while Ray and Helga talked.

The topic of conversation was mainly dope—what kind they had smoked, what had been the best ever, what kind they wished they had— as well as their mutual friends. From what Melanie could absorb, people were either playing around, being left, ready to split up, or had wound up in the loony bin at Napa. Some women had jobs, most as secretaries or at the refinery, supporting their men or children, although one, Marilyn, was an assistant manager at a boutique, and she—Helga said, chuckling—gets by on mood elevators; she stops by occasionally to replenish her supply.

In turn, Ray told Helga about Lytton and their trip across country, but although Helga and anyone who was in the room listened politely, no one seemed genuinely interested. It was as if all that really mattered was what was happening in Helga's kitchen and within the larger scope of the city of Richmond. The outside world had no reality. The baby fell asleep against Helga's feet. Picking him up, she carried him to the living-room couch and covered him with a light blanket.

After several hours, Ray bent over and picked up his guitar. At this, Helga clapped her hands together eagerly, looking more animated than she had all afternoon.

"Well, it's about time! Wait—first we have to smoke some of this special Gold I've been saving just for this occasion. Nobody need mention to nobody else that I've got it. It ain't going no further than this kitchen."

When the marijuana was passed to her, Melanie took a few polite tokes, but overwhelmed by its potency, she then declined. In response to Helga's surprised look, she explained that it took very little to affect her. Ray laughed.

"What do you want to do, Helga," he asked, "turn her into an old pothead like you? This lady's a straight arrow, and I'm gonna keep her that way, right, babe?" He squeezed Melanie's shoulder affectionately, making her flush.

Helga shrugged. "Sure, Ray, anything you say."

Melanie went to the bathroom, which had its share of dirty clothes, too, some of which were piled up in the tub, and then walked around the house. Affected by the marijuana she had inhaled and already feeling ill-at-ease with the general atmosphere, she wished they could leave. The smoke hurt her throat in a different way from the cigarettes she smoked constantly in social situations. She felt out of control, as if her body were split off from her mind. To rid herself of the sensation, she drank some cold tap water. She stood sipping it as she gazed out the back window at Helga's yard. In the grassy stretches connecting the houses on either side, several clotheslines had been strung up. As she watched the clothes flapping in the breeze, Melanie felt calmer, as if it were she being buffeted by the sun and wind.

While Ray strummed, Helga rested her chin on her hand and watched his every movement, her fingers holding the new joint they had begun together in midair. It gradually burned down, as did the subsequent one. She regretted this only later and then teased Ray that it was his fault. Gallantly, he fastened the remainder to a roach clip, and they smoked this together, each of them grinning foolishly as they passed it back and forth.

* * * * *

It was late afternoon by the time they left, and in the car Norm sold him, Ray drove them to Sausalito. They peered into the store windows on the main street and then strolled along a cement path adjacent to the Bay. The locality reminded Melanie of the Marina Ray had shown her in Berkeley, not far from their building. He pointed out landmarks and said they were only a stone's throw from El Cerritto. An incline of jagged black rocks abutted the shore, and within its crevices tiny gray-green crabs scuttled. After they had walked back and forth a while, Ray suggested they sit on a bench overlooking the water.

"You wasted, Mel?" he asked gently. "Cat got your tongue?"

Melanie shrugged but didn't reply. She felt unbelievably tired. She also didn't know whether the California Ray was now showing her was a California she wanted to see or have be part of her life.

"You were okay about Helga, weren't you? I mean, there was something there once, but now she's only a buddy, you know."

"I liked her okay," Melanie said.

"Currently, Helga's in a tough spot. When I last saw her, she was hoping things would work out with this guy Fritz. She's taken it hard that he left, especially because of the baby. But you weren't uncomfortable or anything, were you, baby?"

Melanie twisted a strand of hair around her finger. The Bay looked so tranquil; she wished she felt the same. "I don't know, Ray. Her situation certainly brought me down. You know—raising three kids by herself, being on welfare, the house such a mess, not that that usually bothers me . . . but she seemed resigned to it, settled into that lifestyle, as if she doesn't expect anything else . . ."

"It's true she doesn't have a lot of freedom right now," Ray said earnestly, "but she's holding it together the best she can. She loves those kids a lot, and they love her." He settled his arms behind his head. "You didn't have a good time," he said flatly.

"Oh, Ray," Melanie cried, "I'm okay. It wasn't terrible. It just . . . it just brought me down a little. You know, the dope, the fact that she deals right in front of her kids . . . don't you understand? I guess I had a different picture of her in my mind."

Melanie reached into Ray's shirt pocket for his pack of Marlboros, shook out two and before lighting them, handed him one. She inhaled deeply and crossed her legs. "I guess what really bothered me was Helga's attitude. I can see how easy it would be to slip into that frame of mind myself. I mean, I come from this line of people you could call failures— smart people who didn't live up to their potential—my aunt, my uncle, my dad. My mother had her own set of problems. They all fucked up their lives, and I could, too. Some people would say I already have. I didn't go to college, and I'm hardly following a career path." She inhaled again. "What's worse is that Helga's smart. That was obvious."

"Well, it's nice you're so concerned, Mel, but Helga's life is not exactly over. She's only thirty-two."

"Yeah, but I don't think people really change much when you get right down to it."

Ray leaned forward and draped his hands between his knees. "You know, it's hard to take in what you're saying because I have a history with Helga. When I got out of the joint, I had no place to go, and she was there for me. She just nodded toward the couch. I crashed with her for six months until I got my bearings."

The years Ray had spent in prison were something Melanie always had trouble digesting. The Ray she knew seven years later, at twenty-seven, was seeking a new life, trying to leave his past behind. Yet it was in the joint, as he put it, that Ray had learned how to play the guitar to overcome his self-consciousness with people, and what she liked most about him was his desire to constantly improve his music along with his genuine concern for others.

"I'm sure I sound judgmental, but I think it's important to do things that can potentially help you grow," she said, flicking her ash impatiently. "I'm not talking about establishment success, but I think it's important to have experiences, learn from them, and then go on. You know, not stay stuck someplace that brings you down."

Restlessly, Melanie crushed out the cigarette she had just lit. She shoved her hands into her pockets and began to pace back and forth in front of the bench. The sun was setting, and its golden-red rays on the water seemed to mock her in their beauty and serenity.

"Well," Ray said, watching her, "I've always wanted to be an inspiration to people, show them other possibilities. I mean, didn't you see how Helga's face lit up when we were describing the Rockies?"

"Damn it, Ray, you want to be everybody's savior! Maybe that's really heroic, but nobody I met today was looking to be saved."

"But Melanie, people fall into holes, and then they can't climb out of them. Do you think it's easy to break out of an environment like Richmond? I was scared shitless the first time I went into Berkeley, and I only went because I thought it would be a gas to see the freaks on the Ave—people with beards and long hair, talking a lot of crazy shit. I certainly didn't expect to be able to relate to anybody. But then I got to talking, and . . . well, I discovered a lot of new ideas. Visiting Berkeley opened up an entirely new world. Marie and Pete were part of it, and that's why they mean so much to me. They didn't just peg me as a Richmond loser. Isn't loving people and accepting them for who they are what it's all about? That's certainly what all the songs say—love is all you need . . . yeah, yeah, yeah, yeah."

"Oh brother!"

"So you work to get all the degrees in the world," Ray continued insistently, "a house in the suburbs, a two-car garage; is that any guarantee that you'll be happier than Helga? You'd just be trading for a different set of problems."

"But you'd be doing something you enjoyed presumably," Melanie protested, turning to face him. "Look, you went to New York. You tried to make it. Was that a waste of time?" Melanie shivered. "Oh jees, Ray, can't we go back now? The sun's set, and I'm freezing."

Before he could reply, she began walking in the direction of the car. Ray followed slowly behind her, and they drove home in silence. Although she glanced at him every few minutes, he continued to stare straight ahead. Eventually, she leaned her head against the car window and shut her eyes.

* * * * *

When Ray suggested dropping by Helga's house one day after school that week, Melanie agreed, fearful that he would continue to assume she didn't like her. These visits quickly became habitual. Because Helga usually said very little and then only when drawn out, Melanie felt she still did not know her very well. Sometimes, tired of sitting at the table, Melanie took walks or lay on the living-room couch, listening repeatedly to Helga's Iron Butterfly and Jefferson Airplane albums.

One afternoon, Mike barged in without ceremony. His girlfriend, Dee, trailed behind him. Mike walked straight to the stove and reheated the water in the saucepan to make himself a cup of coffee. Helga watched with a grin on her face as Mike filled his cup half full of sugar and creamer and then gestured to Dee. Dee shook her head and, smiling wanly, took a seat at the table.

"I don't think I could get down a thing," she protested, grimacing. She pushed her long black hair away from her face to reveal blue, unfocused eyes. Like Mike, she wore a leather jacket, blue jeans, and a turtleneck jersey that completely covered her arms.

"You must be Melanie," she said, turning toward her. "We heard Ray had a new old lady. It's good to finally meet you. Mike worships the ground Ray walks on, so don't let his attitude bother you. We're on our way to pick up a balloon, but we stopped off on purpose hoping you guys would be here."

Mike reached into Dee's jacket pocket and pulled out a pack of Marlboro Golds. He dropped into a chair and faced Ray. "Well, if it isn't Mr. Wonderful himself. Decided to grace this part of the country with your presence for a while? The only way I heard you were back was through Helga's grapevine. Too hot-shit a musician now to look up an old friend?" Without waiting for a reply, Mike took a sip of coffee, cursed that it was too friggin' hot, and then extended his box pack to Ray.

Ray lifted out a cigarette and lit it elaborately, blowing a smoke ring into the air. "I was planning to get around to it," he said, laughing.

Mike had raven black hair like Dee's, but instead of lying smoothly on his shoulders, his stuck out, giving him a wild, electrified appearance. When he stretched, muscles rippled beneath his tight-fitting jersey. Although Mike was not significantly taller, Ray seemed dwarfed in comparison to him; as they talked, Melanie imagined that Ray's voice had descended in pitch.

Mike grabbed the wall phone and proceeded to make a series of calls. During each he spoke so loudly and belligerently, it was impossible for the others to hold a consistent conversation. Dee sat nervously twisting her hair in circles with one hand while she chain-smoked with the other, her fingers tapping the ash so frequently, it looked as if she were typing.

"Don't hand me that crap, you fucking sonuvabitch; this arrangement was set up over two weeks ago . . . I said don't fuck with me, dick-head . . . no, I won't take it easy . . . My woman's sick. She's gotta have something tonight." Snapping his fingers at Dee to light him another cig-arette, Mike nearly ripped the phone cord in two as he swung around. Finally, slamming into a chair, he handed Dee his cup, and said "Don't worry, it's under control. Bastards!" Helga sat with her eyes lowered, grin-ning to herself, and watching Dee. Mike suddenly grinned, too, trans-forming his face.

"Man, nothing ever fazes Helga! Fucking, fucking slimy pricks! I'd like to line up every one and shoot *them* up . . . one by one—every pasty, motherfuckin' arm. Kapow! Kapow! Kapow! Did you know that dealers are the scum of the earth, Melanie?" he asked, acknowledging her for the first time. "If you want to experience pure evil, there it is. You ask my buddy Ray here if that's not the truth. You don't know it, maybe, pretty woman, but lover boy here's been strung out in his lifetime. And old brother Mike sat and held his hand. I bet you don't believe I would do that, right?" Mike blew smoke from his nostrils while he appraised her with his eyes. "Don't laugh, Ray, I've got a long memory. Well," he said, pausing, "I hear you and Melanie think you have this traveling thing all sewed up. Maybe Dee and I oughta give you a little competition. How about it, babe? Want to see the country? Ray shouldn't think he's got a monopoly." He swung his arm out, catching her bottom with his hand.

"Shit, Mike. You made me spill the coffee."

"Hey, high school girls aren't supposed to swear." Mike took a sip and stared coldly at Melanie, running his eyes over her in a hostile fashion.

Ray chuckled. "Watch out, Mel. He's giving you the evil eye. The original body snatcher. Hey, lay off my old lady; she's not your type."

"Yeah, that's true. Pretty, but looks too smart by half. Myself, I like my women dumb, so they don't talk back. Right, Dee? What's your opinion? Is Ray's new old lady good looking? Answer like an obedient girl now."

Dee shrugged and said, "Sure," but Melanie could see that she was close to tears. Shortly afterwards Dee excused herself to Helga and asked if she could go lie down on the couch. Mike fired questions at Ray about their trip and about Lytton, and although her head began to throb from the abrasive sound of his voice, Melanie simultaneously realized that Mike was the only person they had met at Helga's who seemed genuinely interested in what Ray had been doing during the year he had been away from Richmond.

When they drove home, after dropping Mike and Dee near Telegraph to meet their dealer, she confessed that she liked Mike, although she told Ray she could never imagine being his girlfriend.

Ray hugged her appreciatively. "I'm really glad, Mel. Mike and I go back a long ways. We even wanted to marry the same girl, but she couldn't choose between us. I found out when I was back East that she married somebody else. I think Mike took it really hard. Maybe that's the reason for the heroin. He gets a charge out of acting hard-assed, but, actually, he's one of the most vulnerable people I know. He liked you, I could tell. Most women he doesn't give the time of day, despite what he said about liking dumb women. Mike's too smart for his own good, if you ask me—it brings him nothing but heartache."

"You really love him, don't you?"

"Yeah. Yeah, I guess that about sums it up."

 # *Four*

On the way home from San Francisco one evening, where they had been visiting a man, Mark, whom Melanie had known in Manhattan, Ray picked up two hitchhikers who stood beside the on ramp to the Bay Bridge. Mutual acquaintances had introduced Melanie and Mark when she had finished high school, and she had been drawn to him immediately because of his extensive knowledge of art and literature. Spongelike, she had been eager to absorb what he could teach her. Now, after a separation of two years, she had met him and his recently acquired wife, Giselle, accidentally, while shopping at the Berkeley co-op.

For their first date, he had taken her to see Luis Bunuel's film *The Exterminating Angel.* Afterwards, on the subway ride back to the group house where he lived, Melanie had felt depressed and was unusually silent because the film had affected her deeply. Watching her intently, Mark told her that she looked like a junkie because she never kept her mouth completely closed. Interpreting his words to mean that he found her weak and unattractive, for the remainder of the evening she had felt as emotionally paralyzed as the characters in the film. The characters' lives were at stake, but they could not summon the will to save themselves. Drawn to him despite herself because of his unconventional personality and apparent understanding of her innermost thoughts, Melanie continued to date him.

During sex, as Mark pointed out the classical lines in her figure, the varying pink and white shades of her skin, he made her see herself differently. His voice and the strong touch of his mouth and hands were mesmerizing. She found herself able to think of little but him, believing naively that he was her guide to greater self-awareness. However, the closer she tried to get to him emotionally, the more he withdrew, disappearing for weeks on end without explanation. Eventually, he stopped seeing her altogether.

When they met in the co-op, Mark embraced her delightedly, as if greeting a very dear friend. Melanie introduced him to Ray, who was with her, and although Mark raised his eyebrows at her and smiled sardonically, the four of them subsequently met for dinner. During the meal, to prevent a rekindling of her former feelings for Mark, Melanie had focused most of her attention on Giselle.

This particular evening had passed quickly and pleasantly enough. They had sat drinking green tea in Mark and Giselle's living room while comparing life on the East Coast to life in California. From there, they had moved to the topics Ray most enjoyed discussing, especially when stoned: Why was there a universe at all? What was the purpose of their lives on the planet? What was the nature of love? Although the room overflowed with potted house plants—asparagus ferns, rubber plants, Christmas begonias, as well as an abundance of variegated coleus—it was otherwise furnished austerely with low-to-the-ground black wooden tables and a matching black rocking chair. Apart from the rocker, there were no sofas or chairs, so the four of them sat cross-legged and barefoot on a thick-piled, white shag rug.

Giselle sat in a half-lotus position across from Mark, smiling calmly and evidently listening closely to the conversation, although she seldom spoke herself. Giselle was studying at the San Francisco Zen Center, and Melanie wondered if the calm she projected was attributed to her meditation practices or if it was her natural personality. Midway through the evening she rose and, with graceful, dancelike movements, set before them a platter of sliced mangos, papaya, pineapple, and passion fruit, lightly sprinkled with lime juice and cinnamon.

Weary of Ray and Mark's energetic and she felt pointless debate, Melanie wandered around the room, gazing at the black-and-white photographs on the walls, remembering with a pang Mark's passion for photography. They had spent many evenings looking at photographs, he beside her on the couch in his living room, explaining nuances and craft. She rifled through the cinderblock bookshelf that stood in a far corner of the room. Nearly every volume had a spiritual-sounding title, although there were also books on Western history and photography. Giselle had disappeared into the kitchen with their cups and plates. Eventually, Ray picked up his guitar and played several melodies of a gentler nature for them. Mark closed his eyes, as if settling into a meditation, and continued to sit trancelike for over ten minutes after Ray had finished. Finally rising, he wordlessly kissed Ray on both cheeks, his dark brown, nearly black eyes shining fervently, and whispered, "Far out, man. Far . . . far fucking out," the passion in his voice rendering an uncharacteristic, dramatic beauty to the normally crude expression.

When they left Steiner Street, where Mark and Giselle rented the bottom floor of a townhouse, Melanie brooded about Mark, recalling evenings and nights spent with him and the passion and joy this had brought her. She realized there was no way they could have remained together, but his presence still had the power to hurt and confuse her; she was grateful that soon he and Giselle would be moving up north to Oregon or Washington. Melanie hardly noticed when Ray stopped the car and two hitchhikers climbed into the back seat. When he tried to engage them in conversation, Melanie turned to look at them. It was a man and a woman, and the man had his arm around the woman's shoulder. With his other hand, he was caressing her leg, moving steadily up her thigh. Catching Ray's attention, she grinned slightly and then returned her gaze to the reflections the bridge lights made on the water. Lulled by the car's noise, the darkness, and the many cups of herbal tea she had drunk, she fell asleep.

She woke with a jerk. Dimly, she assumed Ray was dropping the couple somewhere, but turning around, she saw that they were still in the back seat. The woman was giggling at something Ray had just said.

"Hey, Mel, Jim and Mona need a place to crash tonight." He touched Melanie's leg. "I said they could use our love seat; I didn't think you'd mind. They had this other arrangement, or Mona did, on Sacramento, but we just drove by, and nobody was home. Is that okay, hon?"

Melanie shrugged and looked more fully at the two people behind her. Jim had long sandy-colored hair pulled back in a loose pony tail and a lean, Nordic face with a scant beard. His smile was disarmingly apologetic as he directed it at her. She mumbled, "Fine," and got out of the car, remembering the many kindnesses people had shown her and Ray during their trip across country.

When they were on the sidewalk beneath the arch, she further appraised Mona under the street light. She was petite, and her blonde hair was cut in a bouncy pageboy. She contrasted oddly with Jim because— while he wore jeans and a ragged sweatshirt—she was dressed in a fleecy-looking sweater and straight skirt and wore stockings and high heels. Melanie thought, looking at her, that Mona probably worked in an office or was a teacher because she was dressed like the instructors they had at Lytton. Mona nodded hello, smiling slightly, and the four of them walked to the front door.

Ray took out beers from the refrigerator and at Mona's request, because she had seen him carrying in his guitar, played a few songs. Jim kept running his fingers along the sleeve of her sweater, saying it felt just like fur, man, she was a goddamned pussy cat. Mona meowed plaintively, and their subsequent giggles ended in a lengthy kiss. Melanie curled up in the rocker, as usual, with her legs crossed; the others gathered around the window seat. Ray played "Spanish Boots of Spanish Leather" and then "There But for Fortune," which made Mona exclaim wildly and beg for more. Ray glanced at Melanie, who, lulled by the music, was drifting back to sleep, and suggested that perhaps they should turn in; it was rather late. Melanie took sheets from their makeshift linen closet of two deep-set shelves next to the kitchen while Ray and Jim pulled out the couch. When Jim and Mona slipped into the bathroom together, Melanie threw her nightie quickly over her head and slid self-consciously between their own sheets. The room had never appeared so small to her.

Light from the walkway shone faintly through the transparent curtains, so although the room was dark, shapes were still visible. Melanie lay still and, while she waited for Ray to come to bed, thought about Mark and Giselle. She recalled the vapor that rose from the cups of green tea, the whiteness, the intense quiet. Her thoughts were broken by the sound of giggling, followed by Mona and Jim's shifting around on the couch. The bedsprings began to creak, and although the love seat had been pushed up against the window seat as far as it could go, it was only a few feet away from their own pullout bed. Melanie felt as if Jim and Mona were literally in bed with her. Ray moved beneath the covers and, reaching for her, pressed his body close to hers, running his fingers along the backs of her thighs. After several minutes, Melanie opened her eyes and shook her head.

"It's no good," she whispered. "Not with them here."

Ray continued to stroke her, pushing his body harder against hers and whispering it doesn't matter, but as she remained inert, he finally turned on his side.

The rhythmic bouncing on the love seat increased. Melanie moved as far as she could to her side of the bed and dangled her arm toward the floor. She felt like punching something and as the creaking continued, accompanied by soft moans, she sat up abruptly. Pulling the blanket up to cover her chest, she lit a cigarette and sat staring at the darkened window in front of her. The moaning grew louder and louder, coming now from Jim as well as Mona. Ray moved restlessly against Melanie's thighs. Although she could feel his erection, she only drew harder on the Marlboro she had lit. Finally, tears pricking her eyes, she stubbed the cigarette out and closed herself into the bathroom. She sat on the toilet seat, crying with fury at this couple she felt had invaded their apartment, taking advantage of Ray's good nature and now exciting him by their lovemaking. Jim's mocking eyes and amused smile flitted before her vision. After a few minutes, Ray came into the bathroom and, kneeling beside her, bent to kiss her face.

"You're just turned on by that bitch's moans," she cried in a loud whisper. "I don't want to get off because of a couple of uncouth strangers. How dare they think they can just come in and screw on our couch? Yuck!"

Ray held her face in his hands and forced her to look into his eyes.

"Mel, they're just fucking! We screwed on people's couches when we were traveling, too, in case you forgot. I know we were way more considerate, but to tell you the truth, it's hard not to feel turned on. Aren't you? You're shivering, baby. Come back to bed. You're making yourself miserable over nothing. It's just our animal nature, after all."

"That slimy guy, too," Melanie muttered. "He gave me the creeps from the first, but thinking he can just walk right in here and screw his chick . . . oh!" The outrage made Melanie angrier and angrier. She could hardly breathe. "Make them leave, Ray. Make them leave, please!" She buried her damp, flushed face in her hands and yanked violently at her hair, as if she wanted to rip out every strand.

"No, *I'm* going to bed," Ray said. "I can see that you just want to get worked up, and I can't stop you from doing that, but I don't have to agree with you. I'm sorry, but I can't kick them out, not after telling them they could stay here. You do whatever the fuck you want, Mel."

He shut the door firmly behind him. Melanie continued to sit on the toilet seat, sobbing wholeheartedly. She didn't want to listen to another woman's orgasm—was that wrong? Was she just being too uptight? Weren't Jim and Mona using them, treating them both disrespectfully, or was her thinking distorted? Melanie was further confused by the desire that flooded her body, in odd conjunction with her disgust at their behavior. She *did* want to make love to Ray; she was excited, despite herself, by Mona's noises. She blew her nose violently and then stood to look in the mirror. Her face was tearstreaked and bright red and she felt ugly and unlovable.

She sat back down on the toilet seat and forced herself to breathe deeply while screaming silently at the critical voices in her head. Goose bumps formed on her arms, and her body ached with discomfort. Melanie rose and opened the door. She saw the glow from two lit cigarettes, but otherwise the room appeared quiet, so she tiptoed to bed. Fearful of touching Ray, she lay on her back, uncomfortably aware of the sensual feelings flooding her body. Without knowing exactly when, she fell asleep.

* * * * *

When Melanie woke the next morning, she assumed by the quality of light in the room that it was late, but when she glanced at the Baby Ben on the night stand, its hands read only seven-thirty. She had woken from a dead sleep with the sense that long stretches of time had elapsed. Gradually she recalled, point by point, the events of the previous evening: Jim and Mona climbing into the car, Ray's friendliness, his later irritation toward her, and, chiefly, her own fury.

Turning over, she saw that she was alone in the apartment. The love seat was still pulled out, although the sheets and blankets had been tossed in a heap on the window seat. Jim and Mona were gone, and so was Ray. With a flash of anger, Melanie realized that he was probably driving them somewhere else. She flipped back over to keep the couch out of her direct line of vision and stared instead at the alarm clock. Its regular ticking felt oddly reassuring; the thin, gold minute hand clicked consistently, always moving in the same direction, without pause. She wished that she could feel such certainty.

Was it right or wrong to be angry with Mona and Jim for intruding that way? Right or wrong for her to feel stimulated by their lust? Had Mark ever really cared for her? Would she ever feel as calm as Giselle? Did she belong with Ray? Asking the questions seemed futile, but surely someone, or something knew the answers! Once by a deserted reservoir in Connecticut, during the space of a single day, Melanie felt she had had an inkling of what it felt like to be not self-conscious, felt that momentarily, anyway, her questions had been answered. Upon awakening in her sleeping bag, she had observed the sky growing lighter and lighter until it turned to the bright fullness of real daylight. She had sat, almost without moving, staring at the ground around her, watching insects crawl by carrying crumbs and bits of decayed matter, meandering in patterns she was convinced must be purposeful, though incomprehensible to her. Bees had sprung from flower to flower; the wind had periodically stirred the trees. Melanie recalled thinking that there was nothing else she wanted to do, nowhere else she wanted to be. Normally obsessed with the belief that everything was painfully transient in life, she felt, for a moment, that she had glimpsed eternity.

Later, back at the apartment on Ninety-Seventh Street, she had begun a poem about the development of that day, depicting the earth's gradual awakening through a series of dancer's movements, but she had never gotten past the first stanza, illustrating dawn. Hungry for such contentment, she had voluntarily put herself into natural situations where it might occur, but that exact sense of attunement she had felt with the world at the reservoir remained mysteriously elusive. Because she had taken mescaline, she assumed that maybe it was impossible to have such an experience naturally; chances were it would never happen again.

Melanie had a recurrent dream: She was standing in a subway car, clutching one of the black straps that hung from bars parallel to the ceiling. The train burst in and out of tunnels, moving from darkness into the garish light of the station's stops; an express, it traveled down a middle track and rushed past the local stations. Melanie only got a glimpse of these stations as she went by, disconnected from their platforms by a series of barred, closed lanes. Although exhilarated by the speed at which her train was whizzing by, she felt strangely disappointed at not stopping, as if, perhaps there, *there* it would be: The answer, the clue that would bring her the clarity she sought in life—a person, an experience, a definitive realization! Yet sealed within the tight metal doors of her own car, she could not escape, could not leap across the tracks to investigate these possibilities. As she descended, finally, into the last dark tunnel, she felt an unbearable sense of loss. The dream had recurred several times, and each time she had woken disturbed and in tears.

The outside door slammed shut. Then Melanie heard a key being fitted impatiently into the lock and watched as Ray pushed open the door and came in; he was out of breath, his hair was uncombed, and his shirt was tucked loosely into his pants. With a frown, he took off his jacket and threw it on top of the pulled-out convertible. Folding her arms across her knees, Melanie rested her chin on them before speaking.

"Well, I had the opportunity to experience universal love, and I blew it. I suppose, knight that you are, you carried the poor travelers farther on their journey."

Ray lit a cigarette and flung himself into the rocker.

"You know, Melanie," he said in the tone he used when trying to convince her of something, "maybe they were inconsiderate, but they were obviously so hot, they weren't even aware of our presence. They left so early because they realized you had gotten upset . . . Mona did anyway. She was very sweet and apologetic. She said, being a woman, she could understand your feelings. Evidently, this Jim was just a one-night stand; he took her breath away, she told me, and she just couldn't resist. They met in a bar somewhere in the city. I took her out to Oakland after dropping Jim near Telegraph. She's moving into an apartment above Lake Merritt after the first of the month." Inhaling deeply, he let out the smoke in a long, blue-gray stream. As Melanie continued to sit motionless, he asked, "Are you listening, Melanie? Listen! Mona's a nice person. You'd probably like her if you gave her half a chance." He reached to flick his ash, which had grown quite long, into the ashtray. "Look, babe, I'm sorry. I guess it was a mistake; I realize it, okay? Do you forgive me?"

"I'm sure she's the salt of the earth. Did you get her phone number?" The words were out before she could stop herself. Melanie pulled the covers around her shoulders and mumbled "Sorry" before asking him for a cigarette. Ray lit one for her and then came to sit on the edge of the bed.

"I don't know, Ray . . . to me they were two jerks who saw they could take advantage of your good nature. It's hard for me to trust people the way you do; maybe I'm wrong." Her chest heaved with rekindled anger, but, as suddenly, it dissipated. "I'm sorry, too. Maybe I overreacted. Come here, honey." Ray moved closer, and Melanie pressed his face gently against her breasts while she stroked his hair.

"People are nice if you give them half a chance," he said in a solemn tone. "You think you can tell just by looking at someone whether he or she is trustworthy or not, but that seems terribly unfair. Personally, I don't believe that first impressions are everything. Melanie," he said, pulling his head away, "you hardly give people a chance. I wish I could change that in you." He cupped her chin in his hand and squeezed it sternly before smiling at her.

Melanie lay back against the pillows in disgust. "I expect people to act with consideration, with honesty, morality . . . oh hell, maybe my standards are just too high. What would a generous person have done last night, Ray? Said here, take our bed so you can have a better time—more room and all." She took a drag from her cigarette and stared moodily past his head.

"I suppose this is what I get for robbing the cradle," Ray said. "I'll have to wait until you grow up a little, become less intolerant." Grabbing her, he pinned her arms down on the bed.

"You just don't want to admit you were conned," she laughed, struggling to free herself. He squeezed her wrists more tightly and forced his mouth against hers, drowning out her threats that she would bite him if he wasn't careful. Rolling over and over, they finally fell heavily onto the floor. Without releasing her, Ray whispered against her neck that maybe it was time for breakfast.

* * * * *

The novelty of living in the studio dwindled. Now, more often than not, they left the bed unmade and pulled out all day. Library books piled up in the living room; pots and dishes frequently sat soaking in the sink until either Melanie or Ray decided to tackle them. Many nights they bought carry-out Chinese food or stopped for enchiladas at a Mexican restaurant a few blocks from the apartment on San Pablo Avenue.

Some mornings, she and Ray overslept and, after lingering over breakfast, walked to the Berkeley Marina. They strolled together the length of the wooden pier, arms wrapped around each other's waists, hands hooked into each other's jeans pockets, stopping now and again to lean over the railing and gaze at the Bay or at San Francisco in the distance. In November and December, rain or fog hid both the city and Marin County, but the moist air rushing past her face, picking up and swirling her hair in circles made Melanie feel alive. She liked to breathe in the dank-smelling water and see the fishermen's bloody, shiny catch heaped in buckets beside them on the pier. Here was where life and death truly met.

She and Ray always walked to the very end, to the ghost pier, fenced off because it was damaged. Being at the farthest possible point made them feel they were at the prow of a ship, at the forefront of things; although when the view was blurry, Melanie felt as if she were staring into nothingness. The Marina reminded her of the piers near One Hundred Twenty-Fifth Street in Manhattan by the Hudson River. Her grandmother's apartment building had faced Riverside Park, and as a child, she had often wandered down to the piers, attracted by the boats and the slight insecurity of the swaying boards, although the water was oily and foul.

During the week, when Melanie felt she could not endure another day of typing and shorthand, she purposefully stayed home so she could go to the pier as, similarly, when in high school, she had deliberately cut classes to do something more to her liking. Perched on the piled-up black rocks beside the pier, listening to waves slapping against the pilings, enveloped in a blurry sky, she felt content with the world.

Most weeks, though, she went to Lytton. The course work became familiar, if monotonous. Now she could write business letters, was fairly proficient at the keyboard, and had moved from three-letter words to five and six in shorthand, while Ray knew the rudiments of accounting. She came to know and like most of the students, and sometimes these women joined Ray and her for lunch. But no one suggested socializing outside these boundaries.

One woman in her early thirties, a welfare mother named Bea, who was acquainted with Helga, impressed Melanie because of her determination to make a new life for herself and her two small children. Every morning, unless her babysitter failed to show, Bea came ready to learn. She carried a pencil case crammed with pens and well-sharpened pencils, as if she were still in grammar school, and her loose-leaf binder was the neatest in the class, because she was constantly reorganizing it. In the two classes Melanie had with her—business English and math—Bea sat with her head tilted anxiously, trying to catch every word, and frequently interrupted to ask questions. When she did not understand, her posture—which was always erect, as if in preparation for the position she desired as an executive secretary—sagged reflexively. In their simplicity, Bea's goals—a well-paying job, a car of her own, a house in a good neighborhood—awed Melanie and made her wonder if she didn't take her own future seriously enough.

Most of the time, Melanie felt she was waiting: Waiting for typing practice to be over, waiting for lunchtime, for the weekend, for the course to end. When she and Ray were traveling, she had woken each day eager to see what might happen next, believing that whatever the experience, it was certain to be of interest. Now she more-or-less knew what would happen, and therefore it was only interesting to imagine what might come along after that. It amazed Melanie that she and Ray were still together, especially because of the differences in their personalities. She had seldom been with a man longer than three months and wondered how much time it would take for her to either grow bored with Ray, or feel she had to move on for her own growth's sake. In the past, the man she was seeing and she drifted apart as a matter of course, after both realized their eventual incompatibility, but Ray seemed content. Melanie wondered if, in time, she would be as happy with him as Marie and Pete were with each other.

Late in December, when they joined Marie and Pete on Shattuck to see a film together, Marie proudly patted her abdomen and announced that she was pregnant. She and Pete had been married six years and had occasionally talked about having a child. Ray had greatly supported the idea, telling them he couldn't imagine more perfect parents; they had already spoiled their Siamese cat, Todd, rotten. On subsequent get-togethers, sitting in the rocker Pete had brought home as a surprise for her, Marie gave them blow-by-blow account of what the doctor recommended, how the fetus was progressing, and how she was feeling in turn. Melanie felt inundated with information about breast-feeding and the Lamaze philosophy of childbirth.

Initially, Pete waxed enthusiastic about the pregnancy, but, gradually, Ray and Melanie noticed a change in him. He had always enjoyed pondering the universe with Ray, but now these discussions increased in frequency; yet, simultaneously, Pete withdrew from the general conversation. He sat smoking dope, without necessarily offering them any, and laughed inappropriately at times. When Marie showed Melanie a package of receiving blankets that had come in the mail from her Aunt Gertrude, Pete giggled and then went off on a tangent about the meaning of the word "receiving." Marie frowned at him, but saying nothing, she rewrapped the blankets and went to make tea. Besides refusing to smoke with them, Marie now and then excused herself, claiming a sick headache, something she had been prone to in her early years of marriage. On the sofa, she sat close beside Pete and frequently reached for his hand, pressing it comfortingly between her own palms, as if it were a flower she was trying to preserve.

* * * * *

As winter deepened and the rain persisted, Melanie found it difficult to wake up in the morning. She would shut off the alarm and lie in bed, staring out into the room. Under the gray morning light, it had an ugly cast to it, an empty, forlorn appearance, and the secondhand furniture seemed shabbier than ever. On many evenings, she and Ray found themselves watching show after show on an old black and white television set they had purchased at a thrift shop; they even looked forward to nights when they knew three or four of their favorite programs would be on. It was often close to midnight before Ray picked up his guitar, and his playing was perfunctory, as if his mind was really elsewhere, and he had lost the concentration necessary to give to what he was doing. Some nights he fell into silent moods that reminded Melanie of Norm. He sat with his legs propped up on the window seat, staring out at the night, and presented such a remote posture that Melanie hesitated to disturb him. Once they had discussed the events of the day, they often went in different directions: he to read or jam with musicians he had met on campus in the fall; she to curl up with a book or, less often, fiddle with her poems in progress.

Her production had slowed considerably since meeting Ray. The handful of poems she had written since arriving in California—one about a desert sunset, one about watching the candle splutter during their first dinner with Marie and Pete, another about Ray performing on Sproul Plaza—seemed dull to her, lacking in some substantial fashion. Before leaving Manhattan, Ray had made a tape of her poetry set to his music, with the idea of possibly marketing it. But they never produced a second tape, and although they had found the experience exciting at the time, neither of them had tried seriously to do anything with it.

During the now long, tedious weeks, Melanie felt that she was slowing to a crawl. Northern California, along with other unreal aspects she had trouble adjusting to, did not have true seasons such as she had always known. There were no sharp edges; there was a gradual blurring: a cooling of the air, an imperceptible shift from consistently sunny days to ones streaming with rainfall, the landscape changing from gold to green.

> *"It's raining, it's pouring, the old man is snoring.*
> *Bumped his head and he went to bed*
> *and he couldn't get up in the morning.*
> *Rain, rain, go away,*
> *come again some other day.*
> *. . . Ladybug, Ladybug fly away home.*
> *Your house is on fire and your children*
> *they will burn, they will burn.*
> *It's raining, it's pouring, the old man is snoring . . ."*

The Peter, Paul, and Mary song kept running through her mind, like a steady drizzle itself. Melanie did not know if it was the separation from what was familiar, or the seasonal change, or a sense that—along with nature—she was withering, too. Perhaps she had stood still for too long, she reasoned—she who always wanted to be moving on, to discover her life. Had she hit up against a dead end? Ray and she had been in Berkeley for less than six months, and she was barely twenty years old. Didn't her entire life stretch before her?

* * * * *

It was difficult to remember how it began. It began with the shaking—that was definable, but when had *that* begun? *How?* At what exact moment? Was it only the short winter days, the increasing darkness, earlier and earlier, the feeling that winter was encroaching on her, like something physical, something inevitable, moving in with her, occupying her body like a parasite? Melanie felt as if she were driving toward a wall that was suddenly so close, she could not prevent herself from hitting it.

Perhaps it had begun more subtly, insidiously: something that had been lying in wait for a long time, curled up, waiting, waiting for her mind to become fatigued enough not to resist it. There had already been moodiness throughout adolescence—headaches, recurrent depression—these were familiar. The sense of unreality when taking a shower, realizing as she washed her own skin that it should feel alive to her but did not. As she looked at Ray sitting on the window seat or next to her at the kitchen table, at times she felt a inexplicable sense of despair, as if she were in the wrong place; somewhere everything had turned aside, and this path was not what she had imagined it to be. She was on it, but she could not say how or why. It was a little like believing that the world came in the color blue, with all of one's associations linked to that color, and then one day observing a disturbing pinkish cast to things.

The first night had not seemed extraordinary. She and Ray had gone somewhere earlier in the evening—perhaps to a movie—although she did not remember it as a day or night of particular significance. Back in the apartment, they had gotten ready for bed. She slipped on her nightgown and climbed in on her side with a book and a cup of hot tea. It was late January. Ray sat, as usual, on the window seat, strumming his guitar, trying to recall the chords of a song he had learned the week before. The only sounds in the room were his subdued playing, her sips of tea, and the intake of breath as one or the other of them inhaled smoke from their cigarettes. The night had felt unearthly still—yes, she remembered that— as if, were she to speak, her voice would mimic the sound of a coin hitting something hard after falling a long distance. Melanie glanced at Ray, slid her hand between the pages of her book to save the place, and stretched backwards. Simple movements. What could they have provoked? Her throat suddenly constricted as she took another sip of tea; it felt like someone was thrusting an arm in a swift motion down the passage of her esophagus, plugging it so that she could not swallow. As she strained to choke the liquid down, she noticed that, all on their own, her legs were shaking, disconnected from her other movements. She looked again at Ray, but he remained sitting with his eyes closed, plucking the guitar strings. She set down her teacup and instinctively reached for a cigarette.

"Ray, I can't stop my legs from quivering!" Melanie tried to press her legs firmly against the mattress, but the shaking only shifted from her calves and feet to her thighs, increasing in violence as it traveled. She covered her legs with the blanket, pulling it tightly against them; but when they continued to tremble anyway, she jumped off the bed, as if it were on fire, as if it were the cause. Ray laid his guitar down on the window seat and came to sit beside her.

"Sounds like a charley horse, Mel. I get those when my body's tensed up." He put his hand on her shoulder and sat beside her, his other palm pressed against her thigh. As he held it there, his hand vibrated along with its motion. She watched him frown in confusion, but then he smiled. "Don't worry, babe. You're probably just overtired. We walked a lot today; your body's reacting to the strain."

He rubbed her calves vigorously, and the shaking seemed to pause momentarily, but then it was as if the nervousness had retreated inside her and was consuming her being. Her mouth quivered as she held onto his arm and looked fearfully into his face. She sensed a difference in his thinking by the stilling of his arm, though he continued to smile reassuringly.

"What's happening, Ray? Why won't it stop? It feels so weird." She suddenly hugged him tightly, but as suddenly he seemed removed from her.

"Don't be frightened, hon. Let me fix you some hot milk; it will relax you. Try taking some deep breaths." The warmth from his brown eyes penetrated her, like the heat from steadily applied Ben Gay ointment. She tried to smile back, reluctant to tell him also about the strange disconnected thoughts gathering in her mind like so many snipped-off pieces of sewing thread.

"That helped when I had nightmares as a kid. Shit! I feel like one of those chickens that keep moving even after their heads have been cut off." As soon as she said this, her body shook even more violently, and a wave of terror shot through her mind. She felt as if her arms, her legs were dissolving. Ray appeared distant, unreachable, as if he were in a different dimension, while she was marooned . . . where? Thought came in another language, too, a language she sensed desperately he would not understand.

"Maybe you should get up and walk around, stomp your feet like you're trying to get rid of pins and needles. I don't think you should smoke," he admonished, seeing her shake a Marlboro from the pack beside her. She clutched it.

"No, I have to. I'm scared. Something's really wrong, Ray. I can't even talk about it."

Melanie climbed out of bed and walked to the window. Standing, her body continued to shake; she felt as if a great wind was blowing through her. To calm herself, she tried to breathe deeply and reason with herself. Why were her thoughts disconnected—fragments that did not relate to each other? She wasn't stoned. They had not smoked marijuana in weeks, and she never smoked much anyway. Was what was happening an aftereffect, one of those drug flashbacks she had heard other people describe? What she felt had no resemblance to anything she was familiar with; her brain ached as it tried to comprehend. It was blind, overwhelming fear, fear without cause, without identity, without meaning. How could she tell Ray she was afraid when she could not even say of what or why?

He returned with the milk, and she drank it dutifully, holding tightly to his arm with her free hand for comfort. After she set the cup down, he tucked the covers around her and held her, as he had held her the first night they spent together. The last thing she remembered before falling asleep was Ray's face, half in shadow, bent over hers. Her body trembled, trembled, trembled the entire journey into sleep, and because she held Ray's hand, he shook along with her.

In the morning it was over, scarcely real. Pale sunlight poured through the window, through the space between the top of the hedge and the ceiling. It flowed like a delicate spray, liquid honey over their bedspread. Stretching deeply, Melanie turned to touch Ray. She traced lines along his shoulders and back, working her way down to his bottom, loving the yellowish-white light on his skin, as it coated his limbs, eased over every curve. Finally, he faced her, and they made love feverishly, as if their survival depended upon the merging of their bodies. Afterwards, as they lay enveloped in each other, Ray touched her face tenderly, told her how innocent she looked, said he loved to watch her sleep because in sleep she looked so untroubled. And was she okay now? Yes, she thought so. Maybe it *had* only been tension as he had thought. Wrapping her arms around his back, Melanie clung to him, his body covering hers like a shield.

* * * * *

Although the shaking was not as extreme as the first time, it returned, and with it came a restlessness that made her feel that if she settled in one spot, some awful thing might happen to her: she might sink, melt, be otherwise annihilated. Melanie developed a habit of ritualistically climbing out of bed and pacing in the darkness, back and forth across the living room, from one end of the window seat to the other, until, finally, she could fall into a turbulent sleep that left her exhausted in the morning. Day and night began to collide, squeeze together, blur. She yearned for sleep; her body craved release, but her mind, like a guard, forced her to stay awake. If she closed her eyes, she might . . . she didn't know . . . and yet there was a fear of sinking, of sliding down somewhere, a deep, primitive sensation that warned her she must be alert; she must prevent whatever it was from possibly happening. Therefore, as soon as she found herself becoming drowsy, she jerked herself violently awake. Her body began to feel like one long ache, from head to toe. She wanted nothing more than to be stretched out—have each part of her skin manipulated, wrung out, smoothed down, and, likewise, folded up, curled into a fetal position, so that no edges would be vulnerably sticking out. Her mind sprang impishly about, darting into strange, incoherent territories, while her body labored after it, begging it silently to slow down, stop.

Ray massaged her, and she relaxed until his hands left her skin; then she found herself willfully tensing her muscles again. Hot tea, warm milk—all the magic potions from childhood—brought little relief. Melanie found it difficult, once she had finally succumbed to sleep, to rouse herself in the mornings to be on time for Lytton. Some mornings she shut the alarm off without realizing she had done so. Melanie felt certain that her inability to function normally must show. It bothered her when she caught Ray looking at her with worry in his eyes, as if he knew something she was not yet privy to.

She went to the Marina as often as possible. Walking made her feel more substantial, made her think that perhaps she might not disappear after all, especially when she could see her own breath coming in white spurts from her mouth, merging with the rain and mist. The fog lent clarity to her surroundings; the rocks appeared blacker, their jaggedness more pronounced. A bright-colored jacket was startlingly bright, as if it had been pulled directly from a vat of dye. As she stared at the Bay, at the frequently invisible city in the distance, at the occasional boat rocking about in the water, Melanie felt her heart beat, insistent in its reality.

* * * * *

One bright Sunday in February, she and Ray arranged with Marie and Pete to spend the afternoon at Lake Merritt, a short distance from their apartment, and later go to Shakey's for pizza. Upon arrival, they rang the bell several times, but when Pete finally answered, his hair and beard were disheveled, and he was still in pajamas. After hugging him hello, as usual, Melanie asked where Marie was. Pete stared at her and said that the sky was an extraordinary shade of blue, wasn't it? Spring must be around the corner, he said, and then he laughed: spring has sprung, without warning! Before she or Ray could respond, Marie came out of the bedroom, dressed and ready to go, although her eyes looked puffy, as they did when her allergies bothered her. Coming up behind Pete, she asked in a voice she attempted to steady whether he was coming with them. Without turning around or acknowledging her, he smiled enigmatically and addressed the air:

"Would you go with such a woman? With a woman such as that, who is all belly? Who will not permit me to sleep naked because my flesh disturbs her. Who is demanding that I love her face, button face that it is, pale as sand." The words flowed rhythmically, like a poem, and Pete began to chuckle softly to himself, as if pleased at his cleverness.

Marie bowed her head. She said in a small voice that this had been going on all day; she didn't know what was wrong, or how to get him to stop.

"Oh, Pete," she cried, swinging to face him. "Why can't you talk normally to me?" Turning back to Ray and Melanie, she said anxiously, "He hasn't been himself in weeks. He sits up in bed and strips the covers off me, stares at my body in disgust and then leaves. I feel as if he hates the fact that I'm pregnant, but I can't change that now. Oh, what can I do? All he does is talk in these crazy riddles, and for some reason, he's suddenly obsessed with swapping. We've never even discussed anything like that in the time we've been together! I thought he loved me." She glanced warily at Pete, but then, as if even the effort of seeing his foolish grin was too much for her, she lowered her eyes and walked in the direction of the bedroom.

"That's right. Back, back, you whore of Babylon! Take your belly with you. Display it for the commoners." He watched her shut the bedroom door and then brushed his hands together with satisfaction. "Well, let's go. Let's go for the picnic."

She and Ray could only stare dumbfoundedly at him. While they stood there, Pete lurched toward Melanie, making as if to grab her breasts. "My, my dear, what lovely mammaries. May I touch one please?"

As he stumbled blindly against her, Melanie in turn staggered backwards, putting an arm up to shield herself. Swiftly, Ray came between them, and holding Pete by the shoulders, Ray sat him on the sofa and crouched beside it. Melanie felt as if she had been frozen in place and, as in the game Red Light, Green Light, would have to be signaled to move again.

"Hey, what's going on, old man?" Ray asked calmly. "What's all this with Marie? She's your wife, you love her; we all love her. Talk to me. This is Ray, your buddy."

Gripping Pete hard, he tried to look into his eyes. When Pete fumbled for the remains of a joint in the ashtray, Ray removed it gently from his fingers. "No, I think we've had enough of that. Talk to me instead."

Pete sat, staring mutely at the floor, but finally, mumbling something Melanie could not hear, he got up and started toward the bedroom door. Marie, as if on cue, came out, dressed now in a terry-cloth bathrobe. Parting it slightly, she offered her body to Pete, crying.

"Here, here's your whore. Here, I'll do anything you want," she said in an exhausted voice, "only please, please, Pete, don't speak to me like that again. We're not strangers! We've been married six years. Please!"

Marie broke into fresh weeping, clutching her robe ineffectually against herself, until Ray walked over and put his arms around her. He pressed her protectively against him, while Pete remained in the middle of the floor, his hands dangling at his sides. Ray guided her to the sofa, and Melanie and he sat on either side of her. Hiccupping, Marie held their hands tightly, giggling nervously now and again in her embarrassment that they should see her in such a bad state. Melanie sat stroking Marie's arm but found herself unable to offer any words of comfort.

"He's been like this for weeks—ever since our last visit to his mother's," Marie whispered, trembling. "His mother's always been impossible. She upsets him anyway, going around as she does . . . smoking constantly, wearing this martyr-like expression on her face . . . She dresses all in black, as if she's permanently in mourning . . ." Marie let out a sigh. "There's a tradition that the whole family has Sunday dinner together at least once a month, all the brothers and sisters. Apart from that, everyone visits as seldom as possible. And she never leaves the house; she hardly goes anywhere. She's never been here, for example; she says 'It's 'too great an effort. You don't *really* want me to make that effort, do you?' I'm not sure why I'm telling you all this," Marie said, flushing, "but I think it might explain what's happening. Lately, all his mother talks about is how she is not certain she will make a good grandmother. She's not certain," and here Marie again imitated her voice, "she 'can withstand the excitement.' Well, on this occasion, Pete was strangely silent, and when we made love that night he was remote. He acted as if I were another woman, as if I didn't have the right to be in our bed." She shut her eyes tightly. "I don't know if it's about the baby coming. I kept hoping he would snap out of it, but he just sits and smokes dope . . . I thought of hiding it, to tell you the truth, since it seemed to make things worse. He's begun cutting work; he talks maniacally about the baby one minute, then denies he's the father the next; he tells me . . . he tells me I put him up to this."

She choked, and they pulled her close. "I'm sorry. I'm just so worried. He rambles on and on about wanting to get close to the universe. He asked me the other night if we—the four of us—could all make love to each other and was angry when I said he was frightening me, that I wouldn't feel right, that if we did, it could ruin our marriage."

Marie's freckles stood out distinctly on her face, damp with tears. Her hair hung limply, and the ends were matted. Ray glanced at Pete, who was hunched over on the dining-room table, his head buried in his arms.

"Phew! What a mindblower!" Ray said. "He must be flipped out about becoming a father or something." He squeezed her hand tightly. "I

think you should call the hospital. You can't handle this alone, Marie."
Marie looked at Melanie for confirmation, and Melanie nodded numbly
in agreement. Marie pressed her fingers against her face.

"Oh, I'm sorry!" she said. "I know I'm upsetting both of you. But
what if he's really going crazy? What if I have to have this baby all by
myself? Pete's never acted like this before. He gets silly and spacey at times,
but even when his mother gets on his nerves, he's never this peculiar."

It was the first time Melanie had ever seen Marie cry. Marie usually appeared calmer than the average person, more good-humored, seldom moody, not even before her period. Her even temper had irritated
Melanie at times because she herself was so prone to mood swings. Marie
and Pete never argued; they always acted placid, lovey-dovey, easygoing.
Pete's favorite expression was "What? Me worry?" after Alfred E.
Neumann in *Mad Magazine*.

They held Marie for a long time. Finally, Ray rose and put a record
of flute music on the stereo, thinking it might have a soothing effect; then
he went into the kitchen and, under Marie's direction, made a pot of
chamomile tea. He brought Marie a cup, along with some toast, and, afterwards, tucked her in bed, because she told them she had barely slept the
night before. Ray closed the bedroom door and walked purposefully over
to Pete, who had remained in the same position. Pete would not lift his head
from the table. Instead, he mumbled that he loved them all and wished they
could understand what he was seeing; it was so profound. He was having
an ego death, he explained, which permitted him to see things in cosmic
terms. Addressing Melanie, he said in a contrite voice, "I don't want to hurt
you. I had no intention of hurting you. You're a child of the universe, a
daughter of the universe. God loves you, and I love you."

"I know, Pete," she responded, shrugging helplessly.

Ray dropped his hand from Pete's shoulder. "We know you don't
mean us any harm, old buddy, but listen, there's a problem here, and we'd
like to help if we can. Maybe you should lay off the dope awhile." When
he got no further response from Pete, he signaled to Melanie that they
should probably go. As they gathered their things, Pete made no move to
stop them, so they left, shutting the door quietly behind them.

Ray drove aimlessly into the Oakland hills. He reached the upper-
most street and pulled into a spot showing a panorama of the Bay.
Melanie slid over to him and laid her head against his chest, listening to
the erratic pounding of his heart. Marie's anguished face kept appearing
before her, and she shut her eyes tightly, trying to erase the painful image.
Ray held her and told her not to worry, that everything would be okay,

but Melanie muttered it was difficult to believe that anything would ever be the same again. She berated herself for not being any comfort at all; it was as if she had been turned to stone. Maybe they shouldn't have left them together; maybe something worse would happen if they weren't there. What if Pete hit her because he didn't want the baby? What if he damaged the fetus? They were both such normal people; none of it made sense. How could something like this even happen? After a while, Ray covered her mouth gently with his hand, saying that she was working herself into a frenzy. He would give Marie a call later. If things got worse, they could contact Pete's brother, Al, who lived a few towns away in Walnut Creek. Everything would turn out okay. Melanie clung tightly to his chest, comforted by the reassurance in his voice, by the security of his arm around her shoulder. Mist from the Bay began to seep into the hills. It surrounded their car, until it was difficult to discern the view of San Francisco or even the nearby trees and shrubbery. The sky darkened. Finally, Ray shook himself, as if he had been in a trance, and, starting the engine, drove home.

* * * * *

Pete stopped going to work; he slept half the day. He walked around the apartment naked and, sometimes, opened the front door like that. When Marie began calling in sick at her own job because she was afraid to leave him by himself, Ray took the situation into his own hands and drove the two of them to the crisis center at the local hospital.

Afterwards, back at the Rosaline Apartments, Marie wept as she described Pete's admission. She had answered a slew of questions about his family history, questions about whether he had done or did do drugs (was it so obvious? she wondered), which she had been afraid to answer honestly, questions about their marriage and her pregnancy. At this last question, she had burst into tears. Pete had been calm during the entire procedure, seemingly oblivious to his surroundings, but in the end the doctor decided to put him on medication and keep him in the hospital for observation.

"I had such intense abdominal cramps, I was convinced I would suddenly miscarry," Marie said in a shaky voice. "I felt so frustrated with Pete's lack of concern, I just wanted to desert him. I mean, he's the one who's been acting crazy. Why should I have to answer all those personal questions? I'm not inside his head; I can't read his thoughts or explain why he's acting as he is!"

Marie kept smoothing her hands over her abdomen; intermittently, she took gulping sips of the burgundy they had poured for her. Melanie was stunned. Why had Pete let everything fall to pieces? The bank, which he had remained with for five years, although he often complained of how much he hated it—his marriage, perhaps his sanity?

It had been easy, because they were a continent apart, to put her mother and the schizophrenic behavior she had witnessed throughout her childhood out of her mind. Melanie seldom wrote to or heard from her mother. She was an adult now, the past was the past; why should it interfere with the present? However, as she listened to Marie describe Pete's actions, memories rose inexorably to the surface. She saw similarities between her mother and Pete: inappropriate laughter, seeing metaphors where there weren't any, disjointed thoughts, and obsessive, repetitive behavior. Thinking about this, she understood Pete's actions over the past months better: his giggles, his constant punning, his seeming detachment. Melanie remembered her mother methodically pulling all the electric cords in her grandmother's apartment from their sockets; and she recalled, also, her mother's terrible fear of medication, her anxiety about doctors and hospitals. She wondered if Pete was as overwhelmed by ordinary, regular life as her own mother had been. Melanie believed her mother had chosen to be different from other mothers, had wanted to be crazy to escape life's responsibilities, had not wanted to be well. It was never entirely safe to be in her presence, and Melanie had avoided her whenever she could.

Because of these disturbing thoughts, it took Melanie a week to gain the courage to visit Pete in the hospital. Although he lay in bed in pajamas, as if he truly was a patient with an illness, he seemed more rational. However, by the end of the visit, Pete avoided her gaze and became restless. Marie, who was sitting in a chair by the window, gathered up her knitting and came to sit beside him on the bed. She stroked his arm as she held it. Taking this as a signal that she should leave, Melanie rose and, hugging Pete quickly, said goodbye.

When she stepped outside, although the day was suspiciously gray, as if it might rain, Melanie felt delivered from death. Darkness and pain were wadded together in a ball upstairs in the ward she had just left, while outside was space, light, freedom. The moans and cries of the other patients she had heard as she passed along the corridor of the ward reverberated in her head. Melanie fought to rid herself of the image of Pete sitting unnaturally upright as she left, resembling an Indian chieftain.

Melanie walked slowly down the long blocks of University Avenue. She passed the cleaners, the co-op, the Chinese restaurant where they bought take-out food, the library, the Taco Bell, and finally the Canned Foods store half a block from their building. She was disappointed to find the apartment dark and empty, to not see Ray; he had not mentioned he was going anywhere. Staring at the unmade bed and the previous night's dinner dishes, along with the breakfast ones, stacked by the sink, Melanie thought guiltily of Marie and the Florence Nightingale behavior she had just witnessed. She threw the covers off the bed and smoothed the wrinkles in the sheet, arranged the blanket evenly on all sides, tucked in the corners, fluffed up the pillows.

Energized by this activity, she filled the sink with hot, soapy water, pleased with the way the shiny dish liquid clung to her hands, creating rainbows as she scrubbed. Each dish sparkled after she had rinsed it and stacked it on the drain board. After wiping the table and sweeping the floor, she adjusted the coleus Giselle had given her as a farewell present when she and Mark had headed for Portland, Oregon. It now framed their own window sill, and lent a splash of color and design to their plain beige-colored kitchen. Melanie felt pleased to be doing something concrete, to concentrate only on the physical world, to put the hospital out of her mind, however briefly.

She stretched out on the rug to do the yoga exercises she had been teaching herself in an attempt to improve her posture, which was poor because of her habit of keeping her eyes fixed on the ground when she walked, and because she was so often leaning over a book, immersed in reading. Through the thin rug, the hard floor touched the rope of her spine inch by inch. Leaning her neck backwards in the position of the cobra, raising herself higher and higher, she gradually lowered her head again until it rested on the floor, while she kept her hands limp at her sides. She rearranged her limbs and tucked herself into a half-lotus position, making a conscious effort to keep her back straight, her palms relaxed on her thighs, and her breath steady. While Melanie was concentrating on her deep breathing, Ray came in and knelt by her side. Her face was flushed and her hair, falling in thick waves over her shoulders, was damp from her efforts. Ray surveyed the room and grinned.

"Well, somebody's been a busy little beaver. Did you visit Pete like you planned to?" He placed his hands on top of hers, which lay face-up on her thighs, and she nodded, feeling the heat from his fingers seep into her own.

"I didn't start dinner," she said, pausing. "I didn't know where you were, and I wasn't sure when you'd get back."

"Oh . . . I ran into Vic—you remember the guy we met Saturday on campus. We played some riffs and shot the bull for a while." He stroked her hands lightly. "Wanna go for Mexican food?"

Melanie sensed that Ray had told her a lie, and she felt pain begin to swell inside her chest. To avoid the sensation, she found herself talking rapidly, uncontrollably.

"Pete's eyes were kind of glazed, but he seemed more like himself, I guess. Marie was as attentive as ever. She saw what he needed even before he asked for something—brought him water, straightened the pillows behind his head, you know. When he grew restless, she sat by him . . ." The pain in her chest expanded, turned to a firm lump the size of a snowball, and she found it difficult to breathe. She stood up slowly and massaged her chest to ease it. "Sure, let's get out of here. I need some fresh air, maybe from seeing Pete in that place. It was scary, Ray. His ward reminded me of places my mother had been—the nurses, the patient's faces—although I tried not to look at them too closely . . ."

The joy she had felt straightening the apartment had dissipated. Ray was changing his clothes, and as Melanie watched him, she felt like crying. She didn't want to go out for dinner. The thought of a plateful of enchiladas, rice, and beans, something that she usually enjoyed, made her feel nauseous. Melanie wanted to ask Ray if he had been with another woman, but she knew that if he had he would probably tell her she was being foolish and reassure her that he loved her, which—since she wouldn't believe it—would only make matters worse.

When they were going out the door, Ray put his arm around her shoulder.

"Don't let Pete's situation bother you, Mel. I'm sure the old guy will pull it together. They'll find out what's wrong and fix it, babe."

Melanie did not reply, so Ray turned her to face him, pressing her body between his own and the hallway wall. "Okay, what's wrong? Fess up. I know you didn't really want to go, that hospitals scare you. Are you mad because I wasn't home? Is that it, Mel?"

His dark, penetrating eyes boring into her own made Melanie shiver. What could she say? She knew what he was like. He had told her shortly after they met that he was irresistibly drawn to women, to—as he put it—the female sex. That it had nothing to do with her, that she was nearly perfect as far as women went.

Melanie smiled at him weakly, ashamed of her thoughts, her lack of trust. She slithered free and took his hand.

"There's nothing the matter. I'm just hungry, I guess. It's been a while since I've done so much housework."

* * * *

The following Friday evening, Ray told Melanie he felt like going over to Vic's to see if anyone was around to jam with. She was tired after a long week at Lytton, so she opted to remain at home. But at midnight, worried that he had not returned and getting no answer at Vic's number, she curled up in the rocker with a blanket and her book, intending to wait up for him. A draft of cold air from the French doors being opened woke her. Sleepily, she watched Ray tiptoe in, remove his clothes, and climb beneath the covers. Soon, she got in beside him, but although Ray opened his eyes and smiled faintly at her, he flipped on his side, away from her, muttering that he was exhausted. Sensing suddenly that he had not been at Vic's, Melanie slid out of bed and sat on the edge of the mattress. She swung one leg back and forth until Ray turned toward her again.

"What's the matter, Mellie? Can't you sleep?"

"I could say the same," she said in a constricted voice. "Why did you come in so quietly, Ray?"

"I saw you were asleep, and I didn't want to wake you, that's all." Ray tucked his arm around the pillow and prepared to roll over.

"No, you didn't *not* want to wake me. You wanted to be quiet so I wouldn't hear you come in. At least be straight with me. Please, Ray, I don't want to be your jailor but were you really at Vic's?"

Ray flipped the pillow up against the wall behind him and lay back against it.

"Well, I guess you don't want either of us to get any sleep tonight. I told you I was going to Vic's. We jammed; a bunch of other musicians came; we drank some beers. You forget time, you know how it is. It was going great, and I didn't feel like leaving." He closed his eyes. "I was having fun."

Melanie bit her lip, wanting to believe him, but a slight breathlessness in his tone made her feel uncomfortable. "Really and truly, Ray?" she asked.

He did not answer. His lashes fluttered rapidly.

"You're lying to me, aren't you?"

Ray remained silent and Melanie covered her eyes with her hands. She felt him touch her shoulder hesitantly.

"Right as usual, Miss Perceptivity. I wasn't at Vic's. Well, I was, but just for a while. Damn it, are you fucking psychic, Melanie? Is it so obvious?"

"Sneaking into bed seems pretty obvious to me," she muttered.

"Were you with *her?* You know, that woman we picked up hitchhiking—old Miss Fuzzy Sweater, Miss Goddamn Pussycat?"

Ray shifted and turned on the bedside lamp.

"Yes. I didn't plan to when I left, but I just had this sudden impulse. I tried to stop myself at her apartment door. At first, I couldn't make myself ring the bell, but then, as if she knew I was there, she opened the door and invited me in. I don't know. I *was* at Vic's; we were getting drunk and bullshitting about the different women we all had known, and then I just wanted her. It's got nothing to do with you, Melanie. Maybe men are different from women that way. Mona gives off this . . . I don't know, as if she really needs and wants it. To a guy, that's really challenging. He wants to be the one to satisfy her. I don't know; maybe it's a power trip or something. Male ego." Ray lit a cigarette and looked at her furtively.

"It's not you, Melanie, honest. Sex with you is great; it's always been great, you know that. I don't feel anything for Mona. It was just a lay. I'm sorry you even found out. I thought you'd be asleep, that you'd never know. Oh, fuck it! I just got possessed or something. Please, babe, look at me. Don't be like this." He reached for her hand, but Melanie sat, unresponsive.

Her face felt hot and moist within her hands. As she listened to the anxiety, the justification in Ray's voice along with his attempts to reassure her of his love, Melanie felt confused. She thought of Mona in her tight sweater and skirt, remembered her sighs and moans. What could she say? She felt as if a boulder had been dropped on her chest, and she could not budge it to rid herself of the weight. Maybe it was true, maybe it *was* better if she didn't know what Ray did. She felt angry that she had been consistently faithful to him when at times she too had wanted to allow herself the pleasure of a moment. Why had she bothered? Should she have? What could this woman possibly think of her, this woman he had wanted her to get to know? That she was a failure in bed?

Melanie rose and picking up a throw pillow from the love seat, she propped it against the corner of the window seat. Although the golden-colored light from the street lamp lit the top of the hedges outside their window, the greenery beneath was dark. The night was quiet, except for the murmur of an occasional car going by on the avenue. The curtains looked gray and filmy, and as Melanie grasped the starchy material between her fingers, she realized they were badly in need of washing. She felt numb, only distantly aware of Ray, who had remained in bed. She thought back to the other times, to the other women he had slept with in the brief time they had been together. The other women she knew of anyway. Three other women, and one he had wanted but she didn't think he had ever gotten. That had been the girlfriend of a man who had picked them up when they were hitchhiking.

She and Ray had stayed with the couple for a few days, and Melanie had been impressed that they both seemed truly happy with their lives. The woman was a reporter, and the man was heavily involved in leftist politics. Ray had admitted to her that he wanted the woman. Then, Melanie had felt good that he could be so honest with her, that he didn't treat her like other women but more as a friend. Now she didn't know if that was what she wanted. It hurt too much to hear these details; hearing them made her feel deficient. Why did she always have to be so understanding? It wasn't fair.

When she met Ray, her life had been at a standstill, which was why it had been so wonderful to take off and travel with him. His suggestion had given her a momentary sense of purpose; there had been no need to think of the future. The moment was all that mattered—waking each day and being alive. Because after you left high school, then what was supposed to happen? Maybe some people, most people, found a ready slot to slip into: a job, college, marriage, children, but she had never wanted her life to be like that—so decided and ordinary. Sure, like most people, Melanie had vague goals: college, a career—although she would not have described it as such—as a poet, marriage conceivably; children maybe . . . being a mother tied you down, but who knew? When high school ended, Melanie took a few classes at CCNY, at Mark's suggestion, but she left, dissatisfied with academic learning. She had always been more interested in what the world itself could teach her.

Melanie glanced at Ray and realized he had fallen asleep. As she listened to the regularity of his breathing, she felt oddly at peace. He *was* there, after all, in her bed. There was no one else she could turn to if she was in trouble, no one else she could depend upon. Her relatives had been there at crucial moments when she was younger, when it had become clear that her mother and father could not take care of her, but now her grandmother was dead. The apartment had been rented to someone else. An uncle, her mother's brother, had a place too small to accommodate her and was frequently admitted to the hospital for his health. Her parents now lived on disability and could only afford a single room in a boarding house in New Jersey. So what did she have? Herself and Ray. If she wanted something different, she would have to go back out again—alone. Now that she had been with Ray for close to a year and had grown accustomed to his steady presence, such aloneness and its potential loneliness frightened her.

So what was the point of fighting with him about Mona, or any other woman he had screwed? Melanie knew in her heart that was all his escapades amounted to, that it was only her insecurity that made her feel jealous. Ray was essentially faithful; he had been good to her, would continue to be good to her. Did it matter if someone spread her legs, and Ray entered them? Did it matter? Melanie had never bought into the idea of conventional morality. What had he shared with that woman? A moment of desire. She understood desire; she felt it as well as he. When Pete had made a pass at her in front of Marie, Marie had not deserted Pete, although it must have hurt her. Maybe she could see Ray's screwing Mona as a single lousy moment in time.

Melanie sighed and let the section of curtain she held fall from her fingers. She thought of lighting a cigarette and then changed her mind. She felt drowsy. Maybe she would go to bed, too. At least she hadn't trembled. The apartment felt still and safe; it was good to just sit staring absently at the warm yellow light on the top of the hedge, at its shadows making slashes across her legs. She continued to sit, thinking idle thoughts that—although they trailed off in all directions—were coherent. She finally rose and slipped quietly into bed, luxuriating in the coolness of the pillow against her face and the contrasting warmth of the bedspread as she pulled it up around her body. Ray's arm was flung across her pillow; as she lay back, his hand curled unconsciously around her neck, caressing it. She let it lie there, savoring the tautness of his bones beneath the warm skin. Gradually, she drifted into sleep, feeling as if she were sinking into a dense field of golden wheat.

When she woke the next morning, Melanie felt rested, as if something important had been resolved in her sleep. She cuddled against Ray in a playful manner. She ran her fingers across his back and nuzzled him with her nose and lips until he woke fully. Pulling him against her, she kissed his face and neck and then began to move her body against his. As they rolled over and over on the bed, Melanie was all smiles, the way she had been when they first met. She giggled as he, in turn, nuzzled her neck and breasts, raining her with quick kisses. Melanie felt as if she were being lifted upwards, ascending to a region of intense joy. She grinned uncontrollably at the ceiling, at the walls, until Ray pressed her to his shoulder and, sated, they fell asleep. The morning light swept over them in benediction; when they woke much later, the previous night might never have happened.

Was that the moment she conceived? She would never know. Her birth control pills had run out two months earlier. Melanie had meant to renew them, have an exam, get a new supply, but the weeks had gone by, and she had forgotten. Because they lived together as comfortably as a married couple, considerations such as these had not seemed that important.

 *Five*

By the end of March, Pete had been released from the hospital. Several days after his release, he quit his job at Wells Fargo Bank and obtained a position as a clerk in a hardware store near their apartment. Informing Ray of the change, he said he "immediately felt more useful." To Melanie—when she and Ray visited them two nights later—Pete seemed more like the jovial person she had come to know. He exuded, as well, a new attitude of inner satisfaction. Because this change was so dramatic, she wondered if his breakdown had been beneficial after all.

Her own nervous spells continued; at least one or two evenings during the week she could count on them descending upon her. After an hour at Pete and Marie's, the place she had previously believed contained a magic circle that would protect her from evil, Melanie found herself becoming edgy. When her legs began to quiver, she rose quickly from the couch and went to the bathroom. Certain that her nervousness must show, she studied herself in the bathroom mirror. Her face did look unnaturally red; her eyes were murky-looking and darker green, showing strange, unfamiliar depths. It frightened her to stare at her own eyes. Would they suddenly reveal the insanity she had feared she would inherit from her mother? She opened the door to the medicine cabinet and noticed a bottle of prescription medicine. After reading the label, which said something about "for anxiety," Melanie removed two and squeezed them into the pocket of her jeans before returning to the living room.

"Marie, have you or Pete ever experienced insomnia?" she asked during a pause in the conversation. "Know any good remedies?" Pete said his phenobarb would probably do the trick. He looked toward Marie, and she hesitated.

"Wait here, Mel," she said after a few minutes. "Phenobarb's pretty strong stuff, but I don't think it will hurt you to take a few of them. It's probably preferable to getting no sleep. They're barbiturates. Does that bother you?" Melanie shrugged purposefully. "The doctor prescribed them as a precaution, in case Pete's anxiety returns."

Although she felt guilty about deceiving Marie, Melanie simultaneously felt a deep sense of relief. If she didn't sleep properly soon, she thought she might go insane. Leaning back against the sofa and taking a sip of her lukewarm tea, she told herself the solution was temporary. The phenobarb could not be *much* stronger than aspirin or Marie would never let her take it. As if confirming her decision, that night Melanie slept soundly and woke refreshed.

The following week, besides working more efficiently at school, Melanie felt less nervous. She thought eagerly of the weekend ahead, when the four of them planned to go to a garden show held at Lake Merritt. Later, back at their apartment, she was certain Marie would give her a few more pills. Maybe life was returning to normal: Marie had not miscarried, Pete seemed happy again about the pregnancy, and Melanie did not think Ray had gone to see Mona after his initial temptation. It was nearly spring. The sunny days she had experienced upon her arrival in California would soon be the norm again. Then one Sunday afternoon, Ray brought home Mel.

"Hey, Mel, this is Mel," he said, laughing as he pushed open the French doors abruptly. Melanie's immediate impression was of a frizzy head of hair and an accompanying scraggly-looking beard. She extended her hand and Mel shook it, while he stared warmly at her. Their eyes remained locked, and when the smile on his lips spread to his eyes, Melanie felt a sudden tremor. In turn, her own smile widened.

She had been recuperating from the flu and at first was annoyed that Ray had brought company home. However, when Ray began playing his usual raga-like tunes, and Mel joined in confidently on the flute he had been carrying when he entered, Melanie felt suddenly exhilarated. So easily did they follow each other's cues it sounded as if they had been playing together for months. When they took a break, Melanie handed them each a bottle of Coors and opened one for herself. Mel told them he had come to the Bay Area only two days earlier. That morning, as he walked around campus to familiarize himself, by chance he had heard Ray playing his guitar. Impulsively, he had begun to accompany him; the rest was history.

"I hope you appreciate how talented your old man is," Mel said, grinning at Melanie.

"I know," she said. She continued to gaze at Mel's baby face and innocent-looking blue-green eyes and then began to laugh. "You look like you just stepped out of a painting by Rubens."

"Oh God, it happens every time," Mel replied making a wry gesture. "You're hardly the first person to point that out. People find it difficult to take me seriously. My wife for one."

"Oh, no. It's cute. I mean, I think it's neat," Melanie said, blushing.

Mel made a mock bow before he gazed skyward, as if appealing to heaven to transform him. "Well, as long as you think it's cute, it's okay then." He picked up his flute again and played a classical melody, gazing tenderly at Melanie as he played. His lips were red and full, and she felt a sudden desire to kiss them. Blushing, Melanie shifted her gaze but not before she caught his understanding recognition of her desire.

They ate dinner at the Chinese restaurant on University Avenue where they usually ordered carry-out and, after discussing at preposterous length the truth or falsity of their individual fortunes, returned to the apartment. They discovered Mel enjoyed traveling, too. He had just returned from Europe, where he had been for six months. He had wandered from country to country, supporting himself by playing his flute, which his parents had worried he would be unable to do.

"Maybe my luck would have run out if I'd stayed longer. For the most part though, people welcomed me with open arms. Being an American gave me a certain mystique, I guess. Hard to believe because of the reputation of the ugly American. Actually, my parents have been very supportive, especially considering the changes I'm always putting them through."

Mel set his flute down on the window seat. "I come from this upper-class Jewish family near Burbank," Mel said, "and first I don't take a regular job, and then I go ahead and marry a *shiksa!* After that, I guess they figured what are they gonna do with me? But my younger brother plays the violin with the symphony, and he's pretty straight. I guess they're proud to have two musical sons, even if only one of them remains in the fold."

Ray and Melanie gave Mel an abbreviated version of their own lives: how they met in Manhattan and their subsequent return to California. Ray told Mel that before leaving for New York, he'd tried to play the L.A. clubs but found it difficult to connect with the energy there. "Maybe we can locate some gigs in Berkeley," Mel said. "Our sound is really in sync."

As they talked further, Mel confessed that the main reason he had come to Berkeley—besides to connect with other musicians—was because his wife, Joan, had left him for his best friend.

"That's why I split for Europe, actually. I just had to clear out altogether. But as exciting and different as it was abroad, I found it difficult to stay away from home. California has this way of calling me back. The U.S. is in my blood, for better or for worse, I guess. Besides," Mel said more softly, with such a forlorn tone that Melanie felt an urge to gather him to her breast, "getting away didn't do much for my broken heart. It kind of goes along with you, if you know what I mean."

They talked all night. At dawn, Mel curled up to sleep on the couch.

When Melanie woke up late in the afternoon, she realized she had not thought once about taking a tablet of phenobarbital. Mel agreed to meet them the following day after they returned from Lytton and his coming became a pattern three, four afternoons a week. Even when Mel did not come, Melanie knew Ray was thinking about him. Mel slept on the couch if it grew too late eventually, although he was ostensibly renting a room in North Oakland near Marie and Pete's apartment. Although he considered himself a street musician as Ray did, Mel had been classically trained in the flute. He owned stacks of sheet music and carried a folder of them everywhere he went so, in free moments, he could practice playing scales.

For dinner they either bought carry-out—with all of them splitting the cost—or Mel ate whatever they had available, whether that was peanut butter and jelly sandwiches or fixings for a more elaborate meal. Garbed in one of the two white, long-sleeved shirts he owned and a pair of khaki pants, Mel looked as if he was dressed to go to a regular office job, although his shirt was never quite tucked in, and his fingernails usually needed trimming. When he and Ray went somewhere alone, she felt as though Ray was being chaperoned. She knew they would either be playing music or trying to arrange a weekend gig at one of the smaller clubs in the area. They played frequently on campus, and when they returned, their pockets rung with change. Melanie thought Ray looked happier than he had in months.

When she and Ray held hands, or if she curled sleepily against Ray's shoulder late in the evening, Mel would smile and nod at them in a fatherly way, as if he were giving them his blessing. If the subject of Joan and his marriage came up, as it did in most of their conversations, Mel's eyes shimmered with tears. Melanie yearned to comfort him. Sometimes, she felt an overwhelming desire to untangle his thick, brown curls, as he had told them Joan did whenever she grew particularly exasperated with his unkempt appearance. Afraid to touch him because of her growing feelings, however, Melanie sat as far from him as she thought safe, and Mel did the same.

* * * * *

One late spring afternoon, Melanie sat in the rocker. She was trying to decide which library book she wanted to read first from the stack on the floor beside her, when she heard the French doors rattle. Ray had left early that morning to help Bea move into a new apartment. Getting up, Melanie peered through the thin curtains that shaded the panes of glass and then opened the door quickly when she saw that it was Mel. They had not seen him for several days because he had gone to L.A. to visit his parents.

Mel entered and hugged her perfunctorily but did not return her welcoming smile. Instead, to her surprise, he sighed deeply. He had never before so seemed like a lost little boy.

"Ray's helping this woman from Lytton move, but he should be back pretty soon," she said. "Wanna wait?"

"Yeah. I think I've walked about all I can walk today," he said, taking a seat. "Have you got a beer, Melanie? I could sure use one."

"Sorry, no beer, only soda. Are you hungry?" She hesitated, as he seemed not to hear her, and then went to the kitchen and poured them each a glass of Pepsi. "You look kind of down Mel," she called to him. "Did you have a bad visit at home?"

Melanie handed him the cold glass. Mel took it but sighed again so heavily, Melanie thought his soul would pass out of his body along with his breath.

"Frankly, I'm a little unhinged," he said. "Joan called today after I got back, and she's really distraught. We talked for over an hour. She begged me to give her another chance. Evidently, Marshall's split, and she's cracking up at home . . . she's back with her parents, you know, which is a truly miserable scene. I'm so confused, Melanie. I mean, I still love her, but I can't go through those changes again."

Mel raised his head and looked her full in the face. His green eyes, changeable and sparkling as the sea, stared pleadingly into hers, and she instinctively touched his cheek to comfort him. She stroked his beard thoughtfully for a few minutes, and then he quietly took her hand and covered it with his own. They had never looked at each other so intently. Melanie could barely breathe; she felt as if she were drowning, but, gradually, she slid her hand away. Though they were as separated as if a fence had sprung up between them, Melanie knew that if she moved slightly, they would make a rush for each other's arms. Holding herself rigid to prevent this from happening, she watched the pain in Mel's eyes deepen. She heard his breath coming raggedly. Mel had told her that he loved Ray as a brother; and she herself had no desire to hurt Ray or Joan, despite being drawn so powerfully to Mel. Mel grinned a little wryly and started to speak but stopped. Shakily, Melanie turned slowly out of his reach. Although they had not embraced, she felt as if something irrevocable had occurred. A strand of warmth and desire encircled their bodies, desire for unity beyond the kindling sexuality, a unity they sensed would be possible with one another.

Mel took a sip from his glass and then in a trembling voice told her about his conversation with Joan. Yet even as she listened sympathetically, Melanie was utterly conscious of Mel's presence and knew he was of hers. She understood his love for Joan, knew how betrayed and confused he felt, yet it did not negate what was happening between them. Finally, as if he could bear the tension no longer, Mel stumbled in a disoriented fashion toward the French doors. Impulsively, Melanie rushed to him and, after touching his soft cheek again, bent toward him and lightly kissed it. He reddened as she slowly withdrew and, smiling, moved his hand to where her mouth had been. They gazed at each other for several long minutes before Mel looked down and placed his hand firmly on the glass doorknob.

"Hey . . . I'll catch you guys later, okay?"

Grinning foolishly, Melanie nodded.

The outside door slammed, and she listened to Mel's retreating footsteps as he went down the walkway. She returned to the rocker and closed her eyes to relive the experience. She recalled the way Mel's lips had trembled when she caressed his face and wished, now that the moment was gone, she had held him close to her body as she had so wanted to do. Melanie pressed her fingers against the rough padded material, kissing Mel repeatedly in her imagination, then wrapped her arms around her body in an attempt to contain her joy.

* * * * *

Focused on these new feelings for Mel, Melanie was scarcely aware of her body, except for the thoughts and daydreams it allowed her to contain. She still had moments of trembling that resembled the jittery lights of a migraine aura. On the nights when Mel did not stay at the apartment, she took the phenobarbital as a matter of course, like a daily vitamin. Each time they visited Marie and Pete, she secretly took a few more pills from Pete's bottle, ashamed to admit openly that the problem was continuing, hoping he would be unaware of the loss. Having the phenobarbital on hand gave her the comfort of knowing that if other remedies—such as the spoonful of molasses in warm milk that Mel recommended—failed, the pill could be counted upon to grant oblivion. However, having Mel's additional presence seemed a safeguard: whatever was attempting to do her in would have to fight doubly hard.

In addition, the mutual—if unspoken and unfulfilled—understanding she had with Mel produced in her a tension that overrode her previous fear. Melanie worried that her feelings showed, that she was acting like a classic person in love. Yet Ray only expressed relief when he noticed her silly grins and manic energy. He told her whatever the reason for the change, he was glad she was happier. If she caught Mel's eye, she knew he understood her behavior perfectly. Sometimes, in consequence, he and she went on laughing jags that had Ray convinced they were smoking dope together on the sly.

Normally, Ray thought about music. He restlessly drummed on the table with his hands, or on her back at night, and picked out chords or rhythms at every opportunity away from Lytton, apart from his daily sessions with Mel. Therefore, Melanie felt free to indulge in her new sensations, without fear of discovery. She had no idea where her feelings would finally take her but found it difficult to feel guilty about them. When Mel smiled at her tenderly, he made her feel beautiful and appreciated, much as Mark had at times when he had praised her observations or the curves of her body. Melanie's thoughts became fixated on their daily contact: Would he come? When would he come? How long would he stay? What would they talk about? Would an opportunity arise for them to touch? Other aspects of her life melted into the background—Lytton, poetry, even Ray. Some nights she woke deliberately so she could gaze at him asleep on the love seat. As she drank in the picture of his closed eyes and a way he had of curling his hands up close to his face, as if to protect himself, a deep sense of peacefulness washed over her.

Her feelings toward Mel, though intense, seemed unrooted in reality or in a different kind of reality. They were more akin to what she had felt at the reservoir looking at nature, composed as they were of such moments as watching him sleep or play the flute. His essence seemed connected to hers in an inexplicable fashion; when they had met she had intuitively recognized this. It was so different with Ray who had overwhelmed her, had literally yanked her into their relationship by the power and need of his personality. Mel drew her to him subtly. Melanie flowed toward him easily and willingly, as she did toward nature, music, literature, anything she found beautiful and meaningful. Their contact was sure, right, oddly innocent.

But because she was so wrapped up in these sensations, Melanie was slow to observe differences in her body, although when her manic energy momentarily ceased, she experienced fatigue unlike any she had ever known. She assumed at first that it was caused by taking the phenobarbital so regularly. Other people she knew who took sleeping pills were often groggy the morning after. She stopped the pills for several nights, but the drowsiness persisted, until she found herself falling asleep as early as seven o'clock in the evening. Although happy to finally feel sleepy, she realized such sleepiness was unnatural; when she began to feel queasy in the morning and dizzy every afternoon before dinner, Melanie grew seriously concerned. Upon reflection, she realized it had been a long while since her last period. Confirmation of her worst fears came when she went with Ray to the health clinic on University Avenue to take a pregnancy test.

In the examining room, the doctor informed her that she was nearly ten weeks. The terrible glare from the fluorescent lighting and the pain from the doctor's exploration made Melanie feel faint. It wasn't real to have a baby, to have a baby come out of her. To have a life inside her, already moving, changing from moment to moment. Melanie bent her head over her knees to prevent herself from passing out. She touched her abdomen tentatively, as if it were a new attachment to her body.

When she told Ray, she could not clearly read his response. His distracted look turned—it appeared quickly—to an excited smile, but was he truly happy? How could they afford to have a baby? What about their Lytton training and his and Mel's music, which was progressing so beautifully? She was only twenty years old! If she had Ray's baby, she would be entwined with him forever. What about Mel, and her growing feelings for him? What about being a poet? What about further travel and being independent? Now she would have to stay where she was, wouldn't she? Just when she was beginning to question whether she should remain with Ray at all. Did she have a choice if she was carrying his child? Like swarms of gnats, the questions amassed in her mind.

As they walked together down the steps of the building and then onto the busy avenue, Melanie's feelings gradually shifted from numbness and fear to a deepening awareness of her own womanly power and humanity. Ray moved closer to her and enfolded her in his arms. She clutched Ray fiercely, awed by the reality that this was happening—*to her, to them*. He was necessary to her; she had to connect to him, to feel one with him, for the sake of what was developing inside her, what was even then being nourished by her.

 *Six*

*A*lthough they discussed it, neither considered the possibility of aborting the baby, as though to do so was unimaginable. Yet they realized the probability, given their situation, that they might have to go on welfare, at least temporarily. Their business courses would be over in five months, and they decided it would be best to complete them. The knowledge could come in handy in the future. Mrs. Duran encouraged Ray to register for the next level of accounting, but he declined, thinking he would have little chance of actually obtaining a business job because of his record. In prison he had gained some sheet metal experience, so he searched the classifieds to find a position in that field. However, because of having to answer "yes" to the question of whether he had ever been in trouble with the law, he was frequently not offered an interview, let alone employment. He told Melanie that his karma was catching up with him.

However, when talking with the group of musicians he jammed with, Ray heard about a part-time apprentice mechanic's position at a cooperative garage in Berkeley. The job paid little, but he would learn to overhaul engines. The other mechanics were hippies, so Ray's record did not concern them greatly, even though he had been incarcerated for stealing a car. With these shifts, the excitement he and she felt about the pregnancy dissipated a little. They realized they were putting themselves on an inexorable track of enslavement. Melanie told Ray that probably explained Pete's breakdown. With a baby on the way and the moral responsibility that involved, Pete must have seen himself working for years to come at the bank, without any possibility of change.

When they lay together at night, Melanie and Ray were more aware of each other's bodies. Ray would stretch his hand across Melanie's abdomen, feel it rise up and down, feel the softness of her flesh, the harder ridge of her navel. She in turn absorbed the heat from his hands, the hardness of his fingers, felt his callouses as if they were an outer thickness protecting the fragility of his blood. In the darkness, they fantasized together about the baby, imagined it in the room, imagined Mel, Marie and Pete, Norm and Kathleen holding it.

When Ray announced the pregnancy, others too seemed to swell with happiness, as if this was the most important thing that could happen to a couple, this continuation of the generations. Melanie felt as if she had been initiated into a new club; suddenly she belonged, was accepted by the world. Though Bea wished them luck, she added that she hoped they could keep it together. Her words lingered in Melanie's mind, and that evening, she asked Ray if they were crazy, if going through with the pregnancy was a mistake after all, something they should stop before it was too late. Holding her securely in his arms, Ray assured her that everything would work out; they had each other, didn't they? Bea was a single parent; it had to be tougher for her.

Melanie wrote to her mother, and, surprisingly, the announcement was received with joy. Her mother didn't ask any questions suggesting that their plans were foolish. Only: Was she going to breast-feed? Did she have a good doctor? Did they have enough money? For a window of time, her mother left her abstracted state and was related to the real world of babies being conceived. She became a mother instructing, sharing from her own experience, carrying on the age-old wisdom. Melanie treasured the letters she received, read them over and over, trying to glean a new sense of this woman who had formerly been a stranger. Now she could say, my mother this, my mother that—as other women did.

Now that they were equally pledged to the physical world, Marie became like an elder woman of a tribe. Their pregnant conditions lessened the differences in their personalities, and their discussions became intensely practical. As she gazed at Marie's swelling body, Melanie knew that soon hers would take a similar form; she would be altered forever. She felt as if she were saying goodbye to herself, becoming a new being.

Like everyone else, Mel embraced the news with seeming delight and, if anything, became more protective of her than Ray, acting more like an older brother than a lover. He told Ray he saw a special flush in her cheeks, a new glow in her eyes. Surrounded by such good will, Melanie felt blessed and consequently wrote feverishly, as she had not in months: poems about watching her belly expand, about Ray sitting quietly on the window seat holding his guitar across his lap, about Mel rising from the sea like a young Neptune, music streaming in a spray, silvery as his flute, from his lips.

Tears came, regardless of how she was feeling at the time, as if they simply needed to pour from her. Her body wanted to be both swathed and bared; she yanked up windows, wrapped herself in covers. Diet became as important a topic as the future baby. Melanie carried home stacks of books from the library, bought fish and vegetables she had never tasted before, thinking they would be better for her health and that of the baby's. She watched her abdomen swell, amazed at the form it was taking, at the growth of her previously small breasts, at the color changes of her nipples, differences in her face, her hair. It was a season of great fecundity. Melanie carried this infinitesimal image within her, feeling sudden pokes and ripples beneath her skin, studying the purple marks that looked like bruises, slits marring the frail whiteness of her belly, like a rape, an intrusion, awed that any of it existed, could exist so close to her, a part of her, a new branch, yet contained. It had its own world, even within her, even then floating in its own galaxy. To be so responsible for that innocent creation! To know that the world could invade it, while she stood by helplessly. Stepping off the curb one morning on San Pablo Avenue, a car hood suddenly pressing like a phallus against her outstretched belly—what could she do about the intrusive cars of the world?

* * * * *

Although Kathleen fussed about what to get for the baby, in the end, she slipped Melanie fifty dollars. "Don't piddle it away on nothing," she warned. Norm paid Melanie more attention, made certain she was fed first at the table and refused to let her drink beer, saying it wasn't good for the child. Melanie found she enjoyed these small ministrations. She felt as if she had earned a degree, had become more legitimate because she was bearing Ray's child. It was good to be cared for, to be protected, admonished. Even when Kathleen told her stories of troublesome labors, Melanie listened avidly, eager to learn as much as possible about this experience, hitherto unimportant.

Summer progressed, and Melanie found a woman obstetrician in Oakland who accepted the state's health insurance, MediCal. At Mrs. Duran's suggestion, she and Ray applied for AFDC and food stamps, which would start when the Lytton program ended. Accompanied by Marie and Pete, they shopped for maternity clothes, layette items, and secondhand furniture. As Melanie folded baby clothes away for later use, she marveled at their tiny size, tried to imagine tucking small legs and arms into them. But the creation inside her uterus seemed ultimately amorphous, unable to be truly imagined. When she thought of the baby, it was as an attachment to herself, not quite a doll but something equally manageable. One held it, dressed it, fed it, took it for walks.

When Melanie thought of her sleeplessness, it felt as if it had occurred in another time and place. She could scarcely remember the source of her fear; now any pain she had was physical in nature, while her mind felt clear and fresh. She felt acutely conscious of her skin and treated it as she imagined she would treat the baby, pampering it, rubbing it vigorously, softening it with cocoa butter.

Two years earlier, Melanie had worked as a mother's helper for a three-month-old infant. When she took the little girl out in her baby carriage, it had been fun, momentarily, to pretend that it was hers, to imagine the smiles she received were for her—the new mother. But it had not all been fun. She was frequently bored and looked longingly out the window, wanting to leave her charge—to go for a walk, buy a record, simply be alone. To ease the hours, and to help the baby fall asleep, she had played its parents' records. Walking back and forth the length of their living room while jiggling the infant in her arms had hurt Melanie's back, but it was preferable to hearing the little girl cry. However, it would be different with her own, wouldn't it? The child, having come from her, would respond to her touch, would know that this was her own flesh and blood, would be comforted naturally by that awareness.

Before she became pregnant, Melanie and Ray had not given the question of marriage much thought. When asked by Ray's father and by Marie or Pete if they saw this happening in the future, they had replied that a piece of paper meant very little. They felt married in spirit, and that was what counted. This was typical of their generation, which wanted to get to the essence of things and did not trust conventions. Melanie had not believed in a formal wedding since junior high school. She and her girlfriends had played a fortune game in seventh grade to try and guess their futures. They folded a piece of paper to form four peaks; the outer folds were numbered, and the inner crevices contained messages. Each girl in turn slipped her fingers underneath the peaks to manipulate the paper and then counted out the number she picked. Stopping, she looked inside to read the message or her "fortune." The messages included the color of her future husband's hair and eyes, the color of her wedding dress, the material it would be made of, the type of car they would own.

Like the others, Melanie had wished for lace or satin, a blonde or dark-haired man, a Mustang or a Lincoln Continental, believing the while that such predictions could conceivably come true. She too had fantasized walking down the wedding aisle with the boy she had been infatuated with. Irresistibly then, as she and Ray discussed the idea of marriage, memories of these dreams returned. An idealistic part of her wanted the romantic simplicity expressed by the *True Love* comics she had read in grammar school. The power of fate was a mysterious ingredient that

Melanie could not quite discount. When she and Ray had met, she had longed to find her twin star, her soul mate.

The only difference in their relationship was that they were going to be parents, but would their child be considered illegitimate and be tainted in some way if it didn't have Ray's last name? Melanie began to dream about a possible ceremony. It could be outside, in nature, and they could choose meaningful words. Mel could play the flute for them. Melanie wanted it to be on her birthday, as that day had always felt special to her. Her own mother had gotten married on her birthday, the first day of summer. In July Melanie would turn twenty-one, and although she would be quite pregnant by then, it seemed appropriate to have a summer wedding, with all that summer evoked of warmth and abundance. Ray suggested being married in the Berkeley Rose Garden, knowing that roses were Melanie's favorite flowers.

At Ray's friend Vic's suggestion, she and Ray went to see his minister, who claimed he only married people he felt God had destined to be together. But after talking to them individually and together for several hours, he informed them that he did not think they were suited. In good conscience, he could not unite them. Appalled at this judgment of their relationship, they relinquished their plans, and Ray suggested that maybe they should just go before a justice of the peace.

They purchased plain white gold bands at Milen's, a large discount jewelry store in downtown Oakland. Melanie's was too large and slid up and down on her finger, although as her pregnancy advanced, it began to fit like a vise. Ray rarely wore his because it got grease on it at the garage. Melanie already had a silky blue and green maternity dress she thought would be suitable for the occasion, and Ray intended to switch from his work clothes into a regular shirt and pair of pants before the ceremony. Because their slotted time was in the middle of the day, Ray planned to go to the garage, take off early, and then return to work after taking Melanie home. These practical arrangements lessened the specialness of the day for Melanie, and therefore she did not want any of their friends to attend. At the last minute, Ray invited two acquaintances from Lytton so they would have witnesses.

Her birthday arrived, bright and sunny, with a typical Berkeley summer blue sky, after the morning fog lifted. The night before, Ray helped her ease off the ring she had already been wearing so he could place it on her finger during the ceremony. As she took the short bus ride by herself to the courthouse, Melanie could hardly believe it was her wedding day. The floor-length, peasant-style dress she wore now dipped up and over her full breasts and abdomen. While waiting for Ray, she imagined that the other people waiting eyed her peculiarly. She kept looking at the clock on the wall, seeing the seconds and then minutes slide closer to one o'clock. Ray finally arrived, disheveled and out of breath, and ran to the men's room to wash up. He had not had time to switch out of his mechanic's uniform, and Melanie could not prevent herself from glaring at him. She sensed the judge's eyes on her protruding belly and the embarrassment of the two witnesses who had come at the last minute, so she stared fixedly at a spot in the middle of the judge's robes.

Flushed and angry, Melanie swayed as she mouthed the words: to be together in sickness and in health, to take for loyal wedded husband, till death do you . . . her throat constricted. She could barely whisper her responses, could hardly take in what she was hearing. This was suddenly very serious—these were serious words, this meant something, to be standing there repeating these responses to Ray, and to the greater world, in the person of the judge. Her hand trembled when Ray tried to put the ring on her finger. When it would not fit, and he placed it instead in her palm, she was convinced this was an omen.

Within minutes, they were in the car, driving home. Apologetically, Ray said he had to finish overhauling a car he had been in the middle of working on when he had realized the time. "I'll be back as soon as possible, Mellie," he said, kissing her goodbye. "Let's eat out to celebrate. I guess that'll be all we can do for a while. I wish I could take you on a honeymoon, babe."

After he left, Melanie felt tired and numb. She stretched out on the love seat, with one hand protectively covering her belly. With the other, she caught up and then let drop the band of white gold until it fell on the floor accidentally and rolled beneath the bookshelf. Melanie tried to reach for it, unsuccessfully, and stood staring at its brightness in the dark space. Lying back against the cushions, her face moist with tears and perspiration, she gave herself up to sleep.

* * * * *

The course ended. No more bus trips, no more walking up the stairs, panting, no more typing with puffy fingers. Mrs. Duran presented them each with a certificate from the state of California the size of, and about as substantial as, a piece of typing paper. Then Melanie's days were spent waiting. Although they could no longer make love, Ray held her close in bed, stroking her belly, tracing his fingers over the purplish-blue lines that ran like streams from her navel to her vagina. He played the guitar softly next to her abdomen, speculating on whether this unknown being would have musical ability. The baby elbowed her vigorously in her sleep. With the aid of their case worker, Ray enrolled in a new program, WIN, a work/study arrangement that would teach him how to fix transmissions.

The last month of her pregnancy they spent largely together. They walked in the evenings because it was cooler and stopped frequently to rest, like elderly people. To ready themselves for Melanie's delivery, they attended an exercise class at the YWCA, where they practiced the Lamaze method of childbirth. Marie, who had delivered a boy, Jon, two months before, threw her a surprise baby shower. Mel, Marie and Pete, Bea, and Dee and Helga—looking terribly nervous and out of place in Marie's living room—embraced her and showered her with blessings, like the good fairies did for Aurora in "Sleeping Beauty." No wicked, uninvited fairy arrived to cast a spell.

And then there they were: she and Ray in the hospital, in position, waiting. Melanie's cramps increased in intensity; she felt pressure down her thighs as the baby's head descended. Ray counted the minutes of her contractions conscientiously. The hours crawled past until evening when, after working and working, her body trembling with effort, Melanie gave a last shudder. Her entire body suddenly gave way, helplessly, as she was taken with the pain, unlike any other pain she had felt. A mask was lowered over her face; she heard the mention of forceps. Ray's hair became a dark brown blur, and as Melanie squeezed his hand as if she might break it in two, she spun out into space. Darkness descended completely; the next thing she knew she lay in bed, covered by white sheets. Beside her was Ray, watching her come to consciousness. After a few moments, he placed the baby in her arms. It was a girl, a dusky rose and yellow girl, with dark lashes gracing her downy face.

Melanie could not believe the extent of her feelings toward the baby, the sense of recognition she felt, the desire to trace with her eyes and fingers each inch of skin, to hold each finger and toe in turn. She was certain that the baby's dark eyes looking up into hers were equally caught, that they were strung together in a genetic necklace. The first weeks, it was as though she, Ray, and Lise were on their own island. Time lost meaning; it might be day or night—what mattered were the imperceptible changes in the baby's patterns.

Their few visitors remained only long enough to deliver presents and exclaim over the delicacy of Lise's features. Although Ray talked to his father on the phone, Norm and Kathleen never made the trip to the hospital or, afterwards, into Berkeley. Helga sent a box of baby clothes she no longer needed with Bea. As each person exited, it was as if he or she were another balloon on a string that Melanie was releasing, sending it into space, without concern for its destination. It was as if everyone belonged to another world, a world that no longer concerned her. Her sphere had shrunk.

Content with Ray's presence and the baby's warmth against her body, Melanie felt no desire to go anywhere; she wanted to remain in bed, with blankets tucked around her, hot tea or warm milk beside her on the night stand. As she stroked the downy hair, the equally downy cheeks, she felt unbelievable surges of cramping emotion shoot through her body, felt her uterus shrinking, constricting, returning to its normal, dormant state. Melanie marveled at her newly flattened abdomen and touched the folds of previously stretched-out flesh, amazed that what had been inside was now outside her, was there in her arms. She loved to watch Ray's slender body curved protectively around the small, bundled-up form of his daughter. Her past felt remote, as if it had happened to someone else, though she wondered if anyone had held her as she was holding Lise, had felt toward her what she now felt. Life itself seemed incredibly wonderful and mysterious. Ray left to go to the bank, to buy groceries, but then he was always back again, genie-like by her side.

Sometimes when the autumn sky darkened, Melanie felt as though she were spinning out of control, a repetition of the sensation she had felt when the anaesthesia mask was lowered over her mouth during delivery and she had tried but could not fight its suffocation. She would doze off after nursing, with Lise still on her lap, and would as suddenly jerk awake, feeling as if she were falling somewhere and had to catch herself. She cried uncontrollably, tears for no apparent reason, and had sudden moments of anxiety. But Melanie had little time to examine these behaviors or understand them, to think about herself, Ray, the future. Everything centered on Lise, and there was only now—wide, expansive now.

* * * * *

Two weeks after Lise was born, Melanie stepped outside, cradling her baby in her arms. The air was fresh and cold, misty from the Bay and a recent drizzle. As they drove past the familiar streets, Melanie was aware that she was no longer separate, able to shift and move at will, but had to always consider Lise's movements. She noticed the barren trees along the freeway to Norm and Kathleen's house and felt a sense of barrenness herself. But turning to the warm body asleep in her lap, absorbing the surging heat from the car's heater, aware of Ray driving more slowly, more carefully, she felt a renewed sense of well-being, of excitement, of purpose.

Norm and Kathleen opened the door to their house when the car pulled up and, calling welcomes from the doorway, ushered Melanie into the warmth of the house. When all their wraps had been removed, Kathleen reached greedily for Lise. She swayed, bent over her, cooed, and Melanie had to restrain herself from reaching a hand to stop her. Lise was so pretty, Kathleen exclaimed—like a rosebud, just like a rosebud, those dark eyes, that blush of skin, as if she's wearing makeup, darn it! She bounced the baby up and down in her arms, kissed her head repeatedly.

"Why I might just try to steal her away," Kathleen said, spinning in a circle. "Yes, you just loves your Katie, loves your Katie, don't you? Let's have a smile, just an itsy bitsy smile. Oh, she's done it; would you believe it, Norm? She gave me a smile. I bet it's her first one!" she crowed triumphantly.

"Nonsense, Katie. It's probably just gas; babies don't smile this early. Well, are you going to hold her all night? When does the proud grandpa get a chance?" He winked at his son.

"You can take her but don't drop her, you big oaf. I bet you don't even know how to hold a baby."

"I'll have you know I held all my kids, and gave bottles to them besides, smarty-pants. Come on, hand her over. If anyone's gonna do any dropping around here, we know who that will be." Norm gave her a dark look. "I told you to leave that liquor alone until after they had gone. But would you do it?"

Kathleen froze. Silently, she handed Lise to Melanie and then walked with her head up to the bedroom. They stood uncomfortably, listening, as she broke into loud sobs once she had shut the door. After a few minutes, Melanie said, "Maybe this isn't a good time. Should we come back tomorrow?" She dropped onto the living-room couch and held Lise to her chest, cradling her against what she felt could be an explosion.

"No." Norm sighed heavily. "Goddamn my fool tongue anyhow. But you saw it," he said accusingly, "you saw how she was swaying, nearly dropped the damn child. Had to have her whiskey," he muttered under his breath. "Christ! You came with the baby and come hell or high water, we're going to see it. Just stay now! Kathleen'll be out in a while, once she finishes having her pout. She just wants attention." He straightened up. "As for myself, I think I need a beer. What about you two? You want some coffee, Melanie? Son?"

Ray went into the kitchen with his father. When they left the room, Melanie pressed her face hard against Lise, fighting back the tears that sprang like knife points from her eyes. She listened to Kathleen's wailing from the bedroom and, rising, walked back and forth, holding onto Lise as if for protection.

"Here you go, sweetheart," Norm said as he placed a tall glass of milk on the table. "Now what about food? Remember, you're eating for two. You're breast-feeding, aren't you?"

Melanie nodded, feeling unwilling to admit the fact to this weather-beaten man, unwilling to hand her child over to his calloused hands. In penance, she extended Lise. "Would you like to hold her now?"

Norm turned away, making a sour face. "No, Kathleen's right. It's been a long time since I've held any babies. I might be too rough; sometimes I don't know my own strength. You keep her on your lap. Damn! If I could just get that woman to shut up, there might be some peace around here. I warned her and warned her." He pounded the table with his hand, making Lise's eyes fly open, and she began to cry. "Oh, now look there, I made the little precious cry."

Norm bent over her. "There, there, precious, you don't want to cry," he said in a husky voice. "Grandpa's not really a mean guy." He patted her face gently, his big hands hovering like giant moths around her. "You're a little sweetie, ain't you? Gonna break some man's heart someday."

Melanie felt ashamed that she had ever thought Norm could hurt Lise. She glanced at Ray, who, to her relief, was smiling, and then she began to talk about the baby, thanking Norm for the clothes and baby blanket he and Kathleen had sent to the hospital. Standing, she handed Lise to Norm, and this time he took her, set her on his lap and talked to her jokingly, while she stared up at him with her dark eyes. He picked her up and held her against his shoulder.

"Let's go look at the birds," he said. "You want to hear something pretty?" He walked over to the bird cage and lifted the cover, startling them. As the two parakeets fluttered about, he whispered to them coaxingly, shaking the cage with one hand, turning Lise's face toward the swinging bar. "Looky there. One's still got his eyes shut. Come on, budgie, open up for baby," he cooed. "There, now isn't that a pretty sight?"

Melanie knocked tentatively on the bedroom door and heard a sharp intake of breath.

"It's only Melanie, Kathleen. Come see the baby." She waited a minute and then opened the door. Kathleen sat on the bed, staring down at the rug. Her face, when she lifted it to Melanie, was smeared with tears and mascara, and her hair was mussed. Like a child who had just been beaten and was expecting further blows, she flinched as Melanie tried to wipe away some of her tears.

"You see how he treats me; you see it, don't you?" she whimpered. Melanie sat beside her on the bed and patted her shoulder. "He's such a hardheaded man. Such a mean man. My husband, he would never, he would have nev . . ." She broke into fresh weeping.

"Come on, Kathleen. Nobody's angry with you. Ray and I want you to see Lise. Please. Dry your tears and come out."

"Oh, I look a mess. How can I? And I got specially fixed up, all fixed up for this visit, just like I do when Norm and I go down to Joe's for a couple. I wouldn't drop the baby, Melanie, you know I wouldn't. Why, I have six grandkids, and I never, never . . ." Kathleen rose unsteadily and looked at her face in the mirror above the dresser. She began to giggle. "I do look a fright, don't I? I better do something about that. You go back to the living room. Just give me a few minutes." Melanie knew that besides straightening her hair and redoing her makeup, Kathleen would find time to take a swig from a hidden store of Seagram's, but she removed her hand from Kathleen's shoulder and nodded that it was all right.

Kathleen's entrance was subdued, but soon she flitted her eyes coyly and penitently at Norm until he grudgingly grinned back at her. Finally, he rose and, pulling her roughly against his side, gave her a resounding smack on the bottom that made her shriek. She went into the kitchen and brought out a cake she had bought for the occasion and sloppily cut piece by piece until Norm, in frustration, took the knife from her and did it himself. Then she poured coffee that he had made beforehand. As they ate, the atmosphere lightened.

Kathleen and Norm shared with them their own parental experiences—Norm laughing and teasing Ray about things he had done when he was small, Kathleen saying what handfuls each of her children had been and describing in detail what she called their pranks. When it grew late, Norm offered them the living-room couch, which pulled out into a bed, but Ray said no, they had to leave; he was starting training in the morning. With their arms around each other's waists, Norm and Kathleen stood watching raptly as Melanie bundled Lise up to take her out into the night air. They exchanged goodbyes and Melanie and Ray promised to bring Lise again the following week, although Ray teased his dad that he really should come see them in Berkeley. It wasn't that big a trip, they really should. Back in the car, surrounded by darkness and the foggy windshield, Melanie felt once more as if only she, Ray, and Lise existed, detached from the rest of the world.

 *Seven*

When the baby was two and a half months old, they moved to an apartment on the fifth floor. In the new studio, there was a walk-in closet big enough to hold Lise's crib, which enabled them to tuck her in at night, draw a thin curtain across the doorway, and be afforded privacy in the main living area. Ray obtained a position at AAMCO Transmissions in Daly City. This involved a long commute across the Bay Bridge, so Melanie was by herself with Lise from early in the morning until dark.

One day faded into another. Melanie felt lonelier than she had anticipated and looked forward eagerly to Ray's arrival each night. Mel, who had stopped by frequently while Ray had still been home, left to go traveling in Mexico with another musician of his acquaintance. Joan had returned to Berkeley more troubled than ever, and their attempted reconciliation had ended with her flight to a commune in San Francisco. Mel said it was just as well that he make himself scarce; it was time to move on anyway. But with his leaving, Melanie's loneliness increased.

By nightfall, when Ray stepped through the door and reached for Lise with his blackened hands, leaving smudges on her white diapers, Melanie was grateful to turn her over to his care. Ray ate dinner, and then they played Yahtzee or cribbage or sat together watching television, with Lise beside them strapped in her infant seat, or on one or the other of their laps. On weekends, Melanie ran to the library to replenish her supply of books. Because she was frequently interrupted in her reading, she began to check out mysteries, thinking they would not absorb her attention as greatly. For weeks on end, she read Erle Stanley Gardener and Agatha Christie, quickly exhausting the small library's supply.

Occasionally, in a burst of energy, she cleaned the entire apartment, but the next day she failed to make the bed and left the dishes in the sink. In a padded rocker similar to the one in their former apartment, Melanie sat looking out the window as she nursed Lise. She developed a habit of munching on sunflower seeds while she watched game shows and other daytime television. Fixated on cracking open the shell, tasting the salt, enjoying the crunch of the meat inside, she found it easy to wade through a third of a bag at one sitting. Afterwards, sated, she would feel bloated and stare at her body as if it belonged to someone else. She thought the lines of her stretch marks looked like tears in her flesh that now served no purpose, and she hated a new thickness she saw in her face, as well as the brown spots that had not faded after delivery.

Although she began to feel as if she were fat, Melanie could not stop eating. She felt equally nauseated and obsessed by food. Her interest in cooking waned because she felt no desire to prepare anything that took thought or energy. Hamburger Helper meals, Shake 'N Bake pork chops or chicken, and cold ham and boxed Kraft macaroni and cheese—which only required boiling water and stirring a few ingredients together— replaced their previously more varied, healthier meals. She cringed at the prospect of chopping vegetables or rinsing lettuce leaves. Two or three nights a week she asked Ray to bring home Chinese food.

At her baby shower, Melanie had been surprised to receive a box of perfumed soaps and bath oils, because most of her friends did not use such toiletries, preferring to be completely natural. It had surprised her further that the giver was Marie. Now, turning the package over in her hands, admiring the pretty covers on the tiny bars of soap—one had a border of roses and displayed a dusky-looking flamenco dancer—and inhaling their perfume, she understood Marie's faint chuckle at the time. As Melanie held the sparkling balls of gold, red, and green oils— deeply-colored as Christmas ornaments—up to the light, she realized . . . of course! They were to wash away the urine, the spit-up; they were the transforming agents.

One night after Ray came home and sat watching a show, Melanie indulged with a bath. And it felt like an indulgence. Excitedly, she watched the foaming of the bath oil as the water level rose in the tub. When she stepped into the warmth and steam, the water felt immediately silky and soothing; the bubbles rose around her, covering her body, enclosing her, nurturing her. She closed her eyes, pretending she was a 1950s actress, one of those women who took just such baths foaming with iridescent bubbles. Her hair was pinned up, as Melanie's was, and she always received a phone call from her lover right after she had settled herself in the tub. Acting piqued, the woman would daintily step from her luxurious nest of bubbles and next be seen with a towel wrapped discreetly around her, tiptoeing toward the phone. After minimal conversation, she would make kissing sounds into the receiver and then submerge herself again. On the screen, the bubbles never diminished during the interim; like foam sprayed on windows at Christmas time, once formed, they seemed permanently stuck.

Melanie's bubbles, however, soon dissolved, exposing squares of thigh and belly and dark, smoky-looking water that accentuated the paleness of her white skin. She rose up and down, sinking the back of her head into the water, then pulling it out, enjoying the sense of aliveness this brought her as her wet hair clung to her head. Yet something prevented her from lingering. After staying in for less than fifteen minutes, Melanie wet a washcloth with fresh hot water and pressed it against her breasts, her neck, her shoulder, the renewed warmth penetrating her chest, and then stepped from the tub. Although when she got out she felt clean and relaxed, Melanie felt a little let down. There was nowhere to go—no elegant dinner party, no lover's bed; somehow the bath oil, along with the glamour depicted in the movies, hinted at these things but then failed to deliver. The reality instead was the drabness of the apartment, with its sickening olive green couch, books and clothes scattered on the floor, the draft from the ill-fitting front door. Although removed from the noise of the front entrance way, the new studio was smaller and more cramped. Melanie was accustomed to the height of Manhattan apartment buildings but here she felt trapped being so far from the ground. Instead of the greenery of the hedges, the view was of the tar-covered roofs of buildings and the parking lot of the Canned Foods store.

After taking the initial bubble bath, Melanie felt no inclination to take another. When she came upon the bath oils in the cabinet as she reached for something else, they interested her as much as a tin of Band-Aids would. For that night, despite her feeling soft, clean, and perfumy, had been like most of their nights together. The transmission work and his commute exhausted Ray; when she noticed how tired he was in the evenings, she felt guilty. It was difficult to believe that taking care of a baby required so much energy; it made Melanie wonder if something was wrong with her that she should feel nearly as tired as Ray was at the end of the day. Over dinner, Ray talked about transmissions and engines, of what a customer had said or done, of what work awaited him the following day. Melanie tried to listen sympathetically, but she found it difficult to pay attention. Although she wished they could discuss something else, she could think of nothing to say, other than that Lise had slept for a long time or had held her head up more firmly than the day before. Occasionally, she and Ray made love, but he often seemed preoccupied, and she did not think it was because he was infatuated with another woman.

The car—which they now depended upon—broke down completely, and she and Ray went one Saturday to look for another secondhand one at the wrecking yard Norm managed. It was not the first time she had seen Norm's work place. During her pregnancy, when Ray had been at the cooperative garage, he had often stopped by to chat with his father about automotive-related questions or to see if he could locate in the wreckage a needed part. Sometimes, Melanie had accompanied him.

Norm held court in a trailer set up in the middle of what appeared to Melanie to be piles of heaped-up junk. Car bodies, in all degrees of decomposition, lay on their sides; some were completely rusted through, others had only one or two doors hanging on their hinges. Tires were thrown together pyramid-style; windows were either nonexistent, cracked, or smashed. Melanie found herself wondering about the history of the various vehicles — pickup trucks, four-door sedans, convertibles, even Cadillacs—how each had met its fate and come to rest in Norm's yard. Cars were piled on top of each other—multicolored and stacked as they were, they reminded Melanie of the peddlers' caps in the children's book *Caps for Sale*. While Ray and Norm transacted business or sat drinking coffee poured from Norm's king-size camping thermos, Melanie wandered about the yard by herself, feeling as desolate and useless as she thought the cars were. She carefully avoided the sharp objects and glass that lay in her path, changing directions when she came up against what appeared to be statues of brokenness.

It amazed her that Norm seemed to know each car personally. When a customer asked Norm if he had such and such a part, Norm would automatically go to the right vehicle and pick the part out easily from among the probable thousands that lay there. This was why they came to Norm in the first place, because he knew the drivability or non-drivability of every car on the lot. Because the trailer was usually hot and stuffy and filled with smoke, winter or summer, Melanie preferred to be outdoors rather than sit in its close quarters. Inside, she found herself staring inadvertently at the half-naked woman on the calendar above Norm's work space. Now that she had Lise with her, Melanie did not think she should subject her daughter to the possible danger of falling and getting cut, so she and Lise remained inside the trailer.

As they spent more weekends at or near the wrecking yard, they saw less of Marie and Pete—who lived in the opposite direction—and more of Helga, because her house was five minutes from the yard. Helga never seemed particularly interested in Lise, although she always smiled at her and held her for a few minutes upon arrival. She was more preoccupied with her own child, who was now walking. But as Melanie watched Ray laugh and kid around, downing one Colt 45 after another throughout the long afternoons, she realized he was happiest at Helga's.

Unexpectedly— because up to that point their Richmond acquain-tances had never come to Berkeley—these same people now began to drop by their own apartment. They would come after Ray returned from work, mostly men Melanie did not know well and felt uncomfortable with. She found herself setting extra places for dinner, although she did not partic-ularly view the men as her company. They cursed a great deal and, besides offering Ray dope, brought six-packs of beer with them, which they jok-ingly said was their contribution to the lady of the house. As they sat in the tiny kitchen playing Yahtzee or cribbage, Melanie paced back and forth with Lise. She would look at someone's hand or throw of the dice but then, feeling in the way, would return to the darkened living room.

To break the monotony of her days, she went to visit Marie, although taking the bus now seemed a monumental effort. The long ride, with its numerous stops, had previously meant nothing to her and, in fact, had been a refreshing change of scenery. However, after getting herself and the baby dressed, packing a diaper bag, checking that she hadn't forgot-ten anything essential, and hoisting Lise into her front pack, she felt exhausted. To have to repeat the procedure after a stay of only a few hours hardly seemed worthwhile.

Even going for her monthly checkup at her obstetrician's, whose office was farther than Marie's apartment, was a day's worth of activity— activity that seemed increasingly difficult for her to perform. Surprisingly, her insomnia returned. After nursing at night, Melanie would stare at the ceiling, wide awake, unable to fall back asleep. Constantly fatigued, she dragged her body around, not certain whether she could make it up a street block at times; she, who had previously walked miles at a time, could not believe how her body was failing her. Her doctor gave her sleep-ing medication, but after the first tablet, Melanie refused to take another. The night she took it, as she struggled to get up for Lise's feeding, she felt strange—as if she didn't belong to her own body—and afterwards sank into a dreamless sleep.

During the overcast, wintry afternoons, to help lessen the time until Ray's return, Melanie took from the coat closet the heavy, faded stroller they had bought, packed Lise in with blankets to keep her upright, and walked with her to the nearby playground. It was in a small park three blocks away and had a set of baby swings, a seesaw, and a slide; sur-rounding these were several benches, encircled by stubby hedges. Melanie sat on a bench, pushing the stroller rhythmically back and forth with her foot, while she stared at the toddlers being pushed in the baby swings. She began to recognize a few of the women, but if one nodded in a friendly way, Melanie lowered her eyes, afraid to acknowledge the invitation to step out of her isolation. She could think of nothing to talk about, and felt as if she had lost the natural ability for social intercourse. Only with Lise was she fully present, could she be tender and gentle; only Lise could elicit a smile now and then. Simultaneously, Melanie began to experience such deep sadness, it was as if she had been torn open, as if a tear ran from her chin clear down to her legs, and her exposed innermost workings were being filled with intensely frigid air.

When one of the mothers smiled, she wished that she could respond normally— say hello, comment on the weather, or on their mutual children. If only the other woman would persist, she thought, she could probably reciprocate. But she never did. The mothers spoke instead with each other. As Melanie listened, she felt alienated. She was not interested in brands of diapers, in sales of children's clothes, in how well Sherri was walking, although these topics were certainly relevant to her own life. The time when she had written poems, read literature, listened to music seemed to have occurred a long, long time previously; perhaps it had never happened or had happened to someone else. Not to this person who trod slowly up and down the street, who had to rest on park benches, who was attached to this other human being like a Siamese twin. As she gazed at the watery sky, at the lemon yellow sun straining to break through the rain-filled clouds, Melanie felt as if winter had descended so completely that the sky would never again be bright and blue.

She could not remember when she had felt so alone, so lonely. In the past she had enjoyed being alone. Some places one had to be by oneself, such as at the Marina at night, sheltered within the bowl of the sky, the stars themselves embracing one in their austere clarity. Or lying on the floor, listening to Beethoven's Seventh Symphony, sound pressing against every pore. The spent feeling afterwards, the music simultaneously weakening and strengthening. But now this child was always present; it was a music that went with her, a double persona, a twin who answered to her thoughts, a perpetual mirror attached to her shoulder blades. Lise's very cry was inside her skull; it emerged from her own psyche. Where did a child fit into silence, into a private inner world?

As she had once stroked her own belly, now she stroked Lise's face and hair, outlining with a tremulous finger the cheeks, the nose, the eyebrows. She felt purely animal. It was as if she was reduced to only physical actions— bending, stooping, tasting—and was immersed in odors of urine, feces, perspiration, blood. Equally connected to leaves, soil, natural things. The texture of the day seemed heightened—feet pressing against the ground, skin's sweat and fatigue—yet her mind shriveled. It sank into Agatha Christie's words as her body had sunk into the bubbly bath oils, sank into sleeping, eating, sleeping, eating, until she felt like a gross, physical thing, a slug inching along. Wrapping herself in the blanket of the apartment, closing its walls tightly about herself so that the very light coming in the window in the morning seemed an intruder to her womb, Melanie wondered if, in some ghastly paradoxical fashion, she had become a baby herself. Had she been reduced to an infantile state, afraid of the dark, of loud noises, unfamiliar people and places?

Melanie tried to communicate with the small bundle in her arms that stared up at her so solemnly, with such a direct, dark gaze, yet she was afraid to infect its innocence with her own desperate sensations. The excitement of pregnancy, the glow she had been enveloped in had completely vanished. There was only the reality of the apartment: a suffocatingly narrow space from which she longed to escape. Getting up, changing Lise, nursing Lise, eating breakfast, dressing Lise, on and on, without variance, without strength to create a variance. She began to stare at dirty dishes, powerlessly, at dust balls, as if they were merely interesting objects on the floor. She did what was absolutely necessary and lived for the weekends, when Ray might take her for a drive. Even if it was only as far as the grocery store or the Marina, without her having to make an effort, her world expanded. But the more time she spent alone with Lise, the more Melanie was flooded with memories of her own childhood. She began to think constantly about her mother, her grandmother, the women in her life.

A legacy of failure seemed to have been transferred to her, had been genetically passed on, like her father's green eyes, her mother's round face. Her grandmother's Riverside Drive apartment had always been cluttered, from as far back as Melanie could remember. In the rare photograph of, say, a Christmas or Thanksgiving dinner, the table appeared elegant, displaying as it did a lace tablecloth and an old-fashioned centerpiece of Father Christmas in his sleigh. The crystal chandelier hanging above the table suggested finery, along with the candelabra on the wall above the dining room's marble fireplace. But around the edges of the table shown in the photo there were hatboxes, cartons, clothes on hangers that had been draped out of the way for the picture's sake, pieces of unnecessary furniture. These were present, although the picture chose not to focus on them. On the table was the mismatched china—plates, bowls, cups, which would have shown their chips if seen more closely. One room had been filled from floor to ceiling with once-serviceable furniture. When Melanie read Dickens's *Great*

Expectations, his gruesome description of Miss Havisham's rooms reminded her of her grandmother's apartment.

One year, when she was seven or eight, Melanie's army cot had been set up in this room stacked with furniture. In the darkness, she had seen crags, mountains, odd shapes that might come alive; her dreams had been vivid, as overpowering as the pieces themselves. The dark-paned windows in the room allowed scant light, pale yellow light, as if from a street lamp's glow. That had been the year of most nightmares, exiled amidst those bureaus, end tables, and lamps, shut off from the normalcy of the other bedrooms, which, though cluttered, did not begin to compare.

And her mother, who had fled to her former home because her husband had not been able to support them, fit this strange setting. She wandered about aimlessly, dressed in a winter coat despite the season, stringing words together as if they had relevance to each other—connecting phrases that made little sense to whoever might be listening. Melanie had grown accustomed to the muttering, the ceaseless talking in the night, had stared out at her mother's shadowy form as she sat smoking on the window seat across from the big double bed that occasionally held her father as well, when he was not too drunk to spend the night. Upon his arrival, Melanie was relegated to a small couch near the door, which, in contrast to the bed, felt cold, hard, strange. When she slept there, she always had the impression that at any minute she could fall to the floor because although she leaned inwards, toward the musty folds of stiff material, clutching at it, she found nowhere to secure her hold. Curling her small fists into any crevice, she would try to make her body even smaller, small enough to fit back into the womb. But as a rule, she had lain in her mother's bed, had luxuriated in the vast expanse of it; no matter which way she turned, there was more space. And at the window was her mother, smoking, muttering like a strangely comforting lullaby.

Yet her mother was an object of fear: that roving, mumbling person could suddenly slap, or tie Melanie's hair in knots, could impulsively take her on a pointless journey. Conscious of her insanity, even at a young age, Melanie had avoided her as much as possible, had clung to her grandmother, or remained alone. She sought her own amusements with books and dolls, creating her own universe full of fantasy. Now, as she rocked and nursed Lise, these thoughts surfaced, and she felt the weight of being a mother, felt that she herself might want to wander, might dissolve into her own inner space and be unreachable.

She felt it was vital to do everything as perfectly as possible. Keep Lise clean, dressed, never wait too long to change her diapers. Even if the apartment was neglected, Lise never was. Lise went to sleep only in Melanie's arms. Melanie rocked and rocked her after nursing, waited for the small lashes to flutter down, close over, waited still longer, barely breathing, before she stopped the rocker, got up so gradually she hardly moved, made the seemingly eternal walk across the room to Lise's crib, and then lowered her down inch by infinitesimal inch, her chest tight with conscious effort. If Lise stirred when her body fell gently against the crib sheet, Melanie would place her hand on the small back, patting gently, gently, until she felt she would break with the strain. When she was certain Lise was truly asleep, then she would bend herself painfully upward, standing there in the dark, afraid of the least whimper, and inch away again, exhausted. It was always her fear that Lise would cry out, and the process would have to be repeated. Melanie did not know why she took such care. Perhaps it was because, with Lise, she could correct her own past, be what she felt a mother should be. Sometimes, the strain of perfectionism was too great. If Lise cried, and Melanie was especially weary, rage swelled inside her. She felt like hurling Lise across the room. Instead she cried silently, tears falling over the mounds of her cheeks as she bent again, patting, patting, circling and circling Lise's back with her palm while simultaneously, helplessly crying, feeling as though any minute her legs would give way.

Melanie used her voice so seldom during the day— or used it only for crooning one- or two-word sentences—that to have or listen to a conversation with Ray began to seem impossible. Only she and Lise existed. Like Lise she was speechless, had not found speech yet, was only discovering the world, and it was as though it did not seem important to speak. When Ray came home at night, his sudden entrance seemed odd, as if by accident he had stumbled into the wrong apartment.

The further she sank into this state, the harder it was to rise from it, until when Ray talked to her, she was afraid to answer him, fearing what she said would sound incoherent. Sometimes, after she had spoken, she wished she could recall her words, certain they must have been strange, although Ray never indicated they were. Melanie felt like a too full, boiling pot of water, ready to overflow. Yet all that poured forth were useless tears, tears that went nowhere, that didn't heal her, but instead washed over Lise, until she felt they were one combined, sobbing being. The darkness began to fill her mind again, as it had it seemed so long before, those other nights when she had so desperately sought sleep. How could she escape it this time?

Melanie tried to remember happier times to escape the weight pulling down her being— times when she and Ray had hitchhiked, pleas-

ant moments from her childhood, novels she had enjoyed, movies, trips—
but it was as though all color in her world had been abruptly switched off.
The days seemed putrid gray or filmy brown, as if covered by layers of
dirt. Was it the apartment, the drabness she faced daily? Yet it was outside, too. If she went to pick up a carton of milk, she felt fearful and could
barely respond to the friendly comments and smiles of the salesclerk. Only
after she entered the Rosaline Apartments again did she feel safe.

When she washed Lise's hair, scratching the tender scalp with a
comb to erase cradle cap, she felt that she had transferred that scaly-look-
ing, grayish-white disease to her. She thought back to the times when her
uncle, who, trying to take up the responsibilities her mother and grandmother could not handle, had washed her own hair. How much fun he
had made it, how he had made the experience an adventure! For her it was
another chore to complete, another seemingly impossible duty she was
self-consciously, fraudulently fulfilling. Melanie did not feel like a legitimate mother, no matter how perfectly she tried. If others saw her, they
would know she was only playacting. That was why the women in the
park never approached her; they realized she was alien.

Her uncle had seemed so sure of what he was doing, so adult,
although he had read what to do in a magazine. Melanie would sit on a chair
before the sink, looking into the bathroom mirror, while he combed through
all her tangles. Inch by inch of hair turned from snarls to silky strands as he
patiently tugged through each, making up puns as he did it, to distract her
thoughts from the stinging pain she felt in her scalp. Then came the sham-
poo, the vigorous scrubbing of her scalp until it tingled, and last, the rinses:
first warm ones, as the article said. Then cooler, cooler, cold, until her uncle
announced they were approaching the North Pole. Afterwards, the warm
towel, the cool drops of water on her neck, the laughter, the praise as combed
out again, dried and fluffed out around her face, her hair glowed and shone.
It had been so cozy, sitting in the bathroom together, feeling as if they had all
the time in the world, her giggles at his puns, his deep laugh and twinkling
blue eyes. Why did she never feel that way with Lise? No actions came confidently, surely. No guides—and she read bits and pieces of them all, from
Baby and Child Care to *How to Parent*—made her feel as though she were
doing the right things. She was stumbling in the dark. Sometimes it felt so
dark she could hardly get up in the morning, or upon opening her eyes, keep
them open the remainder of the day.

Part Two

"I can't see my reflection in the waters;
I can't speak the sounds that show no pain;
I can't hear the echo of my footsteps;
Or remember the sound of my own name . . ."

Bob Dylan
"Tomorrow Is a Long Time"

One

Red blotches spattered the walls—brick red, blood red. The color darkened, spread like a stain on a handkerchief; amoeba-like, it formed squiggles, distorted shapes. Crying—faint at first—mounted, intensified. She was inside the chambers of a heart, a crying heart. The cries increased to sobs, yet the redness lightened to rust, rose, pink, white—the exact hue of early morning light. The crying rent the air, persisted until its urgency woke her. Her eyes fought their way open. Gradually she realized that she was in a room; she identified its corners, its dimensions. It was her living room. She was Melanie. Like the smell of burned toast, the colors lingered in the air.

Melanie turned on her side, away from the light streaming through the window. She pressed her hot cheek against the cool pillow and listened to the crying, as if she could not understand its cause. Abruptly, she clutched her nightgown close to her body and pulled herself up from the mattress. In the crib, Lise lay tangled in her blankets; her face was strained and red, and her dark eyes looked at Melanie accusingly. Melanie lifted her gently from the covers.

She changed Lise's dripping wet diaper and then sat by the window to nurse her. As Lise fiercely, hungrily sucked, puffing out her cheeks with concentration, Melanie felt the usual twinges in her nipples. When her milk let down and began to spill into Lise's eager mouth, Melanie's foot began to jiggle up and down uncontrollably. Pressing on her knee to steady herself, she reached with her free hand for a sip of water, but her hand shook so violently that water spilled onto her lap. It was like receiving a sudden burn. Melanie gingerly slid a cigarette from the pack on the sill, lit it with a quick, practiced maneuver, and took a deep drag that, momentarily, stilled the agitation in her body. Lise's red hands were the same shade as the oppressive redness in her dream. They clawed at her. Melanie shuddered.

The winter sky showed the same overcast gray-white haze that had persisted for weeks. Melanie glanced at the Baby Ben next to Ray's side of the mattress. He usually left at six-thirty; the clock now read seven-thirty. Seven-thirty, she thought, trying to calculate the hours left of the day. She longed desperately to move, to leap from the rocker, but she only shifted position and gave Lise her other swollen breast. Melanie was amazed that, tense as she was, any milk came out.

"Oh, little baby blue," she crooned sadly, "what's gonna happen to me and you? I feel so . . . so . . . so . . . there's no way you can understand what I mean, is there? No way at all," she whispered. Lise made gurgling, wondering sounds in response as the thin, bluish milk trickled from the corner of her mouth. Melanie wiped it away with her finger, still conscious of the shaking in her legs, ready to ambush her, to take her unawares if she should attempt to sit holding Lise quietly against her. She got up and strapped Lise into the plastic infant seat on the kitchen table. She flicked the radio knob to on, yawned, and then took orange juice, eggs, and bread and butter from the refrigerator. After popping two slices of whole-grain bread into the toaster, she began to carefully poach the eggs in a pan on the electric stove.

The radio was playing "Summertime," and Melanie accompanied the singer in a reedy voice. *"One of these mornings, you're gonna rise up singing . . . spread your wings and take to the sky . . . But until that morning, nothing can harm you. So hush, little baby, don't you cry . . ."* Tears stung the corners of her eyes, and Melanie impatiently wiped them away. She visualized herself with gigantic wings, a huge butterfly soaring in an equally immense blue sky, elevated from the heaviness of the earth, taken up somewhere, anywhere . . . released.

She buttered her toast, poured a glass of orange juice. Lise had begun to whimper, so Melanie placed a rubber elephant that squeaked when it was pressed into her hand. Cringing at the loudness of the commercial that came on after the song, she lowered the volume on the radio and sat down to eat. She cut into one of the eggs with her fork but stopped as a sudden wave of nausea swept over her. The eggs were utterly smooth and shiny-looking, like eggs made of rubber or plastic. They reminded Melanie of the pictures of food displayed in coffee shop menus. A vague worry that the eggs might *not* be real, that they might even be poisoned, came unbidden into her mind, and she drew back violently from the thought. Impossible! I just made them; I made them myself, she told the insistently teasing voice in her head. Gingerly, Melanie took a bite of toast; it tasted dry and then oily as the butter met her tongue. She put the piece back on her plate and, shoving her plate to the side, buried her head in her arms on the table. Dear God, what the hell is happening to me? What the hell is happening? Melanie tore her fingers through her hair and cried until the sleeves of her nightgown were wet and strands of her hair clung stickily to her face.

When her body shook less with the violence of her feelings, she lifted her head. The white sunlight, filtering through the thin curtains, made the table, the walls, Lise in her white infant seat appear unnaturally bright. A beam of rainbow light hit the side of her orange juice glass as she picked it up to take a drink. The pleasant coolness of the glass beneath her fingers made her feel like crying again, but as she drank, as the cold, acidic liquid poured down her tight throat, a memory flashed across her vision.

She was sitting in children's court in midtown Manhattan. Before her eyes, two police officers grabbed her mother's arms and dragged her across the courtroom. Twisting and turning her body, her mother screamed for them to release her. Melanie numbly realized that they were taking her mother somewhere because she was crazy, but she was unable to get up, to stop the men from hurting her. Directly afterwards, Melanie had taken the subway back to her fourth-grade classroom.

Melanie cried out—a pathetic whimper, like a wounded animal. The memory persisted, continued to flash against her vision with all the frenzy of a strobe light. Her mother had always accused them of poisoning her and checked her food before each meal to see if anything had been put into it. As a child, Melanie had watched her slice open the crust of a piece of toast and run her finger along the edge, checking for a possible pill. Once there had been one, put there in desperation by Melanie's grandmother to stop her incessant talking. When her mother found it, she said nothing but removed it carefully, as if it were an inconsequential crumb. Then, laying the uneaten toast aside, she lit a cigarette and took a sip of black coffee, staring at them all with darting eyes.

Melanie shut her eyes tightly and pressed her hand hard against her forehead. Her body, her thoughts, the trembling, these awful thoughts insinuating themselves into her brain, hiding in the corners, tormenting her—was this what had happened to her mother? Was she going to go crazy too? Fear tumbled over her in thick waves. She stamped on the floor. Get outside! Clean the apartment! If she could keep moving! If she could only stop thinking! Melanie realized with dread that in a few hours she would have to nurse Lise again, and that meant having to remain still.

She forced herself to wash the dishes, although she felt detached from her hands as they held the sponge. Standing upright felt strange; Melanie was convinced her feet would melt into the linoleum or slide uncontrollably sideways, as in a funhouse room. She got dressed, mechanically, washed her face, combed her hair, but barely looked at the mirror, afraid to meet her reflection head-on for fear of what it might reveal. Maybe these sensations were part of a flashback, maybe she was permanently scarred from having taken LSD and mescaline. Maybe the insomnia and trembling had been only the beginning. Maybe this was the end. The End. Like the Doors song: *"This is the end, my only friend, the end . . . The end of ev'rything that stands, the end. No safety or surprise. The end. I'll never look into your eyes again. Can you picture what will be? So limitless and free. Desperately in need of some stranger's hand. In a desperate land . . . waiting for the summer rain . . . "*

She covered her eyes. No . . . not that, please. *Please.* Melanie released Lise from the infant seat and put her on the living-room rug with the elephant and a plastic set of keys. She cranked open the window and stuck her hand out, but the air on her arm was cold, and she shivered. After lighting a cigarette, she turned the television to a game show. Despite her resolution to keep moving, Melanie started watching it. When the program ended, she sat through *Gilligan's Island* and then *Flipper.* Then it was eleven o'clock, time to nurse again, and Lise, grunting on the carpet, was growing fidgety. Melanie picked her up and, putting her on her lap, slowly undid the buttons of her blouse. Staring at Lise, who murmured softly to her hands, held them out in the light, examining them, Melanie felt as though she and Lise were the same person, as if the breaths they took individually merged. She carefully, slowly slipped Lise onto her breast. Okay, twenty minutes, little one, she muttered. Twenty minutes, ten at each breast. She pressed her feet firmly on the floor. Then we'll go for a walk. The fresh air will make us both feel better. Up and down the block several times and then home again. Home again, home again, jiggety jig.

Ray had asked her: How do you spend your days, Mel? Doesn't Lise sleep most of the time? Although he did not say this critically, Melanie felt he was accusing her of being lazy. Ray had a right to be confused. There he was, five days a week, replacing transmissions; and here she was, with only the responsibility of an infant and a small, very small, apartment. She could not even handle that much. Why did it take such effort to move? Or when she moved, why did she have to immediately rest? She ran the carpet sweeper over the rug but then the next day, the rug needed to be swept again, as if the dirt blew back immediately. She did the dishes, and there they were—zap! back in the sink. Melanie wished she had a magical tool to make the work do itself; perhaps she could endure her life if what she did could feel like a game, a reassuring, rewarding, pleasurable game. But now her mind seemed utterly lacking in creativity.

Ray was exhausted when he came home, so Melanie did her best to not trouble him, to act cheerful. She listened while he told her about his day, but she had little to say in return. The silence afterwards could be long and deep, could last until one or the other of them decided to go to bed. Ray held her when she cried, as she had the night before, suddenly, in the middle of nursing Lise, as she had felt the trembling creep up her legs; but even as he hushed and soothed her, she saw his worried expression, saw he did not understand. Did she? She could not explain why she was crying. Sometimes his face seemed to say: Is this what I have now? Is this my life? A job I don't particularly like, a long commute, and a wife who cries and cries for no apparent reason? Melanie found it impossible to explain what was happening to her. In a confused way, she realized that she wanted to be rescued, but rescued from what? How was her life so awful?

On the television screen, an energetic-looking young mother proudly lifted up her baby in its Pampers. Her kitchen was three times the size of Melanie's. It was clear of dishes and mess, and the counters gleamed. The mother seemed to be declaring: I can do it all! I have a neat house, my baby is content and dry in his Pampers, and, to top it off, I'm refreshed and happy! No one's kitchen counter or floor could be that clean, Melanie argued in her mind. How can that woman have such a small baby and not look tired? In her loose-fitting blouse so she could nurse easily, Melanie felt fat and slovenly, like a slattern, and old, old, old, as if her life had already lost its zest. She imagined she was a middle-aged cleaning woman avidly watching soap operas during her brief moments of rest, taking seriously the actors' lives, feeding on their trumped-up emotions.

Lise had fallen asleep against her. Carefully, Melanie lit a cigarette and stirred the burnt-out match in circles in the crowded ashtray on the windowsill, piling up the ashes methodically in one corner. She told herself that she should put Lise in her crib and then sweep the floor and make the bed, but she could not move. Instead, a nursery rhyme popped into her head. As a child, she had loved to recite rhymes while she traced their old-fashioned letters and the pictures of characters like Simple Simon or Miss Muffett in a leather-bound copy she had discovered on her grandmother's bookshelf. Although some of the rhymes had been rather sinister and nonsensical, they had penetrated her psyche and came unbidden, chant-like to her mind at odd moments. They had sparked her early interest in poetry and make-believe.

Eventually, after dressing Lise in a warm outdoor sleeper, she took the blue metal stroller from the closet by the front door. She struggled to push it apart with her hands, because it was old and rusty and came apart only with force. Melanie bounced it unsteadily down the four flights of stairs, holding the bars tightly as she turned each corner, fearful the stroller would slip from her grasp. Down would come baby, cradle and all. Cruel mother drops baby down flight of stairs, claimed she lost control of stroller. She could imagine the *National Enquirer* headlines.

The weather was still cold, but when the February sun touched Melanie's face, she leaned into it as a worshiper, hoping it would warm her clear through. She took Lise up the street, into the neighborhood away from the main avenue, where it was quieter, toward the playground. Her building was the only apartment building on the block; mostly there were dilapidated one-level stucco houses, though nearly every house had a garden of sorts in front. In spring there were tangled nasturtiums and an abundance of wisteria, making the entire street smell fragrant. Even in winter, some homes were covered by vines that bore clusters of white and purple flowers like those in front of the Rosaline Apartments, but the trees were barren except for a few stubborn leaves that hung precariously on their branches. There was no one around. Melanie pushed the stroller along, cigarette in one exposed hand, mittened hand clutching the metal bar. At the playground, several mothers stood talking in a group; another pushed her child in the baby swings. She chose a bench that faced the others and leaning back, closed her eyes. When she opened them again, the sun had gone behind a cloud. Melanie stared at the clouds; they looked thin and vaporish, and through them the sunlight was yellow and watery. The world felt dead. Dead. Winter sun, white sky. Yes, it was winter, even here in sunny California. There was not even the sound of birds. They must have all migrated, Melanie thought. Lines from one of her favorite poets, Rilke, sprang into her mind. It was the first time in months she had thought of poetry. "*O trees of life, when will your winter come? We're never single-minded, unperplexed, like migratory birds. Outstrip and late, we suddenly thrust into the winds, and fall into unfeeling ponds . . .*"

Shivering violently, Melanie rose, although she had been at the playground only ten minutes. She began to walk farther up the block, but then, as if compelled, she stopped. Her fingers clenched the stroller bar. Where was she? Her surroundings seemed blurry. The houses rushed in and then receded like ocean waves. Melanie felt a sinking sensation in her stomach, a scream at the back of her throat. Was it out? Had it sounded? No, I can't scream! I must go home; I must take Lise home. Why was she standing there instead, leaning over the stroller? It's only a few blocks. A man walking his dog was coming toward her. He stopped and, smiling at Lise, asked Melanie if she was all right, did she need help? Mutely, she shook her head. Did he ask because she looked strange? He hesitated but then left, leaving her feeling weaker than ever. How could she manage this? It was such a long distance. As she walked slowly in the direction of the apartment building, the sidewalk appeared to be melting, the concrete grains turning back into liquid cement. I'm not normal, I'm not normal. This doesn't happen to normal people. Oh, please, just let me get home; let me get Lise home.

When she reached the door of her building, anxious to feel something solid, Melanie leaned her cheek desperately against the wooden door as she searched for her key. Inside the hallway, her landlady stood with her two toddlers. Melanie smiled weakly as the woman opened the door for her, but she did not talk, afraid of what her voice might reveal. Panting, she tugged the stroller up the steps. Beneath her jacket, her sweater was soaked with perspiration, and her skin felt clammy. She pushed Lise to the middle of the room, put the brake on the stroller and flung herself onto the mattress. Like Alice in Wonderland, she felt she was walking in circles, confused by this terrifying world she was suddenly inhabiting, which had no clear or familiar landmarks. Her body shook with uncontrollable sobs. Melanie mashed her face against the pillow to muffle the sounds from Lise, tore at her pillow, clutching its substance desperately, as if, like a life raft, it might prevent her from drowning. The clock hands read two-fifteen. Ray would not be home until seven o'clock, perhaps later. It would be dark already for hours. Things were always worse at night. The sky, like a crow, perched over her, filling her mind with such deep darkness, it was as if light did not exist.

Melanie pressed her fist hard against her damp forehead. She wished she could crush in her skull, stop thought from entering her mind altogether. Instead, she rose and unstrapped Lise from the stroller, changed her diaper, re-dressed her. Lise was already half asleep; her head dropped heavily on her chest, and Melanie wondered, as she laid her down for a nap, how Lise could not be disturbed by the misery she was witnessing. She covered her with a blanket and then lightly stroked Lise's rosy cheek. When she thought of how lovely Lise was, how innocent and ultimately unprotected, she began to cry again.

With tears streaming down her cheeks, Melanie removed her own hat and jacket, and threw them over the back of a kitchen chair. She made a peanut butter sandwich, mechanically wiping the peanut butter to each corner of bread as she had been trained to as a child. Maybe the problem is that I'm not getting enough liquids, she told herself; nursing mothers are supposed to have lots of liquid. And maybe the smoking is upsetting me, Melanie sighed, although I can as easily imagine quitting as stopping breathing.

She chewed the crusty bakery bread, forcing herself to swallow each bite, and then washed it down with two glasses of milk. She glanced out the kitchen window as she ate, instead of at the food. The sky had gotten very cloudy, and she wondered dimly if it would rain, another of those drizzles that lasted for weeks—steady, misty, fine-needled rain that turned the universe into a cloud of mist and damp. *Rain, rain, go away. It's raining, it's pouring, the old man is snoring. Went to bed and he bumped his head, and he didn't get up in the morning . . . Rain, rain, go away, go away, go away . . .*

Melanie reached for a bag of corn chips from the kitchen cupboard and poured another glass of milk. She brought them into the living room beside her armchair and flipped the television on. *The Dating Game* was on, and a sexy-looking blonde sat in one of the chairs, laughing and sliding her eyes coyly at the camera and at the host. Mesmerized by the woman's mouth and by the slender legs she kept crossing and uncrossing, Melanie watched for a few minutes before switching the channel to a western. The repetitious sound of shooting and Apache warwhoops lulled her to sleep. She woke to Lise's crying. Wake, sleep, wake, sleep; Melanie did not know if she was dreaming or awake. She carried Lise out from her crib and lay with her on the mattress. Lying together side by side, Melanie felt as though she and Lise were like the pair of heads in the M. C. Escher painting *Bond of Union*. Like those lovers suspended in space, their brains were coiled around each other, eternally, irrevocably bound.

❦ *Two*

Marie guided Melanie through the double glass doors of the hospital. At the reception desk, a perky young woman welcomed them, but as her warm brown eyes sought Melanie's, Melanie's sought the floor. She could not believe she was there, where Pete had been the previous year. And here was Marie, again playing Florence Nightengale. Yet who else had there been to turn to. Marie had not even questioned her but had assured Melanie she would be there within the hour. Had her voice sounded so awful? Now Melanie stood mutely as Marie explained to the receptionist the symptoms Melanie had described brokenly.

"It sounds like you could be having a diabetic attack," said the sweet red mouth.

Melanie let out her breath. Of course, diabetes runs in my family. Why didn't I think of that? Yes, let it be that; let it be physical, please let it be physical. It was the prayer she always whispered to herself when confronted with illness. When she had suffered blinding headaches in high school and had gone for an exam, she had been dismayed that the doctor had been unable to find an organic cause. Rather than pursue other possibilities, she had simply taken more aspirin. But now maybe? She glanced momentarily at the woman's sympathetic face and managed a smile.

"It runs in my family. My grandparents both died from diabetic shock," she said as loudly and clearly as possible. If only the rushing and pounding in her head would cease, if the quivering could stop for a minute. Melanie thought suddenly of Ray, whom Marie had called after speaking with her. He had left work, and when he arrived, Melanie had handed him Lise, crying out apologies. She had felt the most dreadful relief, and as the door of their building had slammed behind Marie and her, she felt she had escaped from prison.

The young woman told Melanie someone would see her soon and suggested they take a seat. When Marie sat close to her on the orange, vinyl waiting-room couch, holding her again around the shoulders, Melanie felt acutely uncomfortable. She did not feel capable of explaining what was the matter with her; she could barely understand it herself. As if realizing what she was feeling, Marie patted Melanie's arm, saying,

"Don't worry. They'll take care of you. They won't let you go until they figure out what's wrong."

Melanie knew she had taken a leap. Would the doctor decide that, like her mother, she was crazy? Would it mean she would have to stay there? Would they take her away from her baby? She didn't feel exactly crazy; she only felt she could not control any of her actions. Being out of doors was terrifying; the bus ride had been nearly more than she could bear.

After several minutes, Melanie heard her name called. As Marie's face faded from her view, she felt like turning and running. She stumbled after the doctor who had appeared in the waiting room. What was she going to say? Oh God, he would discover everything! When he shut the door of a smaller room, and she looked up at his impassive face and cold, blue-white eyes, unfeeling as marbles, her fear intensified. This man wouldn't understand anything! Why wasn't the warm lady from the reception desk here? Her she could talk to about the ceaseless trembling.

The doctor questioned her calmly, writing all the while on a lined yellow pad. But as he took in the terror in her eyes and the way her body clenched over onto itself as if she were hanging on for dear life, he laid his pen down and looked directly at her. Quietly, he said he thought it would be a good idea if she remained at the hospital for the night. Could she arrange that? He would assign her a place on the ward (oh, that word conjured up so much!) and would immediately prescribe some medication, because she was having an acute anxiety attack. It was not a diabetic attack. It *must* be mental, Melanie thought with horror.

He was keeping her there. She did not have to go back outside, did not have to prevent herself from screaming. Cars would not veer onto the sidewalk into her; their sound would not crash through her frail skull; the crowds would not smother her. If they did, she would scream, and then, like her mother, she would be bound, would have her arms held, would be twisted, protesting, across a courtroom. She would be committed. Melanie buried her tear-stained face in her hands, aware that he was watching everything she did. She could stay, she could stay! He would help her. That was all that mattered. As she sat, speechless, the doctor left his desk. Passing her to make further arrangements, he touched her shoulder, and this sudden kindness brought on an ache somewhere so deep inside her, Melanie felt she would howl with grief.

She remembered the line of rooms on either side of the hallway. Rooms on either side, little cubicles, little cells. Melanie followed closely behind the doctor, afraid of those openings, those crevices where who knew what lurked, what unimaginable pain. It seemed a long distance from the heavy double doors to the point where the three of them finally stopped—the doctor, herself, and Marie. The room he selected for her was a single one, rectangular, like a coffin. The walls were narrow, the window was barred, and inside stood a single monastic cot. White pillow, white, antiseptic-looking bedspread. Before she left, Marie hugged her tightly. Feeling her friend's tears against her face, merging with her own, Melanie felt a sudden pang as she realized Marie's love for her and her concern.

Melanie swallowed the oval black and green pill a nurse handed her, along with some water in a small paper cup. It was the kind of cup she used to suck Italian ices out of as a child. Then she was alone. With a door that closed, that could seal her off from the world. She was no longer standing in an open field, out in the open, exposed. Melanie sat down gingerly on the bed and wrapped her arms around her body like a straitjacket. Alone with herself, it was as if the past had never happened, as if her existence had just begun. She lay huddled on top of the covers, pain swarming through her. She was losing herself; she was drowning and would never surface. Ray, Lise, Marie, and the doctor she had spoken with had shrunk to distant visions. She could not push them through to the forefront of her consciousness. Melanie prayed in an irresolute manner to be rescued, without really believing anything could save her. She touched the coverlet beneath her, the unlit cigarette between her fingers, desperate to find some reality beyond herself.

The lamp by her bedside produced a glow of warm yellow light. Its gentle, unobtrusive quality reminded Melanie of the dancing golden lights she had seen in the darkness as a child. When lying alone in her parents' big double bed, she had always been able to make out things in the darkness that was never quite dark because of the lit cityscape outside. Objects had appeared like night-sky constellations when she stared fixedly into the room's space: sparklike shapes that had metamorphosed into floating pianos, faces, and animals. Although the shapes were elusive, to her they appeared very real, and Melanie had always wondered if what she was seeing was energy, if energy could be given color and form. She saw the shapes even now in her mind's eye— darkness alive with movement, charged impressions, molecules jumping, flipping their way around the room, vibrating.

Now, so many years later, as she lay on the narrow hospital bed, Melanie was convinced that if she did not hold onto every atom, cling as a baby would to its mother's skin, her body would dissolve, would merge with those dancing lights, and Melanie as she knew herself would disappear. Could she merge with the universe—melt, slip backwards into pre-existence, the state before the womb? What was existence, after all? Yet with all her strength she fought against it. Her breasts hung painfully, full of milk that needed to be expressed. There was a bathroom within the room. Going to the sink, Melanie squeezed a few drops of milk into it with quivering fingers. She watched the blue liquid fall like tears, one by one, dropping into the pale white container of the sink. Like a huge mouth, the sink drain sucked it up. Afterwards, Melanie climbed between the unyieldingly tight sheets and curled into a ball. One by one, her fingers loosened their grip as she fell, exhausted, into oblivion.

* * * * *

The hospital had three floors for patients with psychiatric problems. Melanie, because of the nature of her symptoms, was on the mildest floor, the least dangerous one, the one for patients suffering from depression. Junkies occupied the fourth-floor ward, while the fifth floor was reserved for those who were either violent to themselves or others. When anyone entered or left those wards, the doors were immediately locked again. On the third floor, however, the doors could be pushed open, leaving one free to go as he or she chose. But Melanie had no desire to leave and no interest in what lay beyond them; it was difficult enough dealing with the small space she was allowed. She adjusted gradually to the ward's routine, to awareness of others around her, although during the first days and weeks, there was only pain. The trembling down her thighs and throughout her body continued for many days and nights. It stole her voice so that when she tried to speak, her words came out in a stutter. Although she shivered constantly, she felt more like a fever was consuming her skin, wrapping her in a cocoon of heat. She had never felt so preoccupied by, yet separated from her body.

Instead of feeling confining, the walls of her room sheltered and defined her. The bed became a known object, sometimes fearful, occasionally comforting. Many nights she slept without waking and felt clearer in the morning as if during the night something had been swept out of her system. Inside the confines of the room Melanie felt whole, but when she left it to eat, take a shower, sit in the circle at Group, meet with the doctor, she felt dispersed. Others' realities flowed into her and confused her. At the dinner table she had to be conscious of the three women who sat with her, who might unexpectedly hurl a dish to the floor or speak to her. Although wrapped in the kimono of her thoughts, she needed also to

be always alert to movement. A centerpiece filled with paper yellow daffodils stood on the table, and Melanie concentrated on the bend of each
stem, each petal. She ate mechanically realizing it was necessary to remain
alive, just as she swallowed, without protest, the black and green oval pill
dispensed to her three times a day.

Melanie did not understand what was happening to her; all she
could comprehend was that her feelings were tied up with Lise and the
sense of isolation and purposelessness that accompanied that relationship.
These perceptions had fuzzy outlines, though, while the truth lay somewhere beyond them. Melanie believed that until she could break through
to that inner understanding—as if scratching through a layer of black
crayon to the rainbow shades colored beneath it, something she had done
often as a child—she would continue feeling confused and lost.

Time had no meaning: it was difficult to believe in its passing, in
its capacity to heal. Such understanding would be factual and concrete;
for the moment, she was swimming in amorphous sensations, unable to
grab on to anything hard. Her posture reflected this state: head bent; long
hair falling across her face; eyes that could not focus clearly, that darted
away if they encountered another pair of eyes; back stooped as if carrying
a great weight. Melanie walked as if wanting her body—if she could curl
it tightly enough—to simply continue to turn in at the edges like an
autumn leaf, shrivel until it eventually dissolved to dust. Would there
always be mist before her eyes? Would her body ever cease its inner rum-
bling? Would she at some point be able to stand erect? *Homo erectus.* She
felt like a lesser form of human life, a mass of primal sensations.

The ward doctor she was assigned to was an elderly, heavyset man
with thinning white hair and a florid complexion. She and he met in a tiny
office next to one of the patient's rooms, reserved for therapy on a rotat-
ing basis. Although the desk behind which he sat had an impersonal quality to it, used as it was by many different doctors, and the abstract paintings on the wall were bland, the room became one of the safe places.

Dr. Huston leaned back in his swivel chair or focused on a point
beyond her. He occasionally asked a question or commented on something she said: Yes, and how did that make you feel, Melanie? or Tell me
more about that. They were leading questions, nonjudgmental, open-
ended. At their first session, Melanie expected him to tell her conclusive-
ly that she was as crazy as her mother. When he did not do this, she
relaxed and began to take comfort in being with him; the experience was
akin to sinking into a tub of relaxing warm water, water that, this time,
she wanted to linger in. Sometimes they sat in silence until, as she poked

her cigarette around and around in the ceramic ashtray on the desk, she frantically said something, anything, to break the quiet. He discussed her illness with her, and it seemed marvelous to know it could be defined, that it was something others knew about, a fact, a reality separate from herself.

"Your symptoms tell me that you are experiencing a postpartum depression, although, because of their severity, it is more likely a postpartum psychosis," he said. He then defined this for her, as if it were something quite neat and manageable. Dr. Huston did not seem disturbed by her incoherence. Instead he made what was happening appear oddly rational.

"You were trying so hard to be good, Melanie, so hard to do everything perfectly; it really is no wonder you collapsed. You must learn to give yourself the permission to be human, to fail a little, to realize you are not the be-all and end-all for that baby. It has a life of its own, you know, quite separate from you, besides its own strength and resources.

"Is the medicine working, Melanie? Is the trembling subsiding a little? I've decided—to help break this cycle of depression—to put you on an antidepressant as well temporarily. You see, right now you are locked into something very powerful. If we can lessen the pain with medication—that's its purpose, after all—then we'll be able to truly make progress."

Melanie drank his words in as she drank in the calmness his presence brought her. She accepted his directions, grateful to be led, instructed.

🌹 *Three*

She began to feel better. Whether from the medicine, or the safety of the hospital's boundaries, or from being cut off from the normal routine of her life, she felt the pain imperceptibly ease. Her trembling ceased, her body straightened, her eyes lifted to see the world.

Marie brought her a pot of yellow primroses for the windowsill of her room. It was lovely, each morning, to see the small, perky flowers, to know that beauty still existed. Melanie had explained to Marie that when she tried to read, the letters moved on the page like scurrying black insects, so, to help her fill the long hours, Marie brought yarn and knitting needles. Mechanically, Melanie copied Marie's instructions and then saw, as if by a miracle, a square of pink wool emerge from her efforts. This, too, aided her sense of reality. If she could create, she existed; if she existed, she had power, didn't she?

Ray's visits were more strained and filled her with guilt. He always looked tired, and the habitual dark creases beneath his eyes were more pronounced than ever. When she noticed the Playtex nurser sticking up out of the diaper bag he carried, she felt tremendously sad. Her breasts still leaked milk and felt sore and swollen. But when Ray handed Lise to her, and Melanie tried to hold her daughter against her, she felt terribly agitated. She handed her back quickly, feeling as if she had been scalded by the heat from Lise's body. Lise's eyes were like twin spotlights following her around the room. Eventually, Melanie turned her face from them and stared instead at the white wall, which seemed to visibly vibrate. As if through a glass curtain, she listened to Ray's movements of departure—heard him pack items into the diaper bag, fit Lise into her plastic seat. Then he was behind her, and she felt his hand stroke her cheek. Her face burned at his touch. Later, she wished she had called to him, but it was as though her voice were still underground; even when she wanted to speak, at times no sound came forth. She tried to write him a letter explaining what she was feeling, but the effort of holding the pen and watching the blurry black letters was too difficult. Unable to concentrate long on any activity, she simply sat in her room, and occasionally in the ward lounge. She could not have said what she was waiting for, but she waited, trying desperately to believe that perhaps soon circumstances would change.

Group therapy was held every day on the ward and involved as many patients as were willing to participate. The usual group of fifteen to twenty men and women met after lunch in the dining area. They sat in a large circle, and the proceedings were directed by an exuberant, bearded man named Chris who initiated a topic and then facilitated the session, interjecting opinions or further questions where he felt necessary. His body seemed everywhere at once, eyes alert and intent, sympathetic and aware, and he had a reassuring voice, like Dr. Huston's, though his was youthful and aggressive, reaching out and challenging while simultaneously remaining compassionate. Like Ray, Chris typically pinned a speaker down, repeating what she or he had said, and then inviting comment from others in the group. By the end of the forty-five minute session, his shoulder-length, thick curly hair looked wilder than ever because he repeatedly passed his hands through it as he moved about. His face streamed with perspiration, which he dabbed at now and again impatiently using a handkerchief he swept out of a back pocket of his jeans.

The patients were strikingly different from each other, requiring Melanie to reevaluate her concept of what it meant to be crazy. She found herself increasingly looking up from her lap and listening to and watching the others intently, curious about what they would say and wondering why they were on the ward. When Chris addressed her, Melanie felt obliged to answer, although her voice shook, and she seldom met his demanding eyes. If attention became too focused on her, though, she gazed at the carpet beneath her feet or her own fingers curling and uncurling in her lap. And always, as if she had grown an extra pair of arms, she clutched a lit cigarette and an ashtray.

At times, the painful details of someone's experience diminished and exhausted her. Two women patients in particular affected her like this. They were Eulalie and Deena. Eulalie, who was about sixty, had chalk-white skin and cropped black hair that stuck up from her scalp like crow feathers. She was unnaturally thin and walked stooped over, her bones giving the impression they were twigs that could snap under the slightest pressure. Eulalie's cheeks were so gaunt, they looked as if they had been pressed inwards, while her mouth seemed permanently shaped into the startled exclamation of an "Oh!" Instead of speaking normally, she whispered, and Melanie had to strain to catch her few words. She and Eulalie saw the same doctor, and so Melanie began to feel a bond with her. When Melanie overheard Eulalie tell another patient that Dr. Huston was planning to start giving her shock treatment, she was terrified.

"Are you really going to do that?" Melanie asked Dr. Huston at their next meeting. "Do you think it's right to reduce people to vegetables?"

"I can understand your fear, Melanie," he replied patiently, "and I assure you I am not making this decision lightly. Eulalie has been suffering from a debilitating depression for over ten years, and she has responded to no other treatments. This is somewhat a last resort. What interests me more is that you are concerned about her. That tells me you are beginning to come out of your own depression. You can be involved with someone outside yourself."

"A stone would care," she snorted.

"I'm glad you care," he replied, smiling at her, "but perhaps you are projecting a little of your own need to be cradled and protected. Do you see how that might be the case?"

Melanie could not answer. She sat fiddling with her hair, feeling sickeningly naive. Maybe what he was saying was true, but why did everything wind up coming back to her? Wasn't it possible to care about somebody without it involving some neurosis? When the silence had lasted for a while, Dr. Huston came closer to where she sat.

"Sorry, our time's up," he said, squeezing her hand gently. Melanie nodded faintly in response. She was afraid to look at him and waited until he left before she rose to go herself. Why did it comfort her so that he made the effort to be so gentle with her?

* * * * *

In contrast to Eulalie, Deena was a chubby black woman with a brassy, sarcastic manner. From the first group on, she attached herself to Melanie and harbored her from the stranger patients, who either did not speak at all or spoke only in riddles. Melanie soon learned that patients gravitated toward each other, pulled by a sense of camaraderie. Different people gathered in small clusters, chose to share their meals, or simply sat together, companionably, in the lounge. Deena could usually be depended upon to talk, and she talked about her life openly with the Group. Chris frequently turned to her if there was a prolonged period of silence. Melanie found it disturbing though that Deena's smile looked as if it had been cut out and pasted over her mouth. It seemed rigidly held in place, as if by invisible toothpicks, and when Deena spoke, the smile bobbed along like a sidekick. This looked ghoulish, especially if what she was talking about was anything but cheerful. But when Chris drew attention once to this dichotomy, Deena merely sighed and said she smiled because it was easier than showing her anger.

"What would happen if you showed us your anger?" he asked.

Deena laughed harshly. "Oh, I don't think you want to know. It's better if I smile, really it is. Anyway, I'd rather you focus on somebody else today, okay?" Though Deena's voice sounded brittle, and Melanie sensed suffering beneath the breezy words, Chris merely nodded and addressed another patient. For the remainder of the session, Deena withdrew into the cave of herself, acting suddenly very frigid, as if something icy was forming inside her. She did not show up for Group for two days, and when she returned she was subdued and distant, although the smile remained.

At some sessions, people screamed and shouted or threatened the others to get out of the way unless they wanted to be killed. Melanie—who shrank inside herself from the intensity of the pain—marveled at how Chris would firmly place his hand on the shoulder of the person who was upset, switching chairs, if necessary. He would pat the patient's arm and speak softly and encouragingly until gradually, the patient calmed down. When she herself spoke, her words spewed out in an incoherent rush; they bounced up and down unevenly, stopping and going like a defective windup toy. Melanie was certain no one would understand what she was trying to say. She hated what she perceived as the whiny sound of her voice and fought to control it.

Chris finally suggested that she make an effort to speak up, to try out a louder, more confident voice. When she did, he congratulated her and said didn't it feel better to act like a strong person, whether she felt like one or not? Melanie marveled that such a simple action could make her feel better. However, unless she concentrated, her voice automatically dropped back to a whisper, and she had to be reminded repeatedly: slow down, speak clearly, take your time, we can't hear you. If he pressed her, it made her angry, and she wanted to tell him to shut up, but she said nothing, fearful that he would in turn grow upset and kick her out of the group.

It was preferable to pretend to be invisible. When Chris spoke to her directly or asked her to follow up on a thought, sometimes her embarrassment was so great that she could only look at him with a contorted face and pleading eyes. Yet contrary to her expectations that the other patients would be either angry or bored, they usually smiled encouraging-ly. After several weeks, Melanie began to feel that, although she was with an admittedly strange assortment of people, they cared enough to listen to her. Just as she felt comforted when Dr. Huston patted her on her shoul-der and squeezed her hand, Melanie enjoyed Deena's hugs after their group sessions and her teasing words that once again they had survived Chris's probing.

Memories came of her life before Lise, before Ray. Melanie found herself thinking frequently of her childhood, as she had in the months after her delivery. During her sessions with Dr. Huston, she spoke more of the past than the present or future, and he seemed to want to lead her back, to want her to explore. One morning, he asked her to describe her mother.

"I couldn't really depend on my mother," Melanie said, as she poked her cigarette around in the grey-white mounds of ash, jabbing at a bright orange spark inside the residue. "She got sick before I was born, I guess. I've only known her well during the few short times, when she'd been put on medication. When I was a teenager, I had this fantasy that she would just hold me, that if I were depressed I could lay my head in her lap and she would stroke my hair. You know—the way I stroke Lise's," she said, looking up at him. "But I could never ask her to do that. She was always in her own world, and it frightened me; I never knew what she might do. Once, she took this *West Side Story* record I loved and broke it across her knee because she was sick of listening to it. I threw a shoe at her and ran crying out of the apartment, and then she wouldn't let me back in. I still remember how sore my knuckles felt from pounding against the door. She used to walk around the apartment and unplug everything— the lamps, the toaster, especially the television— because she was bothered by electricity. It annoyed the hell out of me, of course, but you just learned to live with it, you know. I usually just tried to avoid her."

Melanie had begun wearing her hair in two long pigtails. Now, for comfort, she stroked the smooth velveteen ribbons that held them.

"I've always been ashamed of her, even more than of my father. After my grandmother died, the children's court placed me in a boarding school in New York State during my teens, but later on, I was sent back to my mom and dad, who were then in a better financial situation. After I split—I left home at seventeen because they were not exactly a family you wanted to stay with—they were evicted from the apartment, so they took a room in a boarding house. It was filled with creepy residents. I hated to pass them on the stairs or be introduced, always wondering, you know, why they lived there, why they didn't have ordinary lives, whether they would annoy me or accost me in some way. But you know, now that I'm older, I think they were just pathetic old men down on their luck." Melanie lifted her pack of Marlboros and shook it to see if she had enough cigarettes to last the session.

"It's weird," she continued, "because even though I would have liked more normal parents, in some ways I'm proud of them, too, proud they're not mainstream. Besides being a laborer, my father's an artist; he paints pictures of ships and foreign countries. He's funny; he's very intelligent and sensitive. He reads constantly. Toward my mother . . . well, mainly I feel protective, ready to defend her if anyone looks funny at her, as if she's odd—which, of course, she is, I understand that, but it still makes me furious. Other girls' mothers always want to mother me, take me in, but that's even worse. Mrs. Duran at Lytton is like that. I guess that's why I was uncomfortable around her. But I don't know . . . you know, compared to other people's situations, I didn't have it so bad. I mean, I've met people along the way with really bad home lives! They got beaten or had other awful things happen to them. I shouldn't complain. It would have been nice to have a normal family, whatever that is . . . a real family, where people cared what you did and looked out for you . . . it would have been . . . oh, please. . . I can't . . . I don't want to talk about this anymore. Please. Do we have to?" Melanie bent over in the chair and held onto her body as if she felt it would break into pieces.

"It would have been nice to have received love, maybe?" Dr. Huston said into the lengthening silence. "You wanted your mother's and father's, and they couldn't supply it. No one else can replace that important love. You must feel very angry and hurt. Other children, normal children receive love, don't they?"

Melanie felt tears stabbing her eyes. In response, she pressed her legs together tightly. Why did Dr. Huston have to say things like that? Was he trying to rub it in? Fuck it! What good did it do?

"Let yourself cry, Melanie. This kind of crying is healing. It can be helpful. You wanted love and didn't get it. Therefore, you feel somehow as if you still don't deserve it. You do feel that way, don't you? That you of all people don't deserve love?"

Melanie deliberately straightened up in the chair and lit a cigarette. She felt annoyed as she watched her hands shake and took several drags before answering to calm herself. "That's true, at least partly. I want love; I want to be loving . . . I really do. I don't enjoy feeling so alone. I mean, I'm so fucking critical. I go around summing everybody up, and then I have trouble liking anybody. No one measures up, especially not me; I'm probably the person I criticize most. I can't explain it, but sometimes I feel like my true life is slipping away. Being with Ray, being a mother, I feel like I'm going to lose who I am. And yet telling you that makes me feel so selfish. It must mean I can't love anybody or be there for anybody."

Carefully, unconsciously, she steered away from the pain of not feeling loved, and Dr. Huston let her go, let her begin to intellectualize again. But as she rambled breathlessly, running away with her words, afraid to stop, Melanie felt what she said sounded stiff and pointless, unreal. By the end of the session, she sat, exhausted, with her hands lying limply in her lap, barely able to move.

* * * * *

Lying in bed that night, Melanie hungered to be cradled in someone's arms. She imagined she was reliving the grief of knocking on the door: The aloneness on the steps, the feeling that she had to be let in because there was nowhere else to go. Dr. Huston's final words of the session kept flashing at her: "Perhaps it sounds like a truism, Melanie, but without being given a core of love yourself, it is very difficult to give love to anyone else. You are bound to feel cheated, bound to resent the fact that Lise is being given what you yourself wanted. You can't pour from an empty chalice. It isn't fair, but you'll need to find ways to give that love to yourself, dear girl."

Melanie's eyes filled at the remembrance of his kind face, his strong, fatherly voice. He never seemed to change; although she frequently flew back at him in anger, he appeared to become only more calm. "But people love me. Ray loves me. Marie. I've always had friends. I can't say that I've never been loved. Why isn't that enough? And I do love Lise; she's very beautiful. It's not hard to love her. I just can't . . . I just can't . . ." Her words and the sudden rush of anger evaporated. It was so cruel to resent an innocent child who had never asked to be born. Only an ogre would do such a thing. Yet despite her resistance, Melanie felt the truth of what he was saying. She wanted. She wanted so much, and Lise was always taking, feeding off her . . . Could she give out of an empty chalice?

Fretfully, she sat up and tried to read. But although the words on the page were clearer than they had been, the mystery could not hold her attention. In exasperation, she tried a magazine, but after a while, she let it slide from her lap as well. The blank walls seemed to accuse her. You don't have a monopoly on being unloved, Melanie. Whoever did have enough love; what's wrong with you? Oh, shut up voices! I'm tired. All I want to do is sleep.

Melanie lay back down, turned off the light, and shut her eyes, but she continued to turn Dr. Huston's words over and over in her mind. She did want to be loved! But when Ray tried to get her to talk about her fears or other strong feelings, she felt terrified. She felt as if he was trying to get something from her that she couldn't give him, that she didn't have. Looking into his eyes hurt; it was like being probed with a strong light. He was such a stranger now, part of another life she had lived, and it frightened her because she hardly missed him. Melanie turned on her side and breathed in and out until, finally, she drifted into that floating state before actual sleep. Relaxed, hanging in limbo, she felt warm gauzy material enveloping her body. The warmth soaked deeper and deeper into her tissues, and her hands relaxed their grip on the pillow. The next thing she knew, sunlight was touching a corner of the wall.

Four

Dr. Huston spoke of gaining a new perspective, of developing inner strength. She was a chameleon, a sponge absorbing whatever atmosphere she was in; she needed to solidify within herself, develop a strong inner core that could withstand changes outside herself. Rather than being shaped by others, she could shape herself, create her own destiny. The thought was simultaneously frightening and thrilling. How could she create herself, weak as she was? From where could she gain such strength, such power? Yet in some respects, she had already begun; the separation from her ordinary life, even if temporary, made her feel as if she was meeting herself for the first time. She was like a baby in a hospital nursery window—crying, needy, vulnerable, but, equally, brand-new, open to the future. Protected by the safety of the white, womblike walls of her room and by the reassurance of Dr. Huston's apparent confidence in her recovery, Melanie opened her mind to suggestions she heard in Group or during occupational therapy.

Occupational therapy was held twice a week in a large room on the ward. She and the other patients sat together like comrades, craft materials spread out in front of them on tables; they were like factory workers assembling pieces, creating wholes. Melanie found herself trying things she had never done before or had always been reluctant to do when suggested by Ray or Marie, such as tie-dyeing or batik, believing she had no skill for such things. Now, she found herself enjoying the sensuous contact with the wood, the cloth, the glue, the paint. When she squeezed the wet cloth, red and purple dye staining her hands, or dribbled abstract designs with hot wax, Melanie realized she wasn't as incompetent as she had always feared. As she held up a completed project, she marveled that she had done it. It was like being given an opportunity to start life over, with fewer preconceptions.

After OT, she lay wearily on her bed, smoking or simply staring at the ceiling, reviewing in her mind the morning's events, yet the fatigue felt good. She felt heavy, spent, used. Even though part of her could look objectively at her creations and realize they weren't especially polished or finished-looking, what had been fun was doing them, doing them alone and together with others. When Melanie paused in whatever project she was working on and looked across at Deena or Eulalie or Joan, who had the room next to hers, and watched their faces and hands, she noted with pleasure the quickness of their moving fingers, the concentration in their eyes, the occasional smirk of satisfaction. The occupational therapy room was airy and full of light. When additional light poured in through the window, coating the table before her, Melanie felt as if grace itself had entered, an invisible, healing presence.

Occasionally, she stared at what she held in her hands and felt loathing for it. She asked herself: Why am I doing this? This is meaningless. This has no value at all; it's busy work. Then, pushing away the cloth, beads, and paper, she buried her face in her hands or sat enfolded inside herself, watching those around her with suspicion. The familiar sinking began, the unsteadiness, the feeling of being detached from her body, as if she were standing alongside it. On days like that, Melanie kept to herself. She went to Group because it was required, saw her doctor because it was required, but the moments stretched on and on like a pulled-tight rubber band. By evening she felt as if she herself were pulled tight. Then the idea of recovering from her depression mocked her. Should she never think then, consider, question? Did it only work to have a pabulum existence, not too hot, not too cold? When, what, was just right? Even as a child, she had preferred Father Bear's "great big chair," or, as a second choice, Mama Bear's "medium-sized chair." Little Bear's "just right chair" sounded insipid. Ordinary. She did not want "just right," did she?

Careless of wind, sun, rain, she had run out in the middle of thunderstorms, completely drenching herself, not caring for the deadly power of the magnificent bolts of lightning as they tore devilishly across the sky, as if wanting to make holes in it. There was only the tremendous power they conveyed to her that she clutched tenderly, fiercely inside her, that made her want to explode. Could she never have such moments again? Would there be only knitting, working crosswords, making pointless crafts to remind her of her hospital stay? At home, she would wash and feed Lise, put laundry into the machines, change the sheets, wash the dishes. Did intensity call to her only to cheat her? And yet, for the moment, what? Each day. Then the next. When Dr. Huston brought up the future in their conversations, she found herself changing the subject, afraid of where he might lead her. But was it so awful to live day to day, doing the most ordinary things? Didn't thousands of people live that way, the very people Melanie had vowed never to become like? Perhaps they knew better, after all. Perhaps if she formed a shell, every impression would not dent her being.

* * * *

What Melanie most enjoyed, however, was Movement class. This was held once a week on the floor above their ward. It upset her that it meant leaving the ward and tramping elephant-like up a flight of stairs with the rest of the patients. They each latched onto the bannister, although sometimes someone froze halfway up, restricting the flow of motion. Then, a nurse from the ward had to lead him or her back to safety. Twice, Melanie had become stuck herself and had returned, shamefaced, to her room, where for the remainder of the morning she had punched at her thighs in fury and desperation. Why did her body and soul continue to fail her? Why couldn't this useless being called Melanie simply dissolve and be done with it!

But on other days, it was the most pleasant time, mainly because of the music, the music that streamed through her veins and washed out the muck inside her. Mark, the leader, like Chris who ran Group, seemed godlike to Melanie in his appearance, in his strength, in his apparently unceasing ability to give of himself to others. Like the rats of Hamelin, they, the patients, sat in a loosely formed circle, waiting to follow the directed sound.

"Just move to the music any way you like," Mark would say. "Crawl, stretch, wiggle, get down on all fours. Get in touch with your body. Claim it! Lie down, close your eyes; let the music work its rhythms into your minds and bodies. Surrender to any feelings that might arise, and Marta and I will be here if you feel anxious, if you need us. If you want to cry, go ahead! This is a safe place to do that. If you feel like giggling—and you better believe there'll be some funny pieces I'm going to play—let yourself go. We're just human animals after all, and we can be pretty quirky as a species. If there's time, we'll do some psychodrama."

Long shafts of light filtered in from the tall, cathedral-like windows. The music, a Prokofiev piece, began like an ache, a slow, steady beginning, but it was too loud. Melanie felt as if it was smothering her. Beside her on the carpet, Joan, a fragile-looking, petite new patient with dead-white skin, curled away from the sound. She covered her ears, tucked her face between her knees. Other patients made random movements; they picked at their clothes or self-consciously smoothed their hair back. Some giggled inappropriately and then turned away from the others as sudden weeping overtook them. Marie, an older, very refined-looking woman sat with her face to the wall so that no one would know she was there. Deena and Eulalie seemed far away, across the savannah of the carpet. Melanie wanted to be near them, but the distance was too great, and she did not want to make herself conspicuous. Then Joan lifted her face, held it very straight and upright in the pose of a classically trained dancer; her breasts strained against the purple leotard she wore. She began to slither in a controlled fashion to imaginary music, unrelated to what Mark was playing. And, as if inspired by watching her, Mark stopped the Prokofiev, paused a moment in thought.

"Okay, change of plans!" he grinned. "I can see that Prokofiev is making some of you very uptight. We'll listen to some Debussy instead—his 'L'Apres-Midi du Faun.' Of course, this piece is really about a satyr, a Pan-like creature out to do deviltry in the forest. You can imagine you're that if you want to, but we'll pretend it's about the animal fawn, the baby deer. We're meandering through the woods. How do our hoofs feel as they touch the soil? What scents do we smell? The branches shelter us, protect us; now they part a little so we can see the expanse of the meadow . . . out there we can romp, kick up our heels . . . got it? Let's go." He started the record, and Melanie, sitting crosslegged on the carpet, listened intently.

Joan *was* a fawn, on all fours, desire evident in her flushed cheeks, and fixed pupils. As Melanie watched, the music seemed to weave into and out of her body. She looked strangely vulnerable, a young, awkward animal poking its nose into a grassy meadow. Melanie's own body would not move; she was the silent watcher guarding Joan, preventing her from being shot by hunters. Mark's voice continued . . .

"It's early afternoon, breezy, the sun is lighting up the greenery. What do you feel, young fawns? It's spring, you're waiting for something—maybe your mate or maybe some especially delicious tidbit, and it's out there in the grass. As you nibble it, do you feel sun on your flanks, warm, penetrating sun? Let it in, let it warm and relax those wintry muscles."

Mark dipped, rose, pawed and sniffed at the ground, then at the air. He stopped when he realized that Mary, a young woman with wavy black hair, was sitting in the middle of the carpet, sobbing. Marta, Mark's assistant, held her hand. Her features were stretched out of shape like chewing gum, and her limbs were splayed as a starfish's. As the music increased in intensity and swept over her, Mary screamed.

"I'm not a deer. I'm not a deer! I'm not dear. I'm ugly. Just look at me—this ugly, ugly body! I'm a fat cheese, the cheese that stood alone. . . let me out!" Mary screamed again, jolting the atmosphere of the room. Then she sprang up as abruptly as a jack-in-the-box. In response, Joan swayed toward her, raising and lowering her head.

"Don't you come near me, you! She wants to attack me! Don't let her attack me! Mark! Mark!"

Joan stopped beside Mary and snorted at her. Mark kneeled next to them and watched as the two eyed each other. Marta had moved behind Mary, away from her vision. Mary covered her face as Joan swayed dangerously close to her, slithering in perfect time to the music. Other women on the carpet began creeping toward the two, dancing around them like witches who have found a sacrifice. Melanie thought, I want to join in, but I don't know how to dance. My body doesn't move like Joan's. I'm too stiff; I can't move like Joan.

The patients slyly encircled the two women, inch by inch, as though, with one accord, they wanted to pen them in. Mark spoke softly, "What are you feeling, Mary? Why are you letting Joan trap you like this? Do you think she wants to hurt you? What came back to you through the music—what memories, what feelings? Why are you crying? Get in touch with those tears. And Joan, get in touch with your anger. Why do you want to hurt Mary? Who is it you really want to hurt?"

As he talked soothingly, persuasively, Melanie felt as though she were in the pen, although she was on the farthest edge of the group. Hands clutching her knees, rocking her body back and forth, she thought, I do not want to be held by Mark's voice. Why won't he let me go? But I want to let go; why can't I let go? The familiar jolt of electricity shot through her body. She pressed hard on her legs to stop the approaching trembling that was like the chugging of a loco-motive. She wanted to run away; but Mark's voice took her, held her. Gradually, the shaking subsided. His deep, lulling voice washed over her chest, in and out, in and out, cleansing her. Melanie closed her eyes. When she finally opened them, she saw Mary and Joan enfold-ed in each other's arms. Mark had an arm around each of the weep-ing women and was tenderly patting their shoulders. His face was pallid; perspiration matted his eyebrows and the hair that fell across his forehead. Mary moaned softly, like a cow lowing, and Joan was muttering, "It keeps rising and falling, up and down, up and down. I won't fall if I follow its motion . . . rising, falling, rising . . ."

Melanie felt something being lifted out and up, away from her body. She listened to her own breath, husky, soft, and it comforted her, it felt tangible; she must be real because she could breathe, she must be real.

* * * * *

It was another slow procession up the stairs. This time Melanie glanced at the landing, at those ahead of her on the steps, which extended outward like an arm from the ward. Was up and out to be her release? The sun was above her; its light reached down. It was necessary to look up to see it, while her usual point of focus was the ground. This time, instead of dragging herself upstairs like a dead body in a sack, Melanie moved as if she had a spring inside her. She felt light, airy, while, simultaneously, grounded in breath.

When everyone had entered the room and settled in a comfortable position, Mark looked at each person for a few minutes, as if appraising the general mood. Then, he turned toward his slender blonde partner, Marta, with a question in his eyes. She too scanned the group and then nodded, at first tentatively, and then emphatically. Her smile warmed the group, and Melanie, astonished by her beauty, drank in her Scandinavian features, her small-boned elegance, the lustrous platinum-colored hair that enthroned her face.

"Why is the mood so different today?" Mark asked with a laugh in his voice. "What's in the air, huh? *Something* for sure!" He laughed fully, an assured, completely unselfconscious laugh, and several of the others laughed along with him. "Is it because spring is coming? No one should be sick in springtime. The weather's too lovely, especially here in Berkeley."

"Well, maybe today is a good day for what we didn't have time for last week. I think I've explained psychodrama, role-playing, to most of you before," he said. He sat crosslegged next to Marta on the rug. "In psychodrama we replay past events that may have caused us pain or anxiety, events in which we often felt we had no power. Of course, we can't change the past; we all know that, but here in the present, we can say things to the individuals involved that we were unable to previously. And we can certainly change how we might respond in the future. This will become clearer as we go along if it sounds fuzzy now. If anyone simply wants to watch, that's okay. No one is forced to do anything here, but I hope that many of you will decide to participate. Psychodrama is a powerful, strengthening tool."

He stood up and marked off a section of the room, unfolding two aluminum chairs and placing them beside him.

"Here's our stage. Any volunteers?"

Without realizing she was doing so, Melanie raised her hand. Mark smiled and motioned her to her feet.

"Would you like to do a role play—imagine someone in one of these chairs while you take the other—or would you like to re-create a past situation and work through it? It's Melanie, right?"

"Yes," Melanie said hesitantly. "I think maybe the second thing, if that's okay."

"Absolutely!" Mark took her hand and suggested Marta take her other. "Now, Melanie, close your eyes and picture yourself somewhere and then describe that place to us so we can be there with you."

Melanie held their hands tightly, feeling surges of strength, as if their combined power was holding her up. She concentrated until, unbidden, a terrible memory sprang into her mind. Her hands shook as she recalled it. Dimly, she heard Mark's voice asking what she was seeing. How did he know she had seen anything?

"I was on Broadway, walking down Broadway . . . in New York City, you know. My father was holding my hand, gripping my hand and . . ." She faltered.

"Stay in the present, Melanie, as if it's happening right now," Mark said, squeezing her hand reassuringly.

"Wait," Mark continued. "Is he holding it tightly like this?"

"Yes, yes, it hurts. I can't let go."

"What else is happening, Melanie? Is he talking to you? Is there anyone else around?"

"He's very drunk, and he's singing; he's singing very loudly, at the top of his lungs. I'm trying to get away, but he won't let me. He's laughing, and he won't let go of me. People are staring at us; some of them look like they feel sorry for me, and I feel so embarrassed. He's so fat, and he keeps singing this dirty nursery rhyme. I want to let go, but he has me like in a vise. We just . . . keep on . . . walking and walking . . . everybody's staring . . . it's awful . . ."

Melanie felt her body start to shake, and she tried to release her hands from Mark's and Marta's grip.

"Let me go. Please, let me go," she whimpered. "I want to stop. I don't want to be here."

"Melanie, he's hurting you, and you need to tell him that. It hurts to be held so tightly, dammit!" Mark paused. "But I've got you; I'm not going to let you go. I will embarrass you, humiliate you. I'm going to keep singing." Mark began to sing raucously, swaying his body as if he were drunk.

"No, please . . . No! No!" Melanie suddenly screamed. "Let me go!" She wrenched one hand free, opened her eyes wide, stared at the group in front of her, as if she didn't realize where she was, and then began to laugh in amazement. "I'm free. Oh my God, I'm free! He doesn't have my hand anymore!" Continuing to laugh, she looked at Mark questioningly.

"Yes, Melanie, you're free. See? We're not holding your hands anymore."

"I can't believe it. I can't believe I could let go like that. You don't know how tight his grip was!"

"I think I have an idea," Mark said in a serious voice. "And it hurt, didn't it? But you don't have to be hurt anymore. You can let go. You don't have to be anybody's prisoner. You're a strong person, Melanie. You just need to realize that."

Deena came over and, kneeling beside her, held Melanie around the shoulders. How did Mark know that would happen? How could he, how can he know how I am held back, locked in like that, afraid to move? It was difficult to believe someone could see her pain, even more difficult to believe he could express such concern that it be ended. Thrilling to this possibility, Melanie wept silently, joyfully. If someone could care that much if she were well, maybe she could get well.

# Five

*I*n the hospital, time took on a very different quality. It had been four weeks since she had been outside, but to her thinking it seemed much longer. Her former life felt as if it had happened very long before: having the baby, caring for the baby, even being with Ray—all these events were pushed far back in time. When she woke each morning, there was the sense of time passing, as if during each night, she was living many years.

Where the hospital had been the unknown and frightening possibility, now it was the comforting familiar. The outside world was the place that held things such as the tree outside her window, the place from which came the song of a particular bird she began to identify as "her" bird, because it appeared to be the same one by its distinctive trill. One of the night nurses told her it was probably a mockingbird. It woke her while it was still dark outside and sounded as if it were about to die because of the urgency of its song, as if it were singing its last notes. After such intense introduction, its music settled into brief, sweet-sounding chirps that coaxed her to drowsiness and soothed her back to sleep. Melanie could depend upon the bird and the tree to be reliable, but what about the world itself? The outside doors, the street, the corner, the people who might be walking by—what would happen when she appeared among them again? What would happen? Melanie wondered if she would have to spend the remainder of her life stuck on the ward, all the while knowing that was not a possibility. How long could MediCal afford to pay for her keep? How long could Ray watch Lise by himself? Soon, she thought, terrified, she would have to emerge from this cocoon and deal with her real life. To comfort her, Deena promised that when Melanie felt up to it, she would walk outside with her.

After being away for a week at Dr. Huston's suggestion, Ray came during evening visiting hours.

"I'm giving her solid food now. You know, some oatmeal—that Gerber kind in a mix—and baby fruits along with her formula. She eats like a little demon! Sticks out that delicate little tongue of hers, pauses a minute, and then swoops down on the spoon, gazing up at me like a baby bird, and I've got the worms!"

Melanie laughed. "It's great to see you so excited about her. It's good to see you anyway," she said, patting his leg almost shyly, as he sat beside her on the bed. She felt strangely self-conscious, as if she and he were newly dating. Automatically, as if she had pressed a button inside herself, the accustomed feelings of guilt started. He was being especially sweet, which must mean she was a burden . . . she stopped herself.

"Gee, Ray, I guess I'm feeling more normal. Normal! Whatever that means! At least I'm not trembling constantly. Even sitting here next to you is easier, although you feel kind of like a stranger. I suppose that was bound to happen." Ray yawned before he draped his arm around her shoulder. "Are you getting enough sleep?" Melanie asked, reflexively. "Last time you looked dead to the world. I think the new medication is making me sleep better. Did I tell you that Dr. H. has put me on an anti-depressant? Aren't those what Marilyn takes? Mood elevators, right? Oh God, I just realized that! Holy shit!" She laughed and pressed closer to him. "So . . . what's going on besides taking care of Lise? How's old double A MCO? Shit! That was stupid. You're probably not working because of Lise. Sorry."

Ray crossed his legs and stared at the wall opposite them. "I wasn't gonna say anything, Mel, but since you've asked, I had to go back. They were gonna give my slot to a new trainee. I've been taking Lise to my dad's, and Kathleen's been watching her. Don't worry though; it's okay, really. Kathleen won't drink around the baby; I made her swear. She's never drunk when I pick Lise up at night. You know . . . there wasn't anybody else, and when she offered, it seemed like the best solution. Try to understand . . . I'm doing the best I can. I couldn't keep asking Marie, Mellie. She's already helped us so damn much . . ." Ray shifted his position and moved closer to the edge of the bed. He ran his hands through his hair. "I wish you were home, Mel. I know the doctor says you're not ready, but I wish . . . you look great, you seem fine . . ."

He turned to her and took her hands in his. Then, Melanie noticed the circles, the bloodshot eyes. Why hadn't she seen them before? She shrank back as Ray gazed hungrily at her, need pressing out of his dark eyes. Damn it, she thought. Was she here because she wanted to be? She froze because she realized she did want to be here. It felt so much better than being home. She wasn't exactly happier, but the hospital was so rest-ful. Being there made her feel like a person again. Tears stung her eyes, and she looked away. Melanie heard Ray sigh; on the periphery of her vision, she saw him bent over, hands drooped wearily between his legs. He had every right to be tired, to wish she was back, but she had only just begun to think that maybe she could return, could take care of Lise again. Why was she so afraid? What was the matter with her? Why couldn't things just be normal?

"I'm sorry, Mellie, I shouldn't have said that," Ray said sadly. "I know you're sick, that this is nobody's fault. It's just that it's really hard. Do you think I want to leave Lise with Kathleen? I cringe every time I close the door and can still hear Kathleen cooing in that annoying voice she uses, but what else can I do? I didn't want to hurt her pride, and where will we be if I lose the AAMCO position? I mean, I'm lucky because of my record to even have this job." He leaned toward her pleadingly. "Look, I gotta go. Lise needs you, Mellie, you're her mother. Nobody can replace you. I could bring her over to Helga's. I'm sure she'd be willing to watch her, but I figured that would upset you more."

Melanie held out her arms and pressed her face against his palpitating chest.

"Sure I understand, Ray, I do. And I feel better. I know things will get better. I'm just scared that if I leave here too soon, I'll sink into that hole again. It was so scary, and I still don't even understand how it happened. Please . . . please be patient. Jesus, this is so awful. Please!" Tears involuntarily streaked her cheeks.

Ray tilted her face up and kissed the wet skin. He chucked her beneath her chin, and smiled. "My precious baby girl. Don't worry. I'll take care of everything. I just miss you is all. The apartment's so damn empty without you. Especially at night when you're not lying there beside me." Unconsciously, Ray's expression again showed his fatigue and anxiety. Melanie clung to him, as if she wanted to press him through to the other side of her body. When they pulled apart, she offered him her lips for the first time in weeks. Ray stared down at her for several minutes. Then, instead of truly kissing her, his lips gently grazed her mouth.

They walked down the corridor together, and Ray greeted the other patients. As she clung to Ray's arm, Melanie felt like an invalid. When they reached the swinging doors, she carefully kept her feet inside the ward. Through the partly open door, she watched Ray descend the stairs. His body grew smaller as he went farther down, but she felt his eyes still looking up at her sharply. Finally, Melanie turned away, feeling a sense of great weariness. The world outside the ward did not seem real, did not seem like something she wanted. It was too difficult, too complicated; she did not feel strong enough to handle its stresses. Maybe she would never get well. She walked slowly back to her room, and when she passed Deena, Melanie could not even bring herself to smile at her.

Melanie felt as if she were walking somewhere else, far away, and the exertion took every ounce of her effort. She was stumbling across a desert, without even the possibility of a mirage.

Later, however, as she sat in her room before bed, Melanie began thinking about the future. She imagined taking Lise out in the stroller, imagined watching her begin to crawl and reach for things, saw herself letting Lise touch a leaf, hold a leaf in her small hands, and she smiled thinking of it. It was a scene, a possible scene with her family, what Dr. Huston had asked her to imagine. In the morning she would tell him about it. Melanie wondered if that was what had happened to Pete. At some point, was he able to envision life with their baby-to-be? Pete seemed fine now, like his former self. And if he could get better . . . Sighing, Melanie undid the black ribbons that held her two long pigtails, let her hair fall free around her shoulders. She closed her eyes and pulled the sheets snugly around her body.

*****

Daily, Melanie thought about leaving the ward, going outside: whether she could, what it would be like, if she could return without a problem, if she did have a problem what she would do. Dr. Huston told her that when she was ready she would know and be able to handle the change.

The hospital staff planned a trip to Fisherman's Wharf, and Melanie expressed a desire to go, although because it was across the Bay, the excursion involved a long bus ride and crowded conditions. The idea of a planned trip reminded her of field trips she had taken during her boarding-school days; the same excitement filled the air. When she asked Dr. Huston his opinion, he raised his eyebrows but said why not? It was about time she gave herself permission to have some fun.

Earlier in the week, Deena had received an upsetting phone call. Her mother had informed her that because Deena was doing nothing, in their opinion, to get her life together and was a drain on everybody's resources, the family was officially excommunicating her. After sharing the gist of this information with the group, Deena remained monosyllabic for the rest of the session, much as Chris probed.

That evening, Melanie was reading a magazine in the lounge when she heard a scuffling noise and then hysterical laughter coming from the nurses' station. Jumping up, she hastened to the corridor in time to see two nurses holding Deena tightly by the arms. Deena was sobbing and struggling furiously to be released, while another nurse stood nearby preparing a shot to calm her down. Deena's left arm showed several long scratches that were bleeding profusely. A patient standing beside Melanie whispered that Deena had tried to cut one of her veins with a a piece of glass from a Coke bottle. Horrified, Melanie then noticed the bottle lying on the floor; its jagged edges echoed Deena's face, which bore its painful, carved pumpkin grin. Suddenly aware that Melanie was present, Deena lowered her eyes. Melanie tried to call out to her, but no words would come. Soon the nurse took Deena away, and another nurse calmly scattered the gathering. The next morning, Melanie heard that Deena had been taken to the fifth floor.

Now, back on the ward a few days later—because patients were usually sent to the fifth floor for only a short period of time if they threatened or did injury to themselves or another—Deena seemed more relaxed.

"Deena, you scared me to half to death," Melanie said. "Why did you hurt yourself like that? Are you all right?"

"I'm fine, sugar. But I appreciate your asking. The truth is nothing is ever gonna really get better. My mother can go to hell and rot if she thinks I'll ever see or speak to her again. That closes the subject," Deena said with a snort. After a few minutes, however, she volunteered more information.

"You know, the fifth floor wasn't as bad as all that. I mean it wasn't full of junkies—lying around like zombies, nodding out. It's a drag being locked in, but, you know, everybody's in their own world. They just do their own thing, go their own way, and I do mean completely! It was actually kind of peaceful. Nobody butting in, trying to get you to talk all the time, like Mister Wonderful Chris. You can just sit with yourself and try to sort stuff out." Deena stopped and looked at Melanie's face, which still reflected her anxiety. She smiled. "Sweetie, don't look so uptight! I feel a whole lot better. Sometimes it gets too hot, and I just have to blow. Don't take it so personal. You're the one friend I know I've got here; I can't lose your confidence." She put her arm around Melanie's shoulders and hugged her. "Hey, some people mentioned this Wharf plan to me. I'll go with you if you want to try going outside. C'mon, let's try it, Melanie. I think that even though I had my little accident, they'll let me go. If I show 'good behavior' and all. The last time I was in the city, I was with my whole family, doing the tourist thing. Let me tell you, that memory sure can use some erasing!"

The day arrived, and as they went down in the elevator, Deena stood close beside her. Five other patients stood in the small space, including Joan, the dancing fawn. Men and women from the fourth and fifth floors were going, too; as Melanie's group left the elevator, she saw them already clustered outside, smoking. Watching them, she remembered a scene from the movie *David and Lisa*, in which the patients went on a trip to a museum. Suddenly, she felt a deep sense of shame. Everyone would know that they weren't an ordinary tour group; everyone would identify them as strange. This was not anything like a normal excursion. They were freaks on an outing in public. They were misfits, crazy people.

Melanie stopped in front of the outer glass door, unable to move, unable to touch the door handle. It was the same set of double glass doors through which she had entered with Marie, that led to the Crisis Center. The linoleum felt squishy beneath her feet, and she felt a draft as the door opened and closed on the others. As she tried to cross over the line, her legs buckled, and she nearly sank to the floor. Inching out of the way, she leaned against the stationary pane of glass, wishing she could melt into it, dissolve. People were staring at her with curiosity. Dimly, she felt Deena beside her, heard her murmur huskily, "Next time, sweetie. No problemo."

The nurse who had accompanied them in the elevator guided her back upstairs. Melanie felt desperate and panicky, as if she had had her chance and had only proven she was not equal to it, not equal to the reality of the street, not equal to those other people who would be sitting so close to her, not equal to anything! She dragged herself to her room and lay on the bed for a long time with her head buried in her arms. Finally, as if there was nothing else she was capable of doing, she fell asleep.

She was at the seashore and could hear the rushing, breathing sound of the waves. It was deserted, gray, white, cold. A sudden blast of raw, cold air shot through her body. She stood like a statue gazing at the gray-green water, the swollen, heaving waves pulsing up and down—frozen, silent, erect. The tears on her face were engraved, as if on marble, not wet and salty but still, fixed. Gradually her body began to fall forward, and she leaned with its motion until she actually hit the water. Feeling the water on her face broke the spell. Melanie began to swim frenetically, but instead of reaching the shore again, she moved into deeper and deeper water. Soon, like Alice in the pool of tears, there were no visible landmarks; she was completely immersed in water. Exhausted, Melanie lay on her back, stretching her arms and legs out pinwheel-fashion, in surrender. She would never reach land, so she might as well die. Floating aimlessly, she bobbed up and down, supported by the water's buoyancy, held up from beneath. The ocean grew more and more calm; the waves flowed onto and over her face and chest in gentle splashes, as if they were teasingly nudging her, caressing her. Closing her eyes, Melanie relaxed, feeling a smile beginning somewhere deep inside her. It radiated through her chest, her legs, warming her clear through . . . when she opened her eyes, she saw the sun streaming through the window in a thick, tangible ray. It nearly burned her body with its intensity.

She heard a knock at the door and realized this was what had woken her. After she said come in, Dr. Huston entered. He looked at her in silence before saying: "Okay, you're all right. See you later." Melanie started to rise, but he grinned. "No, lie back down; whatever's happening, it's doing you some good!" He closed the door quietly, and Melanie looked around the room. Slowly, images from her dream returned. She shut her eyes again and clung to the warm memories, as she savored the healing sensation of the sun's fingers on her face.

* * * * *

Later that week, however, as she thought about the botched excursion to Fisherman's Wharf, especially after hearing how much fun it had been from those who had gone, Melanie felt depressed. When *could* she leave? When *would* she feel right? She pressed her palms against the window in her room and felt currents of warm spring air. During the long lapses of unstructured time on the ward, she paced back and forth in the corridors, playing mental counting games as she had as a child when crossing over each city block. When she grew tired of walking, she sat in the lounge, rifling through magazines, trying to ignore the ever-present noise of the television.

One morning OT was canceled. In a mood to do something active, Melanie decided to make a collage. Although she had never made one herself, it was something Ray had done to while away a long, wintry evening when they were first together. As she proceeded to borrow scissors, glue, and a piece of cardboard from the nurses' station, Melanie felt excitement gathering inside her. She grabbed a stack of old magazines from the pile on the coffee table and began to search for pictures. The pages felt as smooth as finger-painting paper and were soothing to the touch. At first, Melanie chose only animal pictures— monkeys, lions, cats, a few birds—but then she began selecting faces—men's, women's, children's. It felt strengthening and purposeful to hold the scissors in her hand and carefully cut out each picture. She turned the scissors in a circle as she once had when she cut out clothes for paper dolls as a girl. Melanie realized the process was similar to writing a poem: choose complementary elements, attracted by some intangible linkage between them, and then arrange them. After filling in one corner of the cardboard, Melanie saw, triumphantly, how apparently random choices could make a coherent whole.

She spent nearly two hours on the collage. Other patients came over to watch. Joan told her she should separate the animals from the people, but Eulalie whispered that she thought the variety was nice and that what Melanie was doing was entirely appropriate. Rather than being irritated by these interactions, Melanie found herself considering each person's comments and opinions before moving on to the next section. Chris, the group leader, came in midway through and smiled encouragingly as he saw her working away. When most of the cardboard was covered, Melanie pushed away the scraps and materials and quietly surveyed her work. The collage was less refined than those Ray had made; some pictures bulged a little from where she had used too much glue or had not pressed them down firmly enough, but, overall, the colors and patterns pleased her.

Melanie propped the thick piece of cardboard alongside her primrose on the windowsill so she could see it easily. She noticed that when sunlight hit the paper, some faces virtually disappeared, while others became more sharply defined. One afternoon as she sat gazing at it abstractedly, she became aware that she was thinking in fragments, a process that happened when she felt a poem coming to her. It had been such a long time since she had written that she was nearly afraid to search for a pencil and piece of paper. If she moved, the tenuous lines could dissolve into meaningless refrains. Grabbing a pencil she found on top of her bureau and tearing off a matchbook end, Melanie found herself scribbling what turned into a poem about Lise.

After copying it out in longhand, she typed it on the ward's typewriter, which she felt lent it more substance.

> *Long, black lashes floating*
> *on a rosebud face. . .*
> *fingers cupped loosely over mine—*
> *one hand, one heart.*

> *Oh, darling baby blue,*
> *what will happen*
> *to me and you*
> *if the wolves leap*
> *from the wall?*

> *We rock together in the night-*
> *mare dark—one body,*
> *one blood.*

A splash of black ink, a Rorschach blot, it probably wasn't any good, Melanie thought but, while writing it, something inside her had loosened, reopened. Did being able to write indicate that her sickness was receding? Was writing the tightrope she could use to carry her back to the regular world, to life, to Ray and Lise again? Back to herself. But who was that?

During her next session, Melanie mentioned the poem in passing to Dr. Huston. When he asked if he could read it, she showed it to him and they discussed it. He told her it expressed both sorrow and longing, as well as her perceptions of Lise and their connectedness: They were two children in the darkness, clinging together, afraid of the wolf. However, because she had written the poem, he said she was beginning to create a distance and make a necessary separation from Lise. With his encouragement, in the days that followed, Melanie wrote more. Finally, she handed him lines describing how the sun itself would come to her, that "even in her darkest corner," she would know its "clear, white, weeping joy."

"Yes, Melanie, I think you will come to know that kind of joy, as well as, of course, the more ordinary variety," he said, smiling. "Although our lives may seem to follow a script, we do have some say in what is written there. Your mother went crazy; that was her way of managing, but you don't have to do that. You don't have to repeat the family pattern. Instead, you can choose to be well and let yourself be strong. You *are* strong. Think back to your first night in the hospital, to the state you were in. How helpless you were, how frightened. How to move without trembling seemed impossible. But look at yourself now. At what you've accomplished. Look at the friendships you're forming, how you're helping others. Yes," he nodded, watching her curl her lip in disbelief, "I hear about you from Chris and from other patients on the ward. There's a world of difference. Believe me, Melanie!"

"If there's a world of difference," Melanie answered in a quiet voice, "it's because of you. You helped me understand what was happening to me, helped me make sense of the craziness. That took away a lot of my fear. But I'm still on medication. What's going to happen if I go off it? Won't the problems just return? Won't I be like I was that first night and the weeks preceding it?" She shivered, remembering the agony she had felt. She could not go through that again. "Maybe I've just been incredibly lucky. I mean, lots of people are sick for their entire lives— my mother, for example. I'm still afraid to go outside, and I really screwed up the Fisherman's Wharf trip. What if that just keeps happening?"

Although they spent the remainder of the session exploring solutions, Melanie was unable to believe she was a strong person. It was so difficult to accept Dr. Huston's words at face value. Why couldn't she believe them? Melanie knew he wouldn't lie to her, but she simply could not take in the truth of what he said. Her inability to do so depressed her because she wanted to believe she could control her life. It was true that the trembling had stopped; the awful fever no longer radiated throughout her body. Why couldn't things just keep getting better? He was right, she *had* begun thinking about things outside herself: Deena, Ray, Lise, even the collage—they were separate from her. She and Ray had begun having daily conversations—normal conversations about baby food, her sessions with Dr. Huston, about AAMCO, and what Norm and Kathleen were doing. *Could* she make the transition back to her regular life?

Melanie remembered the Transition section during her labor with Lise. It had been the most painful, overwhelming part, the part that had made her finally lose control of her breathing. Her body had begun shaking, and the contractions had tumbled so quickly on top of each other that it had been all she could do to bear their pain. But within a short time, look at what she had accomplished! She had pushed out of her body a living, breathing being.

 *Six*

*R*ay came to visit and brought Lise and Marie. The two women sat on Melanie's bed, holding Lise in turns, while Ray paced back and forth, touching objects on the bureau and flipping the window blinds back and forth with his hand. Finally, he announced he was going to get them all something to drink.

"Jesus," Melanie said, laughing, "he's a fucking locomotive!" She laughed again, remembering a poem Marie had written about Ray, describing him in constant agitation. It made her feel ashamed, realizing Marie always saw more than Melanie gave her credit for. From the beginning, Marie had reminded her of her namesake, Melanie, in *Gone with the Wind*. When she had first read the novel in her early teens, she had wanted desperately to be like the Melanie described in its pages—gentle, patient, forgiving, a woman who never raged or broke into fits of weeping like the main character, Scarlett—someone ultimately so, so good! The fact that she identified more with Scarlett and reacted accordingly made her feel her name was a mockery.

Like the character Melanie in the book, Marie had a madonna-like quality about her. Now that she was a mother, this quality seemed pronounced. She could nurse Jon for hours, pausing only to nudge his cheek or take a sip of milk from the glass beside her elbow. Marie could even contentedly read while he nursed, a trick Melanie had been unable to master because there never seemed to be enough room for everything on her lap. Marie would smile down at Jon lovingly, apparently completely content, as if she had found her purpose in life. Melanie found it difficult to believe this was the same person who had suffered so during her pregnancy because of Pete's behavior. Sometimes, Melanie thought Marie was a saint in the flesh.

"The visit actually depressed me," Melanie told Dr. Huston later. "Being around Marie makes me feel like a really selfish person. I don't want to be a madonna, but I keep thinking that she's the way a mother ought to be. I mean, Ray's such a good person, too! People sense that Ray will be there for them, and, consequently, they leech off him. His Richmond buddies are always asking him for favors—will he drive them here? Will he loan them money? It's incredible; he never refuses! He came down with the flu a few months ago because he stayed outside in the rain to help somebody fix his car. His philosophy is that he would rather spread happiness and go the extra mile, even if some people take advantage of him.

"I used to think that I wanted to be a good person, too, like Melanie in *Gone with the Wind.*" Melanie shifted in her chair and lit a cigarette, tapping it hard on his desk first because she felt the need to bang against something. "But, you know, I'm not like that. Maybe I never will be. Maybe that's why I wound up here, because I find it impossible to give that much without exploding. I guess I was trying to be the perfect mother for Lise. But I can't achieve it, no matter how hard I try. Is that wrong?"

"Melanie, Melanie, Melanie! Actually, she was rather a nice character, wasn't she?" Dr. Huston said, smiling faintly. "You get into trouble because you tend to compare yourself to other people. It isn't always good to be sacrificial. You're allowed wants and needs, too. If, as you say, Ray became ill through neglecting his own needs, then that wasn't necessarily a good action. Certainly he was not honoring his own body. I agree that it's *important* to try to be a giving person, like Ray or Marie, because the world would be in a fix if none of us made effort in that direction, but giving should not be at the expense of selfhood. But hold on a moment, Melanie. You are always telling me how concerned you are about Deena or Eulalie, or someone else, like Ray or Lise. You brood that you are neglecting them; you're worried they are unhappy, that Ray's not getting enough sleep. Would someone who is completely selfish consider those things? Hmm?"

"Oh, you're right," Melanie conceded impatiently. "I have to admit I like people who go the extra mile far more than the takers—that's for sure—even though being around them does make me feel selfish. Ray never asks for anything in return. Marie never does either. Then it's ironic, because when, or if, they do, I feel put upon, as if our roles have suddenly flip-flopped. Then I go overboard trying to compensate and wind up becoming a perfect doormat, ready to do anything for anybody, whether I like it or not, until, of course, I wind up screaming with resentment. That's happened a million times! But I can't give past a certain point. There's this part of me that always remains aloof. I try to justify it by saying I wouldn't be a writer if I wasn't that way, if I didn't keep something back—that I need that space, that inwardness. Then it doesn't really feel like selfishness."

Melanie stared out the window in an attempt to avoid Dr. Huston's warm, sympathetic glance. She didn't want anybody feeling sorry for her! Jesus! Yet she hungered to be told she was okay, was good, was okay just as she was. She liked when he told her she was, although she felt perversely obliged to disagree with him. Why couldn't she stop analyzing, inspecting, dissecting herself and others? Yet it seemed to be her nature. She had been placed on a treadmill; she was going in one direction and had no idea how to get off or slow down, how to change positions, how to alter her course. It wearied her. She didn't know how to change, but she knew she didn't particularly like where she was.

"When Ray and I met," she mused, still avoiding Dr. Huston's eyes, "I had dreams about being a serious poet, about being true to myself, but I wasn't doing much of anything, really. I only wrote when I felt in the mood—I still do. The future didn't seem very real. I just let myself follow my muse, and poems just kept coming to me. If people ask me what I do—and people always ask you that at some point—I tell them I'm a poet, but it always sounds arrogant to say it, as if I don't have the right to, as if I haven't earned that right yet because I'm not good enough. It's so crazy!" Melanie took a drag from her cigarette and grinned at him.

"In my grandmother's apartment building," she said after a few minutes, "there was this girl I was friends with, Mia. We were both about nine years old, and we talked about everything—boys we had crushes on, dolls we wanted, what we wanted to be when we grew up. We colored together, played hopscotch. Once we were in her room dressing up our dolls, I think, and she told me something that just kind of stuck with me over the years. She had learned it in Sunday school, probably, but that didn't bother me. Mia said God gives everyone a gift, something special that only that person can offer the world, and our responsibility is to be true to that gift. Well, when I discovered that I enjoyed writing, and that I did it pretty well—teachers praising me, giving me A's, and so on—I felt . . . maybe this was *my* gift, maybe that was what Mia meant. So, if I'm not true to it, I'll be betraying something—God, myself, the world . . ."

Dr. Huston shifted in his chair and then spoke softly. "You know, Melanie, you can choose to see this breakdown of yours as the worst possible thing that's ever happened to you. I can see you do—don't look so incredulous! But it's also possible to see what happened as a break *up*, a beginning. You fell down, you became temporarily paralyzed, but now you have the chance to start over. This is an opportunity to make your life different, even if only in small ways. I already see more strength in you. You're speaking out more, you're letting your anger show, you're expressing desires. When you arrived at the hospital, you barely spoke above a whisper, and you didn't complain about anything. You only whined. I know . . . that hurts," he said, watching her wince in disgust. "But think of the power you possess now. You won't always be afraid and exhausted. Do you think I would have given permission for you to take the Wharf trip if I hadn't thought there was a possibility you could have gone? I know—you didn't make it, but that's not the point. You are headed in that direction. If you used half the energy you have in reserve fighting *for* yourself instead of *against* yourself, you'd be such a dynamo, you'd bowl me over!" He chuckled. "Now listen, I have a proposition for you."

Melanie laughed, feeling a little pleased, a little flattered, a little hopeful. She remembered all the songs and stories she had heard about ego death, about beginning over—conversations Ray had endlessly with Pete and Mark about letting go of one's personality and attempting to flow with the cosmos. The concept had always sounded abstract to her, but maybe this was what it truly meant. Melanie listened anxiously as Dr. Huston suggested she attempt a weekend at home in two weeks time. But even as she felt the familiar twinges of fear, the suggestion appeared reasonable. She still had not been able to leave the confines of the hospital building, but she had to try. She simply had to try. If she didn't try, how could she ever get on with her life?

* * * * *

That week Jetta arrived on the ward. Melanie learned that she too was suffering from a postpartum depression. Jetta's baby was only a few weeks old, and the rumor was that she had never recovered from the baby blues that were common following any delivery. Upon meeting her and listening to her singsong chatter in Group, Melanie was surprised that, considering the similarity of their illnesses, she could not identify with Jetta. Jetta was tall and had thin, lackluster red hair and vacant-looking turquoise eyes. She wore a lacy white cape around her shoulders, and when she moved the material swirled behind her so that it looked as if she were flying. Jetta told the group that she was an angel from another galaxy; with the birth of her baby, she had finally been given a special assignment. She frequently stared into space, giving the appearance that she truly was receiving messages from afar. Jetta reminded Melanie of her mother, who also claimed she heard messages. Her mother was constantly "on the line," receiving information, being controlled by it, irritated by it, yet having what appeared to be conversations. For years, Melanie had tried to visualize this "communication line," as her mother called it. Was Jetta experiencing the same thing?

One evening, Jetta's husband and baby came to visit. In contrast to Jetta's Modigliani-shaped body and slightly skewed facial features, her husband was short, balding, and fleshy-looking. The women in the ward clustered around the baby, as they did when Ray brought Lise into the lounge, but Melanie stood at a distance from the inquisitive, gushing group. Even when Deena beckoned her to come see how small the baby was, she declined politely. She was more interested in watching Jetta's husband pour Enfamil formula into a bottle and then feed it to the baby. He and Jetta did not speak to each other, but Melanie noticed, with pain, the creases in his forehead and the bewilderment in his eyes when, with a grand, sweeping gesture, she pointed her child out to the ward in general but then refused to touch it. Later, in her room, Melanie found it difficult to erase the vision of Jetta dancing around the room, singing ecstatically, as if part of a heavenly choir. Several weeks later, prowling up and down the corridor, unable to sleep, Melanie heard the sound of uncontrollable weeping coming from behind Jetta's door. As she listened, she felt a strange sense of release.

Seven

One morning, waking earlier than normal, Melanie lingered in bed. The room grew lighter and lighter, until the shapes in the room became recognizable objects. Particles of dust floated within a bar of light that extended from floor to ceiling. If she waved her hand, they scattered wildly, then settled like snowflakes in a crystal dome. The bird she recognized by its voice was perched on one of the outermost branches of the tree outside; its light gray breast beat furiously as it sang. Sun touched the windowsill, her collage, her pot of primroses. Melanie climbed out of bed and leaned on the sill, enjoying the warmth from the sun on her bare arms. She cupped the velvety petals of the primroses and marveled at their dainty texture. It seemed to her that the flowers were also basking in the light, which made a smile form at the corners of her mouth.

Marie had loaned her a radio, and now, as Melanie turned the knob to on, she heard a guitar concerto by Rodrigo playing softly. The second movement began slowly; the plucked notes sounded like raindrops falling, one by one, from a drainpipe after a storm. Sorrowful notes, in a minor key. Melanie closed her eyes, swaying slightly as the music swelled. She squeezed the sill with her hands, feeling that if she could just escape the heaviness of her body and soar around the room . . . oh, then! She drew the music into herself and sent it back out again with every fiber of her being.

The orchestra triumphantly joined the guitar. Melanie's chest loosened; something twisted inside her. Laughing and crying simultaneously, she realized that today was it. Today was the day she would be able to go outside! Today she would take Deena's hand. Today they would walk together up and down the block. Melanie knew she could. No matter what happened afterwards, she knew that today she could do that much. Today. She sang softly to herself:

> Today, while the blossoms still cling to the vine,
> I'll taste your strawberries, I'll drink your sweet wine.
> A million tomorrows will all pass away,
> Ere I forget all the joy that is mine today.

Melanie stretched her arms to the ceiling as the movement leaped to a climactic finish.

Still exultant from this early morning experience, Melanie arranged to go walking with Deena after breakfast. Two hours later, she stood in front of the forbidding double doors in the lobby like Alice at the entrance to the looking glass. Trembling, Melanie squeezed Deena's hand, and they walked together out the doors, down the steps, onto the sidewalk. She was out. She had done it. The landscape looked surreal, static as a postcard image; but as they marched firmly up and down the block, Melanie felt the ground gradually become more solid. Trees, buildings, cars appeared more and more substantial. By the time they returned to the ward with their arms wrapped around each other's waists, she and Deena had navigated the street three times.

* * * * *

Ray was picking her up Saturday morning. Friday night, Melanie slept poorly. She had grown accustomed to being in the hospital; she was used to her routine, to things being fixed in their places, secure. She felt she was entering a field of tall grasses, and there might be rabbit or snake holes. Although Ray was accompanying her, as Deena had, Melanie knew she was ultimately alone. She felt handicapped. Instead of feeling that she was walking forwards into life, with everything shining clearly before her, she felt as if she was walking backwards, doing everything in reverse, without the benefit of sight.

Now she went outside daily, although still not alone. To have Deena alongside her, even if they walked, as they often did, in silence, helped shrink the enormity of the world: the bigness of the sky, the complicated interactions everywhere she turned, the potpourri of voices, bodies moving, cars shuffling along the street, starting and stopping. The world never rested; it was such an active place! To Melanie, it seemed overly busy, overly loud, although fortunately less personally threatening. She moved with it and within it, as if on a game board, a separate entity clanking along, like the metal shoe or iron in Monopoly.

It was mid-April, the sun was shining, the sky was the vivid blue of an oil pastel. Ray arrived promptly, and at the doors of the ward, Dr. Huston released her. Out of the corner of her eye, Melanie noticed Deena hovering nearby; she moved back and hugged her for additional strength. Often in her life, Melanie felt she was standing outside of herself, watching her own actions. Now, too, she felt as if she was taking part in a drama, experiencing the great leavetaking scene. As she went down in the elevator with Ray and Lise, Melanie felt as if, like Bilbo Baggins, she was going on an adventure. When they reached the street, she looked up toward where she imagined the ward was and then quickly got into the car.

She had not been inside a car in over two months. It felt peculiar to be encased, to have the world—which appeared so huge when standing outside—reduced to slits of glass that permitted only a partial view of things. She wondered if it was how sailors felt who saw everything through portholes. Lise squirmed in Melanie's lap, staring at her inquiringly, as if uncertain of who she was. Melanie patted Lise's hair and held her own body as still as possible as the familiar scenery swept by. When Ray pulled onto their street, and she saw the dangling Rosaline Apartments sign, she felt momentarily afraid. Memories washed over her intensely. The fortlike outer walls seemed more yellow than ever, but sickly yellow-white, like the filling of a cookie. Under the unsparing morning light, the building appeared garish, and it was only Ray's confident move forwards that propelled her inside. In the hallway, Melanie breathed in painfully the pungent scent of cleaning supplies.

When he opened the door to their apartment, however, she found herself smiling. Ray had rearranged the furniture and had draped a brightly-colored afghan over their dingy green couch. On the living-room wall hung a picture Ray had made using colored pens, welcoming her back, and she noticed yellow roses poking from a tall water glass on the kitchen table. After she set Lise on the carpet, Melanie turned toward Ray and leaned against him. They swayed wordlessly together for several minutes. Melanie felt her cheeks grow wet, and she realized that Ray was crying as well. Now that she was actually in the apartment, the experience did not seem like such an ordeal, and she wondered why she had built it up so greatly in her mind. The return reminded her strangely of when she had come home from the hospital with Lise. There was no evidence of the pain she had felt when last within these walls. The apartment was simply an apartment—a large, box-shaped dwelling place that they were temporarily inhabiting. It bore her no malice. She did not have to be afraid.

As she watched Lise grunting on the rug, crawling toward a nearby stuffed rabbit, Melanie realized how much time had elapsed. Ray poured Cokes for them both, and they sat together on the couch. He laid his arm across her shoulder and placed her cool hand firmly in his warmer one. Melanie closed her eyes and lay back against him. She stirred only when Lise appeared, by the whimpering sounds she was making, to be getting hungry. It was a novelty then to use the Playtex nurser, to give Lise a bottle instead of her breast. Holding her in the familiar position, she felt her nipples tingle, although her milk had long since dried up. Melanie realized that Lise no longer pressed so close; this made her feel freer, less pulled-at. They were no longer one, but two. Had Dr. Huston known this would happen? Had he predicted this outcome? It seemed incredible to Melanie that reality could change so drastically. It astounded her that only a few hours ago the hospital had been vividly her reality. Now, having left it, it was already beginning to lose substance in her mind. Could real only be what was immediately in front of her? The hospital, and her experiences there, felt like something she had dreamed about. That afternoon, when the three of them went to the Marina, the hospital seemed even more remote.

Under the clear April light, the water and rocks shone differently than they had during the long, rainy months; this light was soft, soothing, gentle on the eyes. They strolled along, listening to the waves splash against the rocks and watching sailboats bounce up and down in the dense, green water. Seagulls flew in loose groups, screeching at a lone swimmer whose body moved muscularly in and out of the water, close to shore. Now and again, one of the gulls broke from the pack and dove, emerging with a fish flapping in its mouth. It seemed later that she and Ray had spoken to each fisherman, who were out in droves on the pier, had peered into buckets upon buckets of squirming, glinting fish. Melanie half-closed her eyes as she pushed Lise easily along in the stroller, realizing that she had been starved for sun and moisture.

That night after Lise was asleep, she and Ray turned to each other's bodies, explored each other anew. His touch on her skin made her weep, it was so tentative and fearful of hurting her. For a long time they simply held each other until, gradually, they pressed closer and closer and then joined, almost reverently, together. Later, lying with his sperm inside her and his perspiration merged with her own, Melanie stared peacefully at the ceiling. How different, how raw and opened she felt after being alone for so many weeks in her monastic hospital bed. The weekend was a gift, an unexpected blessing, as the morning of hearing the guitar concerto had been. They were moments of grace, lifting her, assuring her, helping her believe that life, and her part in it were possible.

 *Eight*

*A*fter this weekend, the world of the hospital shrunk for her. Melanie marveled that the place that had brought her such relative peace and comfort was now the place she was most anxious to leave. Dr. Huston told her it was analogous to leaving the womb. The fetus needed that liquid environment to grow and develop to the point of birth, but then it discarded its watery home for one of air. The infant needed to move from complete dependence to a state of ever-increasing independence. Similarly, he explained, when she had come to the hospital, she had been in such a weak, helpless state that she had needed to be cared for "completely." But over time, she had been able to stop shaking, had gained more control over her "crazy" thoughts, had become involved with therapy, Group, OT. Now she was ready to move out of the "family circle." Each new venture had made her stronger, more confident; it was akin to a baby's ever-increasing skill at walking. At first the baby moves awkwardly, spreading its legs too far apart or not far enough apart for balance, yet within a month or two, it walks with ease and even tries to run. Melanie, he said, was like a baby—learning how to be herself, testing her limits and her strengths.

"But I don't understand how I became so helpless and dependent in the first place," she protested. "My breakdown came so suddenly, without my being able to control it. What's to stop that from happening again? After all, I was, I am an adult, not a baby. My circumstances haven't changed significantly. I'll still be alone all day with Lise. I'm still confused about my feelings for Ray, still uncertain about the future, about my writing." As she added each item as if making up a grocery list, Melanie felt increasingly dismal. "I know I've come through a lot, but I don't think this is over yet. I mean, Christ! I can't even walk outside alone, even if I have moved outside the family circle, as you put it. I don't think I could stand experiencing what I went through again; I felt like I was losing my mind." Melanie looked up quickly to see Dr. Huston's reaction, to see whether he thought that was what really had happened. It was still difficult for her to believe she wasn't going to go crazy like her mother. The fear had pressed so close. Where was the line between sanity and insanity? She took out a cigarette and then tossed the box back on the desk.

"Well, I wish I could stop these, let me tell you. Now I'll probably never quit! Ray and I have tried dozens of times. Once we succeeded for three weeks, but one of us always starts back up, and then the other does, too." She bit her fingernail thoughtfully. "When I went home, though, there was a difference. I did feel different. When I was feeding Lise, I didn't feel as attached to her. I realized that we were two human beings, separate from each other—that she had her own strength and power. Actually, I felt more like my old self before becoming pregnant. That was an improvement, I guess. It was okay being in the apartment, better than I thought it would be, really—being together, sitting together as a family again. It was even enjoyable!" Melanie laughed. "Maybe there are no absolute answers," she said, grimacing. "I'm always expecting to discover the great secret, to understand everything, but maybe that will never happen, and maybe, for the first time, that's okay. I'm tired of searching for the truth!" she said, laughing again. "Maybe it's only about dealing with things better . . . who knows? Like Chicken Little, I always think the sky is falling. Things won't stay calm for long; I'll be tested again in some more dire fashion."

"That may be the case," Dr. Huston answered quietly. "I don't know your destiny, and I certainly have no pat answers for you, Melanie, although I hope some of my explanations have clarified things for you. However, I am convinced you don't have to return to your identical situation. With your temperament and sensitivity, you may always be predisposed to depression and anxiety. But that doesn't mean those feelings have to occur as violently as they did this time. You may have other pregnancies and births, and you more than likely will not experience postpartum depression with any of them. Postpartum depressions, of this severity at least, are much more common with first deliveries, with the realization of the responsibility of motherhood. In your case, you had poor role models, besides a lack of support from both your families. You are also very young. Each of these factors contributed to the intensity of your experience—besides the strong hormonal imbalances, which, fortunately, we have been able to stabilize with Librium and Triavil. These imbalances may fluctuate and give you more trouble at some times than others, but they will not simply vanish.

"You are also susceptible to depression because of your unstable background. And if all *that* isn't enough," he said, halfsmiling as he watched her shoulders droop, "it simply isn't easy to care for a small baby. You were alone with her a great deal; you had no help, no time off, only at night when Ray returned, and you were trying to do as perfect a job as possible. It would exhaust the strongest of us! I certainly wouldn't take on that responsibility!" Dr. Huston smiled again as Melanie continued to look disbelieving, as if she thought surely she could have coped if she had tried harder. Her features relaxed as he continued to smile at her.

She reached for the pack of Marlboros again and this time lit a cigarette, inhaling forcefully. She looked steadily at Dr. Huston, noting that his face looked clear and untroubled. His body was still; it never moved nervously like hers did. She was always jiggling her foot, playing with her hair, biting her fingernails, fiddling with a cigarette. Melanie wondered what it would feel like to be so relaxed.

"So . . . what can I do to make things go differently?" she asked half-flippantly. "How do I prevent myself from slipping back to that awful state?" It was difficult to say the words. Remembering the past weeks was like staring into a dark room.

Dr. Huston swiveled around and faced her fully.

"For one, I'm not stopping your medication immediately. I do want to wean you from it, but it's important to cut back gradually. Instead of the Librium you are now on, I'm switching you to Valium, a muscle relaxant that will continue to relieve your anxiety. You will be taking between five and ten milligrams a day, which is a lot less than what you currently take. I think you should stay on antidepressants for about a year, until you are fully adjusted to being back home." He cleared his throat.

"Also, I want you to continue therapy for at least a year, for as long as you're on medication anyway. I have a private office located in a church just off Shattuck, on Vine Street; it's easily reachable by bus. And if you like, I can arrange with Chris for you to attend outpatient group therapy. He runs an evening session here at the hospital on Wednesday nights." He grinned as Melanie's features relaxed further, and she began to smile. "It's nice to see the worry leave your face for a few minutes, Melanie.

"In addition to those measures, I think you should have some relief from Lise, at least two or three times a week. Get away, alone, even if it's only for an hour or two. Even if you don't do anything except take a walk or go grocery shopping by yourself." He chuckled, as Melanie's smile widened. "Think all that can keep you from slipping back into that awful hole?"

Melanie crushed out her cigarette and stretched as she realized their time was nearly up. It amazed her that Dr. Huston came up with what sounded like such perfect ideas. He made everything sound like it could actually work. A year was a long time . . . surely in a year . . . where would she be? Things had to get better. "Thank you," she said. "I'm glad you're not just going to drop me."

Dr. Huston came from behind the desk and patted her shoulder.

"Not a chance, dear. You are too valuable a human being."

Blinking back the tears that rushed automatically to her eyes, Melanie picked up her box of cigarettes and styrofoam coffee cup. She mumbled she would see him tomorrow and left the office. As she walked back to her room she passed Deena coming out of the lounge. Her friend waved. Melanie grinned back at her, happily.

"What have you got to be so happy about? Huh, girl?"

Melanie laughed. "They're going to let me out of this place, and I think I might actually make it!" As she said the words, she realized that, for the first time, she believed them.

* * * * *

Melanie spent most of her remaining time in the hospital with Deena. On one of their walks, they discovered by accident a small court-yard within the confines of the hospital building, that reminded Melanie of a cloistered garden she had known in her teens. Although the Fort Tryon Park's gardens had been much larger, affording a view of the Hudson, both displayed a profusion of flowers, stone benches, and pools filled with lilypads and water grasses. A bronze heron stood in the center of the hospital's pool, and Melanie and Deena both enjoyed gazing at its bent, angular body, eternally poised to dive into the water for a fish.

Rivers, streams, pools, water in any form—Melanie had always been drawn to it, although because she lived in the city, she was especially drawn to fountains. Her favorite stood in a piazza in Lincoln Center, between the Opera House and the New York Philharmonic buildings. During high school, she had gone at night just to gaze at the fountain, and it had inspired several poems. She loved how the water lay low, seemingly at rest around the blue lights within its inner concrete rim, and then suddenly spurted up into the darkness, as if it could no longer be restrained. The geyser gradually drifted back down again, in shifts, as it were, but then would as suddenly spring upwards, over and over again. Melanie loved to stand before the fountain as at a shrine, hands deep in the pockets of her coat, face lifted, sprayed with mist. Inexplicably, winter—when the trees were stripped of leaves and seemed doubly dwarfed by the massive structures—was her favorite time to visit. Despite the many lights that shone from the large, floor-to-ceiling windows, the buildings emitted little warmth. Melanie seldom entered them, preferring to stroll between the several tucked-away, bench-lined gardens behind them.

Sitting in the hospital courtyard gave her a similar sense of peace. As if they were each calmed separately by the gently flowing water and the heron's gleaming presence, she and Deena seldom found it necessary to speak there. When they did, it was mainly of experiences they had shared together in Group or on the ward, and discussions concerning their progress. They planned get-togethers outside the hospital because Deena was to be released shortly after Melanie, yet even as they made plans, Melanie sensed the improbability of them happening. Their friendship was based on the hospital stay; outside its walls they might feel strange being together.

Consequently, during these pleasant last afternoons, Melanie tried to fix in her consciousness Deena's high cheekbones and steady brown eyes, her bronze skin that shone like an ad for Coppertone and like the heron itself. Deena was rotund, solid, like a statue of a laughing Buddha. Melanie had always seen herself more as a piece of Kleenex—something that tore easily, that could be blown away by the slightest sneeze—while Deena appeared strong, impenetrable. She realized, however, that for all Deena's seeming strength, she too could be undone by the slightest provocation. Perhaps it was this mutual vulnerability that connected them, although geography alone would separate them. One morning Deena mentioned that she was moving to San Jose to stay with an aunt from a different, less hostile side of the family.

* * * * *

The morning before Melanie's release, her session with Dr. Huston went poorly. She felt as if he were trying to pick out splinters imbedded in her soul. Panicking, she leapt to her feet.

"No, please stop! This is too frightening. I can't, please," Melanie involuntarily cried out. Her chest burned, her heart pounded. Why was what he was saying so painful? It was not as if she did not know what her childhood had been like. Then what was he uncovering? With her, everything was on the surface, wasn't it? Wasn't she as open as a person could be? She prided herself on the fact. Yet sensations had flooded through her that made her feel as if something was about to fall on her head, but from where? From whom? What?

Melanie realized these panicky feelings rose to the surface whenever he asked her to talk about her parents, or about what it had been like for her as a child, although this morning the feelings were stronger than usual. Her usual tone when speaking of her mother and father was detached and slightly bitter, and then, as if reflexively, she would apologize: They couldn't help it, they were both sick; she realized it wasn't their fault. When she did this, her words invariably choked her. Even as they automatically spewed out of her, they felt fraudulent, although she said them anyway. When Dr. Huston would attempt to slow her down or penetrate further, she withdrew, sidestepped, pretended she did not understand what he was getting at. Sometimes, it felt as if he were chasing her, and she had to redouble her efforts at escape. At the end of these sessions, she had burning sensations in her chest as if she were being picked clean by buzzards. Buzzards of her own creation. It was like that now. She felt dirty, angry, raw.

"I don't *know* what I'm feeling," Melanie yelled heatedly before stopping in embarrassment, fearful her tone had been too violent, too strong. "I mean," she began again more quietly, "I mean, they couldn't help it. They had their own problems. How can you blame sick people? They shouldn't have been parents, really. So I didn't get enough love. Lots of people don't. The world goes on. Look at Deena and Joan. They had worse situations than I did! Their families voluntarily cut them off, hurt them, beat them. Deena showed me scars from where her mother whipped her with a cord from an iron. On a regular basis, too! That never happened to me. I didn't have it so bad, really. People have cared about me along the way, lots of people—friends, teachers, my guidance counselor. You know, it was just the way it was. I'm tired of dwelling on it, sick of living in the past. I want to make my own life. I want to be . . . happy, at least sometimes . . . well, maybe . . . no! I don't want happiness; I want joy." Melanie's voice trembled, stopped.

Running, running with her words, as if she had to fill every inch of blank space with sound. Why did she feel so choked? Why was Dr. Huston so quiet? What was he accusing her of? Was she supposed to ruminate forever about her sick parents, the one a drunk, the other crazy? Couldn't she just forget about them? Melanie sat stonily, angry that he would bring up these subjects on her last day. She wanted to say goodbye, to discuss the *future*, for Gods' sake, not the past! Why did he have to keep harping on the past? That was all doctors ever did! Nothing was going to change anytime soon. She had left home, she was on her own, she had her own life, for better or worse. Did she need this? Great! So she had screwed up and landed in the hospital. Now she was ready to get out. Should she be punished forever because she hadn't been strong enough, punished for one lousy screw-up?

Melanie squeezed out her last cigarette. Fuck it, she thought, now I'm out of cigarettes, too, just when I need them the most! Staring miserably at the floor, inhaling so hard it made her throat burn, she decided she just wouldn't respond; she wouldn't even look at Dr. Huston. He had all the answers. He was always so fucking calm, so fucking sure! Melanie heard him sigh and then make a motion indicating that perhaps it was enough for the day. She stared at him in disbelief, her face twisted with pain. Didn't he understand it was hard to go over and over the same stories? Why couldn't he understand how much it hurt to do that? What good did it do to mourn the fact that her mother had hardly held her, had not been anybody she could trust? What *good* did it do?

"Terrific," she snapped, "so you don't give a shit either?" She bit her lip. "Oh God, I'm sorry. I didn't mean that, that was stupid. It's just . . ."

"Melanie!"

Stunned, she glanced at him fearfully. What had she done wrong?

"Melanie!" he said again, even more forcefully.

She squeezed her eyes shut, leaned back in her chair. The tears came slowly, spilling out of her eyes, dribbling down her cheeks, onto her chin. Before she realized what was happening, her mouth tasted salt. Yes, it hurt. It hurt, hurt, hurt! She had a right to feel hurt. She wasn't just being babyish. He was right. She must stop defending, excusing, rationalizing. Was it so bad to feel the hurt? Didn't she have the right? She did.

Melanie heard him rise from behind the desk. He knelt beside her chair, pressed her hand. The warmth and firmness from his palm broke open any last resistance. Melanie felt as though she were cracking apart, breaking apart.

"Yes," he whispered. "Yes, Melanie. Go on. Let it out. Let all those tears come out of you."

Melanie had no idea she could cry so much or cry for so long. Dr. Huston held onto her hand until the tears finally subsided. When she opened her eyes and looked him full in the face, she felt cleansed. Her skin felt cleansed, and she felt relaxed and alive, whole. Melanie saw this reflected in his eyes, in his kind, appreciative glance, and it made her feel overwhelmingly glad.

Part Three

"... My eyes collide head-on with stuffed graveyards
False gods, I scuff
At pettiness which plays so rough
Walk upside-down inside handcuffs
Kick my legs to crash it off
Say okay, I have had enough
What else can you show me?"

Bob Dylan
"It's Alright, Ma
(I'm Only Bleeding)"

One

She got to the end of each day, then each week, although it felt like revving oneself to jump to the other side of a crevasse on a hiking trail. Frequently, when Melanie was small, her grandmother would say, "I'm going to throw you into the middle of next week." Remembering this now, away from the protection of the hospital, Melanie wished this could happen—anything to speed up the pace, to be free from panic, to be farther along . . . to be cured. When she was afraid to take Lise to the park, Melanie went as far as she could before turning back. If she got breakfast down without feeling nauseous, or looked at the dinner she had prepared and it resembled ordinary food, she saw these steps as little victories, games she played against time and fate.

Melanie was amazed by how much Lise had grown in the months she had been gone. Nearly eight months old, Lise now sat by herself, crawled, and pulled herself up on furniture. She pushed toys along the rug and explored them with her mouth and fingers. Her body was no longer bright red, but flesh toned, and she appeared sturdier, less fragile. With the warmer weather, Melanie took Lise out as often as possible. Melanie delighted in her look of surprise when wind blew the hairs on her arms; and Lise was always eager to hang out of the stroller so she could touch flowers and other objects they passed. This heightened Melanie's own awareness of her surroundings. She felt as if she and Lise were both babies, seeing things for the first time. She searched for a larger playground, and in the new park she found closer to campus, she could put Lise down on the grass and let her crawl where she liked. Melanie was surprised that other mothers in the park held their babies tightly on their laps. Like an animal sniffing another on the street, Lise crawled over to these children and touched them inquisitively. Sometimes, they cried or drew back in alarm, as if Lise was of a different species. The mothers seemed fearful, too, although they smiled wryly at Melanie and shrugged, as if to say their babies' reactions were beyond their control. Melanie wondered if it was how she herself had appeared only months before: fearful, closed-off. She enjoyed letting Lise wander off and explore because it made her feel freer herself. When she thought back to her expe-

riences at the former playground, they felt as if they had happened to
another person, to someone so much more fearful than the person she had
become.

Occasionally, because it was a midway point for both of them,
Marie and Jon met her and Lise at the park. Later, back at the Rosaline
Apartments, the two mothers fixed lunch, while Jon and Lise romped in
the living room. Marie and Melanie talked or listened to classical music
to soothe, Marie laughingly said, their overextended nerves. Toward din-
nertime, Melanie accompanied Marie to the bus stop to catch the
Oakland bus, although sometimes Pete swung by to get them in a secondhand car on loan from Marie's parents. Her parents had told Marie
that now that she and Pete had another person to consider, they mustn't
be selfish.

Although Marie had a driver's license, she resisted driving the car,
because for years bicycles had been their main mode of transportation.
Pete had even added a child seat to his bike. Marie informed Melanie with
a groan that the next thing you knew they'd be buying a station wagon. I
guess we all have to grow up at last, sell out, become normal, she said,
laughing, as if she didn't really mind after all. Ironically, finding the afternoons with Marie restful and calm, Melanie wanted more than ever to be
normal, too. She sought to become as like Marie as possible, to derive new
meaning from being a parent. She was tired of feeling outside of regular
life; she wanted to belong.

Because reading mysteries had become associated with her breakdown, Melanie found herself rereading poets she had enjoyed during her
teens: William Blake, e. e. cummings, Rainer Maria Rilke, Le Roi Jones,
T. S. Eliot. Marie also loaned her books from her collection. She told
Melanie she had been rereading the same page of Jane Austen's novel
Persuasion for weeks because as soon as she resumed where she had left
off, she was distracted by either Jon or the ringing of the telephone.
Melanie was amazed that Marie said this laughingly, rather than with the
resentment she felt herself.

One of the poets whose books she borrowed from Marie—
Roethke from Washington State—appealed to her because of his imagery
and the compassion he showed for the human condition. She found herself mouthing lines of his, and after copying a poem she particularly liked
called "Cuttings (later)," she taped it on the kitchen wall. Melanie used it
as a reminder to herself that she, like the young plants it described, was
"leaning to beginnings, sheath-wet." If a plant was able to push through
the hardness of the ground, maybe she could push through her thicket of

depression. During moments when Lise was napping, or at night after Ray returned, Melanie tinkered with the poems she had written while in the hospital. Dr. Huston suggested she bring her poetry to her sessions with him so they could discuss its meaning together.

* * * * *

Located in the upper story of a church, Dr. Huston's office had a tucked-away, cloistered feeling. The room was much larger than the one he had used on the ward. When Melanie seated herself, she felt a plain stretched between them. The building was as still as a tomb, made as it was of cool gray and white stone. In addition to the omnipresent stone, the shadowy lighting and the thick carpet contributed to the sense of serenity and protection. Climbing to the top floor felt like climbing toward heaven.

Each week when she arrived, Melanie felt: this is my moment, my stage. There must be a point to this session. I must prove myself, establish myself—my worth, my existence. I must convince you that I'm bright, that I'm attractive, so, like a sophisticated woman in a film, I will immediately light a cigarette. I will twist it in my fingers, cross my legs, angle myself toward you. Melanie felt she had to prove to Dr. Huston that he had been right to release her.

She appreciated the security of the chair, end table, ashtray, lamp—objects she could name—as well as the desk whose mahogany surface was covered with mysterious papers and paperweights. And behind this magnificent surface, seated in a padded leather swivel chair, was the large boned, balding man with his fleshy red cheeks and neck and white Santa Claus eyebrows.

Although it had admittedly loosened something inside her, Melanie still felt angry about their final hospital session. She felt he had intruded upon her, left her wide open. Questions arose spontaneously in her mind: Why must I talk to you? Who are you that you should know my life? Do I feel like unfolding today? Some visits it was easier to surround herself with smoke, like a protective cloak of invisibility. But protection from what? The silence itself seemed to accuse her, chastise her for existing. How dare she take up space on the Earth?

"I want you to try something a little different today," Dr. Huston said. "Feel up to it?"

The automatic grimace. Must I? Lifting her face to him. Can I do it? Do I want to do it? Do I want to get well, or don't I?

"Here, Melanie, lie on your back on this table. Don't worry, it's matted. There's no danger of falling. If you do, I'll catch you." He rose from his chair to demonstrate.

She was a patient, etherized upon a table.

"This might remind you of the psychodrama you did in Movement class. Let's see what happens, Melanie. I want you just to lie there for a few minutes and then reach your hands upwards, like this, toward the ceiling."

He is so fatherly, she thought, but I won't be cradled. I am mute. My mouth won't work properly. Only brokenness comes out—sighs, streams of smoke, the choked gasps from a frozen voice box. Oh, why am I such a fucking actress?

"Don't be worried. I'm here to help you get past these fears. We need to fight them together."

Melanie climbed up on the table. She lay flat on her back and stretched upwards, reached upwards with her hands. After several minutes she felt oppressed by the ceiling, as if she were pleading with it. Cover me. Hide me from this intense exposure. Cover me.

"What's going on, Melanie? Why do you look upset? What is it you're reaching for?"

"I don't know. Oh God . . . I don't know. I reach, I keep reaching, but . . . oh God! She doesn't come, she doesn't come. No matter how hard I cry she won't come. She won't come to me."

Torrents of loss, kicking and flailing, bars, no shelter.

"Anything else? Stay with your loneliness, your sense that no one is there, that no one will be there. Let it wash over you, fill your chest. If you feel panicky, take in some deep breaths, but try not to run away from what you're feeling."

"I keep reaching . . . but there's no answer," Melanie whispered. Her chest burned intensely. "It's a blank sky. A completely blank sky. I can't even turn over to protect myself. I'm so far away from everything. It's . . . so . . . lone. . ." She felt close to tears and took a deep breath to try and steady herself. The ceiling felt as if it were going to crash down on her, swallow her, destroy her.

"Go on, dear. It's okay. I'm right here with you. You're not alone," Dr. Huston said gently.

"It's so weird. I just remembered something. When I was younger," Melanie continued, "about fifteen or sixteen, there was this graveyard across the street, and I liked to lie there at night. I know that sounds crazy, but I found it peaceful to stare up at the sky, the stars. Milky white clouds usually lit the darkness, so it wasn't as scary as you'd think it would be. For some reason, I wanted badly to penetrate them, see through them, into them, but I never could . . . I don't know. Nothing comes. Everything just feels empty and very lonely. I guess that's how I usually feel. Alone, reaching up, not finding any answers. I'm all alone in the universe, unprotected . . . it's scary. I don't like it. I want to feel safe and happy."

There were no cigarettes, no coy gestures. There was only the reality of herself and the table, only herself reaching up and the sound of Dr. Huston's voice.

* * * * *

The following Thursday, Melanie brought Dr. Huston several poems. She tossed them on the desk as if they were trash. Here—maybe you'll get something out of these. As he read them, Melanie fidgeted in the leather armchair, running her fingers over the brass buttons stapled into the arms. Light from the small barred window flitted unevenly across Dr. Huston's features. Melanie had to strain to decipher his expression.

"One of those is a revision of the poem about Lise and the wolves—you know, the one I wrote in the hospital," she explained. "I can't seem to express what I mean, though. I feel as if the poem is too short, that it needs more lines, that the idea isn't clear enough, but I can't think of anything else to write. Ironically, when I was playing around with it, I suddenly recalled this film Ray and I watched on our trip cross country.

"We had stopped somewhere, either New Mexico or Arizona—one of those Southwestern states anyway—I'm not too hep on geography. This couple Ray met in New York said we could stay with them for a few days if we were in the area. People are friendly like that, I have to admit. They tell you that if you're ever in their part of the world, they'll put you up for the night. People were really generous for the most part. Anyway, we crashed on their living-room couch. Of course, the woman was beautiful, and I could see that Ray was hot for her. What stands out in my mind, however, is this film we saw at a Southwestern museum they took us to.

"The film was about this woman potter—Maria somebody or other—I don't remember her last name. She's an American Indian, and she lived nearby in this pueblo. Ray and I had seen some of her bowls beforehand, and I had to admit they were truly beautiful, even though I'm not especially interested in pottery. But you could see their artistry, you know, the care she had taken with them; the film showed her making a pot from start to finish. What impressed me most . . ."

Melanie paused and looked toward Dr. Huston. He indicated she should go on, so she lit a cigarette elaborately and continued. "Well, you know, what impressed me was that even before this Maria began working, she gave corn to the land in thanks for allowing her to gather its materials. Isn't that cool? She kept saying that she and the clay were in a partnership, that she and the clay were discovering each other. Everything depended upon 'feel,' she said. You had to know when the clay was the right texture, when to add more sand, when to stop kneading, when to dry it, when to know if the temperature was hot enough. Sometimes—and this really got me—she could go through the entire process, and when it came to the final baking stage, the pot could crack or not come out as she intended it to. She considered the whole process with such reverence, such humility and thankfulness. I mean, jees, when I sit and write a poem, I know the inspiration is not necessarily coming from me, that it's a gift, but I don't do anything remotely like that. Talk about humility. That's very humbling!" Melanie threw up her hands.

"Gosh, Melanie," Dr. Huston said, "are you an American Indian? You have neither her heritage nor her training. How can you possibly expect to possess the wisdom and patience she has probably spent a lifetime acquiring, or even do what she does? This smacks of the old comparison game again, doesn't it? She does this so well; therefore, I should be able to. So, why can't I?"

"No . . . that's not it exactly," Melanie said, leaning forward intently. "I don't want to be Maria, but I admired her standards, her patience, her reverence. I wish I were closer to that kind of ideal or felt toward art as she does. I wish I had some 'corn' to offer. But who should I thank? The Universe? I don't know if I even believe in God. Sometimes, I get an inkling of that kind of reverence, that kind of being really centered and present—and you could see it in the way she moved her fingers—there were no wasted motions, but when I try, I certainly don't get results like that and that depresses me."

"You're barely twenty-two, Melanie. I would guess that Maria is closer to my age, isn't she? How can you have the maturity of a fifty- or sixty-year-old woman? You always want to skip the process, which is ironic, considering your desire to experience each moment."

"I'm sick of being so young and stupid," Melanie said. The bows in her pigtails had begun to loosen, and she gave each of them a violent yank.

"I think you have difficulty accepting yourself as you are, that somehow just to be who you are makes you deficient."

"Whatever . . ." Melanie rose from her chair, feeling if she sat there another minute she would explode. What was wrong with having ideals? It was the same old story. Be patient, be patient, be patient. Shit! "We're out of time, aren't we? See you next week." Before Dr. Huston could reply, Melanie opened the door and started down the stone steps.

🌹 *Two*

*A*lthough she had left the session frustrated because she thought Dr. Huston did not understand her, Melanie still could not decide what her *own* definites were, her own ideals and goals, or whether she even had any. What decided if a poem was good or bad? What gave it its value? Was it something she should know intuitively, or could it be taught? Would she ever feel as humble and assured as Maria appeared to be regarding her work, or had the film only shown Maria's best side? Was the rest of her life in shambles? Didn't Dr. Huston think it was good to have idols?

Writing again, reading again, listening to music—all these activities made her feel as if she had regained her mind, made her feel closer to the person she had been before meeting Ray and giving birth to Lise. That person cared primarily about books and writing, even if she had not taken those interests as seriously as she ought to have. Dr. Huston told her it was possible to be a wife, mother, *and* poet. This seemed doubtful, though, because if she was in the middle of a sentence and Lise cried for her attention, Melanie did not want to stop what she was doing. Often, she responded with great reluctance.

She was equally bothered by the fact she was not content with Ray. It was not the first time she had felt uncertain about their relationship, but she felt her dissatisfaction increasing, although for over a month after her release from the hospital, it had seemed as if their love was stronger than it had ever been. Melanie wondered if she would ever feel sure about anything in her life. She was so tired of drifting. When would everything be worked out? When would there be a time without problems or doubts? During lone neighborhood walks, as she meandered aimlessly along the street, arms swinging free, unencumbered by the stroller, she fantasized about being alone again, seeking her destiny. At those times, Melanie felt detached from her existence, as if her life, Ray's, and Lise's were only brushing against each other momentarily in the scheme of things, while her future lay elsewhere.

Yet in the evenings or on weekends, when she and Ray sat drinking coffee at the kitchen table with their feet up and touching on the same chair, Melanie felt content. Then, she was not concerned about the future. Times like those—although not particularly exciting—reminded her of their early months together. Days had spilled into each other as a matter of course. Did she need excitement to feel alive? She had a place to live, even if it was pretty shabby, a husband who loved her, a good-natured child. Why couldn't she be content? During the relaxed, uneventful evenings, Melanie felt as if she were burrowing in, nesting, being grounded in the moment. Wasn't that what Dr. Huston had said she should do? Accept her life, the substantiality of it, accept the peacefulness that came with doing ordinary things.

When she was a young girl, she had ridden the subway regularly and was familiar with all the stops on the IRT and IND lines. She felt secure in the cars themselves, but she hated to wait on the platform and stayed behind the yellow line, peering uncomfortably down at the shiny, blue-gray metal tracks, the dark soot, the blackened walls. Melanie could never say whether it had been a dream or whether it had actually happened, but once she had fallen onto those tracks and landed close to the third rail. She vividly recalled the image of being below everyone, of sensing she would touch the rail and be electrocuted. Yet she also knew she would be unable to prevent this; she knew a train would inevitably come. A cluster of people were crowded around the edge, yelling. Melanie saw the train at the entrance of the tunnel, about to bear down on her. Without warning, she had been lifted by strong arms. Were they her father's? Some strong person had jumped down, had taken her in his arms, had pulled her away from danger, saved her from death. The belief that she had actually fallen and been rescued was so strong, she could never approach a train platform as an adult without fear. She could fall again. Maybe this time no one would be there to rescue her.

Melanie found herself waking suddenly and staring around the apartment, as if it were those train tracks, as if she were trapped in a place from which there was no escape. She had merely deluded herself that danger was past. Without warning, the trembling could begin again; this time no one would be there to help her. An anxious voice inside her whispered: This state of relative contentment is not going to last; this is only a grace period. You will be tried in more difficult and painful ways—to prove what? she asked—to prove you can still suffer. You do not deserve happiness. When these thoughts flitted through her mind like demonic predictions, then Melanie was grateful for the calm evenings. She snuggled into them appreciatively, as she had previously snuggled into the comforting pair of arms that had rescued her from the subway tracks.

* * * * *

The Human Resources Department was sending her a babysitter. One July morning, Melanie dashed around the apartment, cleaning the bathroom, washing the dishes. Melanie knew, logically, the babysitter would not care about the condition of the apartment, but it seemed important to make a good impression. The subject of making a good impression, of pleasing others, had come up during a session with Dr. Huston. Melanie contended that unless she made superhuman efforts, no one would really like or accept her, while he countered that if someone truly liked her, he or she would forgive her so-called imperfections. What they might not be able to stand was her perfectionism! Did it really reflect on her character if she left dishes in the sink to soak, or if Ray's dinner was not ready as soon as he walked in the door? Would the sky fall in if something didn't get done at the exact moment she wanted it to? Why did she drive herself so hard? Melanie wanted to yield to his arguments but remained skeptical, as she had about earlier arguments concerning her strength and beauty. Didn't Dr. Huston believe it was necessary to have standards, to try for one's best? Although she expressed this to him as reasonably and painstakingly as possible, Dr. Huston only smiled and laughed. Then, he threw up his hands and told her she was impossibly stubborn but that this quality would work in her favor someday.

Melanie clunked down the wide, striated, blue-gray steps afterwards in her Dr. Scholl's sandals, feeling weary and depressed. She was tired of arguing, tired of dwelling on her problems; the medication made her feel better, so why did she have to continue therapy? The following week, when she suggested that maybe it was time to quit, Dr. Huston told her that unless she faced her demons, she would never be truly well. She was only beginning to develop a sense of who she was. Why give up halfway to the well? He knew that he was being provocative, but he wanted her to get angry. He wanted her to fight for herself. Didn't she want to try at least? Melanie shrugged. She didn't know what she wanted; sometimes all she wanted was to curl up in a ball. Just be and do nothing. Be left alone. She remembered her previous sluglike state with a feeling akin to envy. Was it better to be left to simple motions, simple animal actions? Consciousness of being was what got you into trouble.

When Melanie talked with Ray about whether she should quit therapy, he was frustratingly supportive in either direction. He told her she should probably continue; it was great to be able to tell your troubles to somebody else. Why not take advantage of the opportunity?

"Honey, you're always so intense about everything," Ray said one evening and reached to hold her hands. "You think too much. You've got to trust life more. Answers don't come in a day, nor should they."

Disgusted, Melanie yanked her hands away. He just did not understand. Why couldn't he see how important these decisions were to her? She lay on the bed, unable to concentrate on the book she had picked up, fuming at what she perceived was his complacency. With seeming regularity, their discussions led to arguments in which Melanie found herself momentarily radically transformed. Frantically desiring to prove her point, she found herself suddenly screaming and throwing objects around the room—pillows from their bed, books, magazines, whatever came to hand. These objects normally landed near the wall or against the sofa— she could never bring herself to aim directly at him, as if afraid to admit he might be the true object of her anger. Yet in those violent moments that occurred once or twice a week, Melanie felt as if she would die, so desperately did she want confirmation for her feelings. Later, as she lay huddled on the bed, weeping, she felt worse because she could not pinpoint why she had gotten so upset. It was as if all the anger she had ever felt in her life was erupting, spilling out of her without restraint. The intensity of her fury made her feel as if she would go blind; it took over all her senses, shot from her fingertips. When Ray held her afterwards and gently chided her for having what he called a temper tantrum, she felt increasingly alienated from him. He told her that she needed to gain control of herself. So what if they disagreed? Melanie marveled that he never lost his temper. Things *did* matter to her. Was that wrong? Was that a reason to be admonished or cajoled?

In despair, she would snatch up her cigarettes and retreat to the fire escape at the end of the hall. This quickly became a place of refuge, a quiet spot where she could sit and relive entire incidents, sometimes many times over. As she smoked and retraced what each of them had said, wondering how things had gotten so out of hand, the misty night breeze and starlit sky gradually relaxed her. Perhaps Ray was not trying to be contrary. Maybe he and Dr. Huston were right after all. But she still wanted to care about things deeply, even if doing so threatened to destroy her peace of mind. When she returned to the apartment, ready to apologize for her outburst, she shuddered when Ray playfully chided her further: She was a naughty girl, she mustn't throw tantrums. It was how his father spoke to Kathleen.

Only after much time had elapsed could she snuggle against him and talk in a similarly playful fashion. Melanie wondered how long they would be able to keep up such a dance. She didn't want to be a baby, and she didn't want him to treat her as one. Despite the seven-year difference in their ages, Melanie had always believed they stood on an equal footing. Now she frequently found herself feeling like the loser, the one who had to apologize, the one who was always in the wrong, the one in the down position. After one of these turbulent evenings, Ray often called from work to tell her she shouldn't wait up for him. He was going to swing by Helga's or his dad's on the way home. The first time became a second, and then a third, and Melanie worried that her temper was responsible for this change. In response, she attempted to be more solicitous. She had never expressed her anger violently in the past, and the intensity of her emotions frightened her. Dr. Huston assured her it was all part of the healing process, part of what would help make her whole.

Predictably, she and Ray had argued about the babysitter. Melanie told him she was worried the girl would not be nice to Lise, or would ignore her. Ray replied that everything would go smoothly; she was making a mountain out of a molehill. She was relieved that when the babysitter, Judy, arrived, she barely glanced at the apartment and was immediately friendly to Lise. However, rather than easing her fears, the outcome made Melanie wonder if she would ever be right about anything again, if she could trust her own judgment. Lise immediately crawled over to touch Judy's hands and face, and Judy laughed and accepted this readily, smoothing Lise's hair back with her hand and murmuring to her. When Melanie observed that she seemed comfortable with children, Judy explained that she was the eldest of five and had been changing diapers since she was eight years old. Her ambition was to be an elementary school teacher, and she was applying to colleges in the fall. Before long, Judy put a sweater on Lise and, after strapping her in the stroller, headed to the park.

Although Melanie had thought about how to use the two afternoons a week Judy's assistance would allow her, on the first occasion she found herself at a standstill. She sat in the rocker drinking a cup of coffee, but then, realizing forty-five minutes had already elapsed, she jumped up and headed for the grocery store. The babysitter was there ostensibly because she had important things to do and needed the three hours to do them. It was wasting precious time to sit drinking coffee, she explained to Dr. Huston later. She knew it was a good opportunity to revise her poetry, but she had never worked in such a disciplined fashion in the past, and to do so felt artificial.

*****

She walked to the co-op, ruminating on her situation. As she glanced at the stores she passed and stared ahead at the view of the campus and hills in the distance, Melanie wondered if she would ever feel at home in Berkeley. The town seemed like such a transient place, a place people drifted into and then back out of, epitomized by the steady stream of hitchhikers lined up along University Avenue, close to her and Ray's apartment. There were often as many as ten or twenty people standing there, and although most were only heading into San Francisco or east on Route 80, others brandished cardboard signs with destinations ranging from Los Angeles to New York. Melanie was aware that many people stopped in Berkeley to visit the now-famous People's Park or to catch up with old friends, then left just as quickly. The Bay Area was a place that embodied memories of exciting times and chance meetings, especially as it drew many people from the East Coast and other parts of the country. But to her it didn't feel like home.

It amazed her after two years that upon arriving she had thought she had finally reached home. If there was a deeper community, if a sense of home were to be found, it was eluding her, although she suspected the possibility remained. Physically, Melanie thought it was a nearly perfect place to be, but she did not feel connected to the people. They were too mellow and slow-moving, not intense and hard-driving like New Yorkers. Ray did not reflect Berkeley to her. He was forever and ever Richmond, rooted there, no matter how hard he tried to escape the confines of his own past, while she would probably always be a New Yorker in her heart. Berkeley would always feel too small, too beautiful, too perfect; maybe she could never make it her own.

"I'm not sure how to explain it, but this isn't a real place," she told Dr. Huston. "Berkeley is a fantasy, a beautiful fantasy, not a town where people actually live and have daily routines. I mean, even Richmond has a definite personality, with its oil refineries and its rows of stucco houses. But here . . . real people, ordinary people don't seem to live here."

"Goodness, Melanie, I live here!" Dr. Huston said, astonished. "Do you honestly believe there's only one Berkeley, one Richmond, one New York? Perish the thought! Numerous people live here who have careers and meaningful, satisfying lives; you simply haven't met them yet. You are so quick to pass judgment. Berkeley is not only the Ave or Sproul Plaza or the Marina. There are faculty and staff at the university; others own shops on Telegraph or Solano; the majority work in Oakland and San Francisco—

businessmen, nurses, teachers, artists. It's surprising that, considering what travelers you and Ray claim to be, you have limited yourselves so much on the home front. You have stuck to your own neighborhood, without venturing out at all. For example, you've never availed yourself of the university, which is certainly close at hand. Why don't you use your two afternoons a week to take a class? Or go at night through Cal Extension. Explore the hills or drive farther—south toward Carmel and Big Sur. I imagine Ray's actually shown you very little of California. California consists of a lot more than Richmond, Oakland, and Berkeley, Melanie, although there's a rich community of intellectuals here in Berkeley. You'd fit right in with your love of literature and your aesthetic tastes."

"And zero education." Melanie grimaced. "Don't you remember me telling you I dropped out of school? I'm always reading, but higher education just doesn't seem important to me. The people you're talking about are all probably highly educated; they would never accept me. Besides, I'm basically a loner; I avoid groups. As far as hitchhiking across the country goes— well, I wouldn't have done that except for Ray. I knew he'd be there to protect me."

"This is all up to you, naturally," Dr. Huston admitted. "I'm not about to tell you how to conduct your life, but keep in mind that such options are available. Don't be such a snob that you shortchange yourself."

"*Me* a snob? That's rich!" Melanie dismissed the validity of his words with a wave of her hand. "I'm about as down-to-earth as you can get. I wear blue jeans and T-shirts; I seldom wear a bra; I walk barefoot— I'm practically a godamm farmer! But the primary thing in relation to what you're saying is that I don't have a degree, and Ray and I are not rich. Ray's working at AAMCO, but we still receive assistance. Things like money really separate people, you know."

"There are different kinds of snobs, Melanie, and poor people can be snobbier than wealthy people. But I can't convince you, can I?" Dr. Huston said, smiling wryly.

"Actually, Ray and I did visit a lady who lives in the Berkeley hills," Melanie interjected, "somebody I met at the hospital. Lynn was there because of a fainting spell caused by anxiety. She told me these spells happened every once in a while, and she would just check herself in until they passed. What a luxury, huh? At the time, I thought maybe she should take it more seriously, you know, get some real help. It seemed like she was putting a band-aid on a puncture wound. At any rate, Lynn and I hit it off because we both enjoy reading and listening to classical music. After I was released, she invited Ray and me to her house for lunch. She has a beautiful house, with a view of the Bay, a huge garden. A real contrast from the flats."

"Were you comfortable there, Melanie?"

"Yeah. There was this weird dichotomy in my childhood—my father could hardly hold down a job, but my grandfather was a wealthy lawyer. So, it's like I know money and the quality of life it can buy, but I also really know poverty. I was comfortable at Lynn's house because it reminded me of my grandmother's apartment in Manhattan—you know, bookshelves fronted with glass, paintings on the wall. She even had a grand piano like my grandmother did, although no one ever played ours! Lynn has very good taste, and I appreciate that. I enjoy beautiful things.

"Anyway, we sat on her terrace eating hors d'oeuvres, gazing at the view, and listening to folk music; she had a terrific sound system. This was during July, and it was a beautiful sunny afternoon. The house was extremely modern with high ceilings and wood paneling throughout. There were a lot of windows so it was filled with light. There was light everywhere, and breezes drifted throughout the house. Yet despite all that beauty and comfort, Lynn had problems in her marriage—her husband's a dentist—and with the rest of her family, so I don't think she enjoyed what she had very much. The truth is, I think Lynn felt sorry for me, and I don't want friendship on that basis. One night later on, we invited her to dinner at our apartment. She was very polite, but I could tell she was uncomfortable. Plus, I thought she was coming on to Ray and who needs that? Especially right now. She's called me a few times, but we never got together again. That's the problem though—I don't live in her world, but I don't like the Richmond environment either, and Marie and Pete's situation . . . well, that's a whole other story. I don't know where I'd be happy, really, where I'd fit in. Sometimes it depresses the hell out of me."

"I'm sure you'll figure out where you belong one day, Melanie," Dr. Huston said.

* * * * *

Apart from Marie, whom she saw only periodically because of the distance between them, Melanie realized she no longer had any real friends. She did not count people in her building, or store checkers, or the produce workers at the co-op who greeted her in passing; the contact between them was ultimately superficial. Ray had introduced her to a few other people on campus, but they had been mainly transients, passing through Berkeley on their way to somewhere else. She had had a few casual friendships with women at Lytton, but she had not followed up with any of them, and now too much time had elapsed. Although she felt more comfortable with Helga and with Ray's other Richmond friends than she had in the past, they remained Ray's friends. This was Ray's stomping ground, and she was still the moody, intellectual outsider from New York. But because Melanie had chosen to be part of his life and had been directed by him in many ways, she found herself less able to act independently, apart from the fact that they now had a child together. It frightened her to imagine seeking out compatible people in Berkeley, whereas in Manhattan acquaintances had developed easily and spontaneously.

Melanie thought with longing of Mel and the period before and during her pregnancy, when the three of them had been so close. Mel energized both her and Ray, and he was someone she could do things with; he had loved going for walks and poking his head into bookstores. The three of them had frequently eaten at Kip's, a local college hangout that sold pizza and hamburgers. With Mel along, it had been less a dinner than an event. Ray would even approve of their friendship, because Melanie thought he had never even suspected her stronger feelings for Mel. But Mel had been out of touch for several months. His last postcard had told them he was traveling again. Disenchanted with the United States, he was headed for Mexico and was considering moving there permanently. Melanie wondered what would have been the outcome if she had met Mel before Ray, whether she would have been happier with him. Fate appeared to be working against her. She wondered if she was where she was supposed to be, if some lesson she did not presently understand would eventually be revealed to her.

During their evenings sitting at the kitchen table, she and Ray talked about his quitting AAMCO and setting up his own garage somewhere now that he had some automotive experience. In crazier moods, they spoke of ditching everything and moving north to Mendocino or farther up near the redwoods. Locate a cabin, go back to nature, raise Lise in an unpolluted environment in the country, either within a commune or by themselves. People they met did such things. Why couldn't they, too? Then Ray could play his music more, away from the stresses of the city. Maybe her poetry would flourish in such an environment. But although it had been fun to dream like this when they had first gotten together, now, when Melanie thought of them in isolation, it made her nervous. What bothered her more was whether she wanted to remain with Ray at all—in Berkeley or anywhere.

☞ *Three*

Several months after her release from the hospital, Ray's Richmond friend Mike invited them to come see the new apartment he had moved into with Dee. Melanie had not seen Mike since her pregnancy, and then only briefly when he had come by to borrow money from Ray. Mike had virtually ignored her, except for asking flippantly how the little mother was getting along. Melanie knew that when she was in the hospital, Ray had frequently run into Mike at Helga's house.

Helga had passed along the information that Mike and Dee had been living in a trailer park with her older sister, Gina, with whom Mike was having a fling. Dee had pressed to move out of the situation, and, remembering the passive, skinny teenager she had met briefly at Helga's, Melanie was amazed that she had gotten her way. In addition, Dee had quit shooting heroin and was trying to get Mike to stop, too. Given the circumstances, Melanie wondered how much longer they would stay together.

On the way over in the car, Ray was unusually quiet. Melanie had persuaded him to drop Lise off at Norm and Kathleen's because she did not know what to expect once they got to Mike's, and she was still uncomfortable in his presence. When they were back in the car again, Melanie turned away from the window and patted his leg, anxious to break the silence between them.

"I realize I'm not acting very eager to see Mike and Dee, Ray, but I don't like Mike's effect on you. You act tougher, and then you both play this game of who can put the other down the most. I mean, do you really enjoy that? You glamorize Mike; I can see it in your eyes when you look at him, as if you believe every word he's saying is brilliant. It just isn't." Melanie touched Ray's cheek, trying to get him to look at her, but he avoided her eyes. "Please, babe, I don't want to fight. I'll do my best to act friendly. It irritates me, though, because Pete is far more intelligent, and he has proven a hundred times more that he's a real friend. You hardly ever get together anymore."

"Pete's still my friend," Ray answered quietly. "I can like two different people, can't I? It's just . . . just that so much has come between us all—his breakdown, your breakdown, our both having kids now. Mike and me go back a long ways, Mel, and I know all his different sides. We've done a lot of shit together. It's hard to ignore him when he comes in my direction. Maybe you see it as foolish, but he'll always be way up there on my list of people I care about and think most highly of . . ."

"I understand, Ray, but I'm afraid he'll never be on mine. I feel nervous every time we see him, and I despise the crummy way he treats Dee. Like she's some kind of slave. He's in love with his own fucking power. See? Whenever I even get close to being around him, I start cursing, too, as if it's contagious! I don't like men who mistreat their girlfriends and whose lives revolve around doing drugs. I want a different kind of life. That's what I want for us, for you, me, Lise. Isn't that what you want?"

"It is. I do." Ray sighed. "But I can see that Mike draws you to him, too, because he's really more than a bully. The way I figure it, you really do like him, but you hate the fact you do. I've read about that; it's called a love/hate relationship. You're determined not to give him a chance because you have such conflicted feelings. Don't spoil tonight, honey. It's been a long time since we've seen him, and I'd really like to have a nice evening. For my sake, try not to have an attitude, Melanie. Can't you just be open-minded and try to get along? Mike and Dee accept you. Why won't you at least try to accept them?"

"Don't worry, I won't spoil tonight, *honey.*"

"Jesus, babe." Ray pulled the car to the side of the road and gathered her in his arms. "You're such a bear, Mel. Come on, give me a kiss." He kissed her fiercely, making Melanie's eyes tear. "Now, are you ready to face the big bad wolf?"

Ray had brought along his guitar, and Melanie decided that to cope with the evening, she would concentrate on listening to him play. She hated the hard edge his Richmond friends brought out in her; she always felt she had to shut down to keep her real self intact. As a teenager she had occasionally met her father at a tavern in Manhattan. While she waited for him, men on the bar stools gave her the once-over. They leered at her and made coarse comments, meant to be funny, about her figure or her imagined popularity with the boys. In consequence, Melanie had developed an intense distaste for all working-class men. Mike made her feel naked and mentally-pawed over, too, and this contributed to her uneasiness in his presence. With him it was worse, because she felt he not only visualized how she looked undressed—made worse during her pregnancy, when her breasts had increased in size—but saw into her mind as well, was aware of every thought she was thinking.

The beginning of the evening went well. Dee was more talkative than usual. She asked her about Lise and motherhood in general, making Melanie wonder if she was pregnant. They sat cross-legged on the floor, and Dee encouraged a small, white mouse to run up and down her long skirt.

"He won't bite, Melanie. Go ahead and pet him. Isn't he cute? We've only had him a week, but look how much he trusts me already."

After a while, Dee scooped the mouse in her palms and put it back in its cage so Mike could give them a tour of the apartment. As Melanie fell behind the others, she thought of the time she and Ray—in their initial excitement about moving into the Rosaline Apartments—had given Marie and Pete a tour. Mike and Dee's furniture consisted of a wooden table, two chairs, and a foldout couch. A mattress covered by a thin, tie-dyed bedspread lay on the floor in the bedroom, next to a pole lamp. Dee whisked away a pair of panties that lay next to the pillow. Mike, seeing her do it, said she was a goddamned exhibitionist; she'd left them there on purpose to give Ray a thrill. Dee turned pale at his words and tried to convince him otherwise, but he only grunted skip it, Dee, I may be old, but I ain't a fool.

When they returned to the living room, Mike straddled one of the wooden chairs and motioned for Ray and Melanie to take the couch. They sank together onto the plastic-coated cushions and slid toward the middle because of the broken springs. Mike laughed and said he hoped they hadn't expected the Ritz. Dee set a six-pack of Colt 45s and a plastic bowl of unshelled peanuts on the table. Mike's hair, wild-looking and ferocious as ever, stuck out at every point, as if it had been teased. Melanie found herself staring at it, unwillingly, as well as at his butchered veins, which were visible because his T-shirt was cut off at the shoulders.

"Looks like your old lady has the hots for me," Mike said, winking at Ray. "She can't keep her eyes off my body. Don't you keep her satisfied?"

Ray laughed. "Lay off, Mike. She's already built herself an attitude about you."

"Do tell. Let's hear more about that," Mike said, looking penetratingly at Melanie, as if she were a gnat or flea he was considering squeezing between his fingers.

Melanie glared at him. "I guess I'm just not used to male chauvinist pigs, macho man," she said, knowing her words sounded absurd even as she said them. Predictably, Mike laughed and muttered, "Gee, Ray, it sounds like she doesn't think too highly of your masculinity. Touchy, touchy. Mustn't ruffle mama hen's feathers. Speaking of, where's the little one tonight? Scared to bring her with you?" He looked shrewd-ly at Melanie, and she blushed.

Looking away from him, she picked up her can of malt liquor and took a sip. The main room was comfortably large, apart from its lack of furniture, combining as it did a living-room and dining-room space. Melanie wondered how they could afford it on Dee's waitress salary. She looked at the vase filled with plastic pink and white carnations in the cen-ter of the table and wondered if Mike appreciated Dee's attempt to create a homelike atmosphere. Mike turned toward Ray and asked him how things were at old double A, MCO.

Dee brought back the white mouse in its cage to give it company, she said, and sat cross-legged on the floor beside it, making kissing sounds at it when it squeaked. Now and again, she jumped up to replenish their food and drink. A trashcan stood alongside the table, and, periodically, each of them rose to dump their shells into it, except for Mike, who, after taking careful aim, shot each shell, one by one, into the metal can, accom-panying each delivery with a "kapow." This caused the mouse to squeak, and, in exasperation, Dee rebuked him. In response he kicked the cage violently with his foot and asked her who was more important, him or the godamm mouse?

Mike hit the bullseye several times in a row before Ray said, half-jokingly, half-enviously, "You've missed your calling, Mike."

Mike bowed and, leaning toward Melanie, whispered in a seduc-tive voice, "Want me to shoot your shells for you, dear?"

On one of her trips back from the kitchen, Mike grabbed Dee and swung her onto his lap.

"Hey, what do you know? It's the peanut girl from the circus." He squeezed her before kissing her lingeringly on the mouth. "Ummm, nice and salty." Dee spluttered and blushed before finally yanking herself away. "No need to get uptight, babe; we're among friends. Aren't you proud of having such a beautiful body? You sure strut enough when we're by ourselves. Turns me on every time, too, like magic. Did you know," he said, addressing the others, "this little girl is a fucking ballerina? She's been taking classes since she was seven years old. I've never seen so many pliés and pirouettes in my fucking life. Miss your dance classes, Dee-Dee? Sick of shacking up with this dirty old man? Getting yourself in shape for a younger guy?"

"Cut the shit, Mike. You know I'm not," she said, looking at the floor. "Why must you embarrass me in front of company?"

"I want you to know that this is a helluva strong old lady, even if she has such a passion for dancing it can drive you insane," Mike said, gripping Dee as she tried to move away. "She kicked this shit for four days straight. Sweat buckets, threw up, beat the floor, practically punched a hole in the wall, but in the end, she licked it. I've seen grown men throw in the towel before she did. My own record certainly bears examination. Yessiree, folks, Dee wins the blue ribbon."

Mike shook a cigarette from Ray's pack and tapped it dramatically on the table behind him. "Well, I know you thought this was a social call, but I really invited you here tonight because I've come to a decision. Dee wanted to show you the place because for some reason she likes you. Can't see why, especially not you, Ray—you motherfucker. But I called you all together because I've decided I'm going to try to kick this shit, too, and I wanted someone to bear witness to that fact. 'Cause this mother's got a hold of me good, and it's gonna be a bitch to throw her off."

Ray grinned, as if he'd heard something like this before. Melanie glanced toward Dee, expecting a similar reaction, but to her surprise, she saw that Dee was crying.

"Fucking women, cry at the drop of a hat," Mike said impatiently. "But seriously, I'm gonna need some people by me, so I hope that fits with your agenda. Melanie's presence doesn't matter, but maybe if you're not home for several nights, she won't think you're trying to make it with another chickadee." Mike grinned nastily at Melanie. "I know I'm on your shit list, princess, you don't have to pretend. Let's have a truce already." As he held out two fingers, Mike looked more closely at her eyes and then suddenly stood up.

"It's stuffy as fucking shit in this hole. Not enough windows, and if it were up to Dee, none of them would even be opened. She's so paranoid someone's gonna break in, she wanted to nail everything shut. Well, what do you say, Melanie? I think it's time we got past all this hatred. Let's take a walk around the complex. I trust Dee with my buddy Ray here."

Melanie rose unwillingly from the couch, but she did want to go for a walk. For over an hour, she had been feeling increasingly panicky. She looked pleadingly at Ray, as if to say, please rescue me from this situation; you know I don't even want to be here. He only smiled and said it was fine, he trusted Mike. It was a good idea to get things straightened out. For a second, Melanie felt betrayed, as if what was happening had been arranged between them beforehand. Dee came over and gave Melanie a quick hug.

"You do look kinda pale, Melanie. Go on. It's okay with me. Mike can be a big comfort when you're in a bad space."

They descended the steps of the garden apartment and began to walk down the street. Suddenly, Mike put his arm around Melanie's shoulder and pulled her body hard against his. The sudden gesture and the strength and heat from his body sent a jolt through her.

"You were scared as shit in there, weren't you?" he said, squeezing her shoulders. "I could tell; I have moments like that myself. I'm probably going to go through them again soon, too. That's why I depend on Ray so much. Strong as she is, it's too much for Dee to handle by herself. Listen, we're gonna walk until the fear passes, and then we'll go back. Just talk to me—say anything that comes into your mind—about Lise, Ray, New York, how you grew up, what it was like in the hospital; it doesn't really matter what it is. Just talk. Are you warm enough? Press closer to me. I'm not really the bastard you think I am."

They walked for what felt like hours. Melanie found herself telling Mike everything. It was a relief to bring her terror out into the open, although she glanced at Mike now and then to be certain he wasn't mocking her. After a while, as the panic receded, Melanie paid more attention to their surroundings, noticed parked cars, people out walking their dogs, women pushing strollers, the crescent moon high up in the sky. She was grateful that Mike didn't break physical contact with her. The strength and calm from his body seemed to flow into her own. How different it was from being with Ray, she thought, where frequently—as much as he made an effort to comfort her—she felt completely alone with her pain.

Abruptly, Mike pulled her to face him.

"Well, I guess the men in the white coats won't have to carry you away quite yet."

They walked back to the building, and Mike opened the glass door and held it for her. Melanie turned to him before entering and impulsively hugged him.

"Thank you, Mike," she said in a tremulous voice. "This really helped me. I'm not sure how, but it did. I appreciate it. I hope someday I can return the favor."

Mike chucked her lightly beneath her chin.

"Have I risen a little in your opinion, Melanie?" He laughed softly as they mounted the stairs.

* * * * *

Because she had promised Dr. Huston, Melanie began to attend Chris's Wednesday evening group sessions. Ironically, she found the people to be more hopelessly sick than the patients she had known within the hospital. Melanie felt as if she were in a place where the troubles were too deep for her, but she made herself sit through the hour and a half sessions.

This Wednesday night, her fourth, Melanie sat in her folding chair around the circle, playing with her fingertips, seeing if she could match each evenly with its mate. Despite this distraction, she felt increasingly morose and kept glancing toward the clock on the wall, aware of every five minutes that inched by. A large-boned woman, Joanne, was talking about her husband, who had beaten her severely the night before. Melanie knew from the previous week that Joanne had a history of suicidal behavior, that this was her third abusive marriage, and that she was on heavy medication. As she watched Joanne push up her sleeve to reveal one of the hideous black and blue marks Luke had delivered, Melanie turned away, thinking, unexpectedly, of how differently Deena would have described the situation. Before she realized it, she muttered under her breath, "Why did you let him do that to you?"

The room grew intensely quiet. Joanne glared at her incredulously, as if astonished that anyone had spoken. Melanie felt like everyone was staring at her, and their expressions were extremely mixed. In confusion, she looked at Chris, the leader, but his face showed neither sympathy nor accusation; it merely reflected curiosity. She repeated her question, this time more loudly, thinking, What the hell? Why should she let herself keep getting hit? Why not leave the bastard? But as she spoke, her voice shook, and Melanie realized the enormity of her words. Of course Joanne must not be able to stop it. If she could, she would. Oh Jesus, she told herself, Joanne can no more stop it than you could make yourself leave the hospital grounds until Deena accompanied you.

Joanne snorted and reached for a fresh cigarette, the previous one having burnt out between her fingers.

"Well, baby, I *do* try to stop him, but he keeps on coming—bars the doors, threatens to take my child away, tells me I'm a loony, and that he'll have me committed again—so you figure it out. I'm just trying to keep the peace. Like it or lump it, he's the father of my child, and Robbie's my only baby." She looked down at her light blue stretch pants and sighed. "I'm not telling anybody I'm enjoying this, get me. Luke's a strong motherfucker, and I don't think I got a whole lot of choices here . . . I know, I gotta quit trying to kill myself, though; you're right. I gotta keep alive for Robbie's sake. The fights scare him to death, poor darling. He just don't know Luke. I mean, Luke gets all hot and angry, he takes some swipes—especially if he's had a few too many—but then he cools off, and there's nothin' he won't do for us. Buys Robbie and me brand new clothes, and I know he ain't got the cash. Takes us to dinner. I mean, when Luke's sweet, he's real sweet, but he's got a temper, and I should know better. It don't take much to set him off. Once I smiled at the paper delivery boy, and I didn't mean a damned thing by it, but boy, was I sorry later. Luke had it figured we was sleeping together, that we was exchanging a secret wink. Fat old thing like me, too. It sure did make me feel good in a way, after the cuts healed. He don't touch Robbie, at least; I mean, if he started in on Robbie, I'd leave him in a flash. It's that simple. That's one thing I simply will not take." Joanne crushed out her half-smoked cigarette, a Benson and Hedges, Melanie noticed, the same brand she had smoked before meeting Ray. Joanne shrugged her shoulders and delivered a twisted smile to the group. "So you see, honey, I know you're new and everything," she said, looking at Melanie with a sharp glance, "but it's just not as simple as should I let him hit me or not."

Melanie stared at her before lowering her eyes. She felt humiliated and inwardly furious. It sounded to her as if Joanne had talked herself into believing things were really acceptable. If she felt so strongly that Luke shouldn't hit Robbie, why couldn't she see *she* was as important? Melanie could only reason that perhaps this Luke guy was a fantastic lover or had some equally fantastic quality to make up for his abusiveness, though from Joanne's description, he sounded ignorant and boorish, besides incredibly jealous. Chris, however, appeared genuinely troubled. He had moved to the seat next to Joanne's and was gently pressing her palm.

"Joanne," he said softly and with a tenderness that surprised Melanie, "I want you to make a promise, here and now—a contract with yourself and the group—that if Luke strikes out at you or even threatens you, you will head straight for the door if you can get there. You will not in turn pick up a razor or take an overdose of your medication. You will remember that you are a valuable person, as valuable as Robbie, as worth keeping alive. I'm going to write this down, and then I want you to sign it."

Chris's voice was as calm and certain as Melanie remembered. She watched him take a pad of paper from his shirt pocket, write quickly, and then hand the sheet to Joanne. When Joanne took it, her hands trembled, and every trace of toughness left her face. Instead, she began to cry, at first soundlessly, but then uncontrollably. As she wept, she gasped that she didn't know if she could hold on any longer, that he was going to kill her, he was going to kill her, and she was so fucking scared.

She cried for some time. Chris held her hand so tightly that his knuckles turned white, but when she subsided, Joanne signed the paper, promising solemnly that she would call for help and not inflict violence on herself. She smiled weakly out at the group and thanked them all in a sweet, humbled tone for helping her and believing in her. Chris then went on to say how proud he was of Joanne's progress in the past several months, that she was really taking strides to help herself, that she had shown up regularly for the group. She was always making sure she had a babysitter, and she had called him right away when she took the medicine and had gone directly to the hospital. Longtime members of the group nodded in agreement.

When Melanie was leaving, Chris hugged her and told her not to worry; she was right, no one *should* allow herself or himself to be hit, and he thanked her for her righteous anger. But as she walked to the bus stop, she felt chastened by what she had witnessed. Compared to Joanne, she wondered if she had any real suffering in her life and wondered, too, if she could ever share her problems with this new group. They seemed so unsympathetic to her and such strangers. Despite Chris's reassuring hug, she felt little inclination to return the following Wednesday; coming there seemed pointless.

 # *Four*

Mike began to visit them two or three times a week. He, along with other Richmond friends, developed a habit of dropping by the apartment after Ray had come home from work and staying until late in the evening. They played cribbage and drank beer, and sometimes, one or the other of them brought dope. As joints were passed back and forth, and the table became cluttered with beer cans, Melanie realized the center of activity had inexplicably transferred itself to their kitchen rather than Helga's, although Helga herself never put in an appearance. It was mostly men who came. Dee seldom accompanied Mike, as if acknowledging it was men's night out, and he seemed not to mind her absence.

Because Ray grew animated and seemed to enjoy these evenings, Melanie was reluctant to complain, although she dreaded the men's arrival. She had already told Ray her feelings about his Richmond friends. If she took a drink or two herself to feel part of things, though, she found it made her nervous all evening. She assumed this was because the alcohol mixed strangely with her medication. Unable to stand being confined within the stuffy, noisy apartment, Melanie developed a habit of sitting on the steps of the fire escape. However as she sat, breathing in the contrastingly refreshing night air, she felt terribly alone and isolated from Ray. She did not understand what pleasure he took in these men's company, what comfort or sense of solidarity it brought him. Their conversations consisted chiefly of mutual put-downs of each other and minute discussions of card play, although sometimes they discussed travel, sports, their women, and other friends. Later, when Ray turned drowsily to her in bed, Melanie felt frozen, unable to express how unhappy the new situation was making her. She was secretly afraid that if things continued, they would precipitate another depression. As she watched him interact with the others, he reminded her of his father, which made her feel, once again, that she was turning into Kathleen. It was as though they were both playing out someone else's destiny rather than their own.

What bothered her more than anything, though, was Mike's constant presence. Melanie had to remind herself again and again that once at least he had been a great comfort to her, because now he virtually ignored her. Mike came nearly every night and stayed long after the others had left. She stayed in the background, appearing only, as Dee had, to replenish food and drink; but the apartment was small, so she was constantly aware of Mike's dominating presence. If she attempted to participate in the conversation, more often than not Mike deliberately cut her out or immediately challenged the points she tried to make. Ray did try to include her—she had to grant him that—but the force of Mike's personality was simply too great. After a while, Melanie quit trying and usually fell asleep while waiting for Mike to leave.

✻ ✻ ✻ ✻ ✻

"Because he's so self-destructive, he wants to make sure everyone else gets pulled down along with him. I can't stand listening to him slice everybody to pieces," she complained to Ray. "He reminds me of this woman's husband in my group, who thinks he can just bully everybody to get what he wants." As she spoke, Melanie felt she could barely breathe. She continued more pleadingly. "Don't you see it, Ray? He's messing up our lives, driving a wedge between us, competing with me for your attention. I can't take his constant company. Once in a while, maybe . . . but this is night after night after night! Jesus! Why doesn't Mike just move in with us and be done with it!"

"I understand, Mel. I know Mike's hard to take after a while," Ray said, smoothing her hair with his fingers. "But I thought you guys were friends now. It's just been so long since we've spent any amount of time together. I mean, I love the guy, and it's hard to see him suffer. Listen, Melanie, he'll move on; I promise you. Mike never stays put long. But I'll ask him to come less often, I promise, I will," Ray murmured into her hair as he pulled her against his body. "Of course you come first. You and Lise always come first."

Melanie assumed Ray had spoken to Mike because for a week, there was no rattling at the apartment door, no shouts from the street below, no desperate phone calls in the middle of the night. Surprisingly, she found the nights dragged by without him. Some evenings, unable to keep still, she paced back and forth, tapping restlessly on the window pane, peering down into the street. So she was startled one morning when she first heard the outside buzzer and then a knock on her door. It was only nine-thirty, and she could not imagine who it could be, except the landlady. At first she did not respond. When the knocking persisted, Melanie picked up Lise for protection and opened the door. Mike stood in the hall. Perspiration beaded his face, and he was out of breath. He brushed past her into the apartment.

"I know I'm not your favorite person, Melanie, but I've got to talk to somebody, and I know old lover boy's at work." The words came out breathlessly.

What could she say? No, you aren't. Get lost.

"I was just going to feed Lise," she said uncomfortably. Then, relenting, "There's some coffee on the stove that Ray made earlier. Help yourself to a cup."

Mike headed toward the kitchen and Melanie frowned, wondering what new aggravation was in store for them, for her. Why would Mike come visit when he knew Ray wouldn't be home? Melanie sank with Lise into the rocker, shook some milk from the bottle she held to be certain the liquid was flowing freely, and leaned back as Lise began to pull at the nipple. She could hear the motions of Mike busily stirring sugar into his coffee and wished suddenly that her blouse did not have a milk stain on the front, and that she had brushed her hair. Oh, what did it matter? she told herself severely. It didn't matter one whit! After all, her morning had barely begun.

Mike set his coffee mug on the floor beside their bed and stretched out on the mattress. Her nightie lay crumpled next to the pillow. As he arranged his body to get comfortable, he moved it gently away from him. Melanie blushed furiously before she turned the rocker to face the window more, wondering if he thought that she, like Dee, was a goddamned exhibitionist. But of course, she hadn't been expecting anyone, had she? Out of the corner of her eye, she watched Mike lean his head against the wall and shut his eyes tightly. His face was full of pain. She had never been alone with him, except for brief moments and when they had gone walking at his apartment. Now that she was married, she seldom saw men without Ray being present. Memories of the few times she had been alone with Mel sprang to her mind. She had been nervous then, too, but so much happier.

Mike took several sips of coffee but then, letting out a sigh, set the cup down and wiped his mustache off with the back of his hand. Pushing himself up from the mattress, he walked to the record player and started flipping through the albums which they kept in a milk crate. He slid out a Kris Kristofferson record, and, after a few minutes, the music oozed like honey into the room:

"I have seen the morning burning golden on the mountain in the skies
Aching with the feeling of the freedom of an eagle when she flies
Turning on the world the way she smiled upon my soul as I lay dying
Healing as the colors in the sunshine and the shadows of her eyes . . .

Coming close together with a feeling that I've never known before in my time
She ain't ashamed to be a woman or afraid to be a friend
I don't know the answer to the easy way she opened every door in my mind
But dreaming was as easy as believing it was never gonna end
And loving her was easier than anything I'll ever do again."

A pulse beat in Melanie's throat. The song always brought on an ache inside her chest, made her long to be the beautiful woman Kristofferson described: loving, loved, strong, needed by her man. Music weakened her. It swelled inside her chest, made her feel as if she could easily break into weeping, especially if it possessed a bittersweet quality. It was too early in the morning to deal with such passion. When the song ended, Mike played it from the beginning, and then again. He listened with closed eyes, and Melanie realized that, like her, he must be an incurable romantic—undone by anything that even hinted of sentiment.

She wondered how long it would be before he began to talk about what had brought him there so early, wondered how long she would be kept in the apartment, listening to him. The day promised to be warm and pleasant, and she yearned to be outside; she had planned to take Lise to the playground. Why couldn't she simply tell Mike that he had to leave, that she had things to do? Why did he assume that, like Helga, there was nothing she needed to do? Were women only alive to wait for men to activate them? Were they supposed to be on hold until their men decided what they wanted to do? Melanie sighed, realizing she had probably given Mike reason to believe she was passive. She hardly spoke in his presence, and, like Dee, she served snacks like an obedient servant. During the weeks when he had visited regularly, she had said barely ten words to him. Did he want another beer? Could he spare a cigarette? Once she had asked him to move over slightly when the three of them had watched *Mission: Impossible* together. She put Lise on the rug and went to get a cup of coffee for herself. Unwilling to encourage conversation, Melanie resisted asking Mike if he needed a refill. Mike finally exchanged the album, *The Silver-Tongued Devil* for Neil Young's *After the Gold Rush*.

After pouring another cup of coffee, Mike fished a cigarette out of Melanie's pack, lit it, and blew out a stream of smoke. He grinned as Lise stared up at the sudden blue-white cloud it produced. She crawled toward him, and he patted his thigh invitingly.

"Come on, that's a girl," he said. "Come to Uncle Mike."

Uncle Mike! That does it, thought Melanie. I've got to tell him he can't stay.

However, before she could budge from the rocker, Mike began talking.

"You know, it seems to take a woman to really understand a guy, Melanie. Women are sensitive to a guy's feelings, they're forgiving; they're more willing to give some shithead—no matter how worthless—another chance . . . It's a nice thing to have a woman's ear, a woman's support. Dee's a sweet kid, but that's just it. She's a kid. That was refreshing at first—her being so innocent—but I can see things are not going to work out. Dee pretends she's tough, but she's soft as whipped butter. It's time to end it for everybody's sake, although I admit I'll miss her. Taken all around, she's pretty damn sweet." He took a drag on his cigarette and blew a smoke ring for Lise.

"You know about pain, don't you, Melanie? I think you could take in just about anything a person told you. Even though you seem naive, I think in the end, not too much would shock you. Because you've faced some of your own devils." Mike crossed his arms behind his head and stared at her. " 'Some are born to sweet delight. Some are born to endless night,' " he said softly. "I bet you didn't think I knew any poetry, did you?"

"I think Dee understands a great deal," Melanie answered, ignoring his question. "She's more mature than a lot of girls her age. But you're right, she is very young."

"I am such a major fuck-up. I finally break free of heroin but then I drink like a fish. I guess I must be simply incapable of change. I used to believe I could get my life together if I had the right woman—that somehow she would be my salvation. One day I would suddenly want the straight life and get it all together, but I'm thirty-three years old, and it just ain't happening. So why put Dee through those changes? She's the youngest girl I've ever lived with; they seem to get younger and younger anyway. What does she see in an old geezer like me? I'm twice her age. She says these really childish things that bug the shit out of me. Take the mouse, for example. Dee can play with it for hours and not get bored. Watching her, I feel like throwing the godddamn thing out the window, it makes me so sick!" Mike laughed humorlessly. "Yes, it's time to end this shit. It's probably been going on too long already. Dee needs a chance to date guys her own age, have a normal life, go to proms, basketball games, get out of this before she's in too deep, too hooked into this shit. What do you think, Melanie? Don't you think it's a good idea for me to pull out?" Lise had climbed onto Mike's shoulder. He caressed her face and then kissed her on the forehead.

"Jesus, Mike, it's obvious Dee loves you. She'd be really hurt if you ended things, especially if you did it abruptly, without any explanation. I mean, she wants to be with you. Don't you think she knows her own mind?"

"Ray's a fortunate bastard, Melanie. You're really true-blue, aren't you? He tells me you are anyway, that he can always count on you . . ."

"I'm sure you can count on Dee."

Mike laughed. "You know, the gods have always smiled on Ray. He's been through so much shit, but he always comes out shining. He's so cheerful sometimes, it's nauseating. There's not a mean bone in his body, while I hate just about everything on two feet. He's one of the few exceptions. I envy Ray," he continued, "you should have seen how worried he was when you flipped out; it's rare to see him cry. I'd like a woman I could feel that way about. Someone I wouldn't have to worry about constantly, make all the decisions for, like I do with Dee. It's better to be surgical. She's been getting weepy and clingy lately; it's uncharacteristic of her. Time to cut my losses before it gets worse. See, you straighten me out, Melanie. It helps to talk to you."

"If you do it that way, Dee won't understand what happened," Melanie repeated. "She'll think that if she only tries harder to please you, she'll make you change your mind." She rose to change the record, which had been grinding away.

Mike's words twisted her, troubled her, flattered her. She felt herself being drawn in by his voice; it lulled her, caressed her. Although they were discussing Dee, Melanie felt very conscious of Mike's masculinity and of the intensity with which he looked at her, as if he was stripping her with his eyes. She was equally aware of his lean, hard-looking thighs as they pressed against the fabric of his jeans, his T-shirt pulled tautly across his muscles, his exposed arms. The nearness of him made her feel slightly faint, and she had to restrain herself from jumping up. Melanie tucked her hair behind her ears, fiddled with the edge of her blouse, ran her fingers along a milk stain, blotting it, circling it. Mike's confusion pulled at something inside her. His intelligence enticed her, and she was swayed by his sudden boyish looks of helplessness and the deep frustration that occasionally flickered in his eyes. She found herself nodding, confirming, smiling, even laughing at his self-deprecating jokes.

After a while, she rose to fix lunch. Before she realized it, it was two o'clock, and Lise, whom she had put down for a nap an hour earlier, was murmuring in the crib. Mike got up from the mattress and stretched. The motion pulled his shirt up, exposing his lean, tanned chest. A scar, whitened over time, marred the area near his navel, and she wondered what had caused it. As if guessing her thoughts, Mike grinned, although he gave her no explanation.

When she carried Lise back into the living room, Mike swung her up to the ceiling, which brought on a cascade of smiles. He then picked up Melanie's pack of cigarettes and shook out several—for the road, he said, grinning. At the door, he locked eyes with her intently.

"Thanks for hearing my bullshit, Melanie. See you around, beautiful." Mike ran his long, slender fingers slowly along her chin and then pulled her abruptly against his chest. His breath felt warm against her neck, and Melanie felt herself swaying closer to him. Before she could decide whether he had planted a kiss on her cheek, he was gone.

She cranked open the windows to try and erase his presence, his smell, his touch. She realized she had wanted Mike to stay. She had wanted him to hold her longer, wanted him to, yes, kiss her. That was just what she needed! It was the exact opposite of what she wanted. She wanted to go somewhere with her life, do something. With Mike—apart from the fact that he replaced one addiction with another—life would be a total dead-end street. But who was she kidding? Mike chose girls like Dee; he didn't want a serious relationship. He wasn't even interested in her! This was all a game to him.

*****

"Why does he affect me so strongly?" she asked Dr. Huston the following day. "After he left, what did I do? Nothing! It was as though by sitting there and listening to him, I spent all the energy I had, limited as it is. I made it to the park eventually, but only my body accompanied Lise. I kept thinking about Mike, turning the morning's conversation over in my mind, feeling guilty about my desire for him. Conversation! I barely spoke. He has such a paralyzing effect on me, and he's cruel; he's really cruel. Now it looks like he's going to dump Dee without any explanation. He's never hidden the fact that he doesn't like me very much, so what am I to him? A substitute for Ray? Why on earth does he want to talk to me and be with me?"

Melanie crossed and uncrossed her legs. She knew Dr. Huston would not answer her. Their time was almost up, and, truthfully, what answer could he give her? What did this new entanglement mean? Why did Mike suddenly appeal to her, if only physically? She had never been attracted to extremely masculine men, what she considered the muscle-builder types. She did not know how to relate to them, and, ordinarily, they were not attracted to her either. Did Mike's vulnerability draw her? Out of all their acquaintances, Mike understood most what she had experienced during her breakdown. Although he needed to talk constantly now, Mike had told her about withdrawing for days, voluntarily shutting himself away from everyone and everything. Melanie understood his need to do this; he understood and even appreciated loneliness. In contrast, Ray needed to be surrounded by people and found it difficult to be alone with himself.

When she left Dr. Huston's office, Melanie felt more restless than ever, although for the entire fifty minutes, she had relentlessly spewed out her frustration. Unlike her usual experience, though, the more she had talked, the less comforted she had felt. What if Mike came again? What if he now came daily, as he had nightly? Would she be worn down by his need, by her own loneliness? By her own desire to be understood? Melanie felt she could not bear seeing him that frequently. She feared, equally, that he would tempt her into some type of relationship, as Ray told her Mike had done with other men's wives. The thought made her feel terribly vulnerable.

The following Wednesday in Group, Melanie brought up the situation. She found she enjoyed getting out at night, taking the bus by herself, sitting alone, being alone. It was how she had felt in the hospital—temporarily restored to herself, an individual separate from her husband and child and the intricacies of those relationships. When she entered the meeting room, Melanie felt nervous and hesitant, although after five months she knew everyone and could essentially predict what each would talk about during the session. Melanie talked very seldom herself, although in the hospital she had shared frequently. In the new group, she felt criticized and misunderstood. Two weeks earlier, when she was attempting to comfort a newer member, one of the regulars, a man named Jim, had yelled at her, "Will you please stop trying to rescue everybody! Take care of your own goddamn problems instead of trying to fix everybody else's."

Shocked and angry, Melanie had skipped the following session, which led to a phone call from Chris, persuading her to return. Chris had not refuted Jim's statement, though, which made her wonder if he believed it was accurate.

Now, before speaking, she unrolled the sleeves of her man-tailored blouse and then re-rolled them.

"I'm having a problem with something," she finally said slowly. Some members seemed to be listening; others were looking around the room or at the floor. The man who had upset her, Jim, sat stiffly, staring ahead at seemingly nothing. "There's this guy, this friend of my husband's, who's been coming by all the time lately. Well, he has a way of making me feel very insignificant, as if who I am and what I think are not important. But now, instead of stopping by only in the evenings the way he used to, he comes in the mornings as well. He's come three times this week, and this is only Wednesday. His being there basically chews up my day, but I'm scared to tell him to leave because he's kicked junk recently, and he told Ray and me he needs to be around people. What bothers me the most is that I'm starting to feel drawn to him. And he's dangerous. I feel like he could swallow me up, and then I'd lose everything! I mean, I've got this fantasy that I'm making some headway with my problems, and now I've got this complication on my hands. Ray just doesn't understand. He does-n't see how poisonous Mike is."

Melanie stopped talking. Several people nodded, and a few smiled encouragingly. She saw Chris listening intently, and Jim was finally look-ing in her direction.

"It's deeper than what's happening with Mike, though, because part of what I'm struggling with is whether or not I'll ever be truly happy. Maybe I really want Mike to keep coming because he fills a void in me. I don't know . . . maybe nobody is ever *really* happy or is even supposed to be, but lately I feel unbelievably dissatisfied, incredibly restless. Not because of Lise. We're getting along great, and the babysitter thing is working out. It's more to do with Ray. I don't know if I even love him anymore, and having this other guy around just makes it even more confusing. The apartment is so tiny, and he's got this really dominating personality. It's difficult to not get overwhelmed by it. I've come through so much, I realize I should be happy—I mean happy I don't tremble anymore, that I'm not scared all the time—but it's not enough. I want more . . ."

Melanie stopped, surprised that she felt utterly confused and mis-erable. Coming to the meeting she had been tired, but not particularly depressed. When the silence lengthened, she became increasingly nervous, and tears pressed painfully against her eyes. God damn it! What was it she *did* want? The members of the circle seemed distant. She felt anchored to a buoy, rocking aimlessly, going nowhere.

"Why not decide what you want, what you'd like to do in life—you know—what your interests are and all," the newer girl she had tried to help suggested hopefully.

Melanie smiled at her wanly. A sense of desperation washed over her. She realized that no one could help her or tell her anything. She turned tentatively toward Chris, but although he smiled sympathetically, he said nothing.

"I know my interests and what I enjoy, but knowing them doesn't make things any clearer!" she cried. "I'm not sure if what I want is a person, a place, a goal, or even happiness. All I know is that I feel driven, restless, hungry . . . incredibly hungry, as if I'll die if I can't satisfy it! Maybe what I'm searching for is some type of communion or completion. I ache, I simply ache for that! Sometimes, I feel as if all I am is just one big lump of pain, as if every cell is massed together inside me, crying. I feel strung apart like a marionette's body. Oh Jesus!" Melanie took a long shuddering breath and wrapped her arms tightly around her body. "I feel stupid even talking about it. But I don't know what to do; I just don't, don't know."

"For starters, you should stop feeling sorry for yourself," Jim blurted out. "You want lots of things to happen, but it doesn't sound like you want to make any effort to achieve them; you want everything to come easily. You act like a baby who wants to be taken care of all its life. Well hell, honey, no one's going to do that for you!"

Melanie felt as if he had punched her in the stomach. She sat rigidly, unable to move a muscle. She could scarcely release her breath. If she could have stopped breathing altogether, she would have.

After several minutes, she muttered, "Forget it. Forget I said anything, asked for anything from any of you. I'll certainly never do it again. Fuck it! Let somebody else talk, some other sucker." Her chest heaved with pain.

"Melanie, if you can handle it, we should stay with this," Chris said quietly. "I realize that you feel attacked and hurt. Jim was not very tactful, but if you can see beyond the pain, there's some validity to what he said. We *can* block our progress with self-pity. It can prevent us from taking charge of our lives when we think we can be magically rescued. The cure doesn't come from outside ourselves; we are our own healers."

"What the fuck is wrong with wanting to be rescued?" Melanie cried. "Haven't I suffered enough? Am I supposed to be enjoying this? Is that what you're telling me? Shit! Jim's always got it in for me. What the hell did I ever do to him? Can't I even express what I feel without being punished? I've never condemned any of you for what you've shared! I only come to this stupid group because I hope I'll receive some answers. Otherwise, why subject yourself to this fucking bullshit?" Melanie began to sob. She felt utterly humiliated and sickened that she had laid herself open to attack and dug her fingers deep into her thighs in an attempt at self-control. But it was as if she couldn't help herself. The tears burst out of her. That's what you get, you fool, she told herself; that's what you get for trying to be open with people. Melanie snatched up her purse and strode out of the room before Chris or anyone else could rise from their chairs.

As she walked home, disdaining the bus because she felt the need for cold air, pain radiated like hot wax through her body. Jim's words turned over and over in her mind, intensified by Chris's affirmation of them. Was Jim right? Was her only problem that she was filled with self-pity? Could it be that simple? Was that all there was to it? Was she alone responsible for her unhappiness? And was there really no one besides herself who could ultimately help her? The idea depressed her beyond belief because it seemed to say that everything depended upon her own strength, and Jesus, how strong could she be anyway! Why did everything always come back to her? Well, whose life was it anyway? As her feet hit the pavement emphatically to expel her frustration, as the evening's moisture billowed around her face, her heart gradually beat less erratically. She felt so destroyed by words, by what others said to her or about her, as if indicted. Why must she feel everything so violently, so physically? Was it true? Was she a baby who didn't want to grow up, who wanted to be cradled and never put down alone, as she had always hesitated to put Lise down until she was totally asleep? But Dr. Huston kept assuring her that she was growing, that she was strong, that she had moved out of the protective womb of the hospital, that now she was on her own. Fuck Jim! Who the hell did he think he was? God?

Melanie kicked at a discarded Good & Plenty box, following it down the street. Except for the time when she had been afraid of the sky darkening, she had always enjoyed the night sky—its deep layers of purple and blue—and now, as she grew calmer and calmer, she let its cool tones wash over her, cool and ease her pained heart. Lights from the city in the distance looked as if they were bobbing up and down in front of her. She walked toward the Bay, toward home, toward the apartment where there was so little space, so little sense of the cosmos. Turning the corner, turning away from the water and toward different lights—store lights, car headlamps— Melanie reached her own dark, tree-lined street and the Rosaline Apartments. She stopped for a minute and looked at the building. It stood alone—vacant parking lot on one side, fenced car lot on the other—an anomaly. The other dwellings on the street were single-family homes or duplexes. They had true gardens, pathways, while this stucco structure had been self-consciously plopped down in the middle of them—an institutional eyesore, faded and ugly-looking, even in the dusky light of evening. It would be right to leave such a place. Ray's mother, having retreated to these apartments, had died there. Alone.

 *Five*

Melanie did not know how to turn her vague dreams into reality, but she decided that a step in the right direction might be to take a class at the university, a night class in writing, as Dr. Huston had suggested months before. The question of leaving Ray, of having a different life began to torment her. Melanie woke to the thought, and throughout the day she continued to turn ideas over in her mind. Even at night, even as she and Ray lay holding each other, even when she ran her fingers tenderly through his curls, she thought about change.

Several weeks after what she considered her disastrous Group session, she and Ray sat on their mattress drinking beer and eating pretzels watching *Mission: Impossible.* When Ray was not looking, Melanie studied him. His face was ravaged-looking, though he was barely thirty years old. He had deep indentations in his cheeks and forehead, and his eyes, like now, were frequently bloodshot, as if he used them too much and too intensely. Although Ray's slight body was still young-looking and wiry, Melanie noticed a resigned set to his shoulders when he scrunched down to reach for a cigarette.

It suddenly hit Melanie that Ray had settled in. Resigned to the present, he would glean whatever pleasure he could from it, whether that took the form of talking or jamming with friends, getting stoned every night, or by having an occasional fling. The rest—the drudgery, the monotony—he would accept as his due of what it meant to be a man and a father. Something in him had died. He was no longer the same person he had been in Manhattan, or perhaps she was only seeing him as he truly was for the first time. But although her desires may have temporarily gone underground, the passion for a meaningful life had not died in her. Melanie did not want to remain in a world of second-rate choices; it was necessary, essential to her being, to find something else. She stared unseeingly at the gray television screen, realizing that for perhaps three years she had been living beneath a coverlet. If she did not remove it, she could suffer a slow suffocation. Melanie barely realized that the show had ended and that Ray had shut off the set, until, turning toward her with a smile, he stroked her leg affectionately.

"Wow, that was intense!" Ray exclaimed. "They get me every time. I never know until the end whether things are going to work out or not." Sensing that Melanie was not listening, he tickled her beneath her knee. "Mel? Mel, where are you? Weren't you watching? O where, o where has my little Mellie gone? O where, o where has she gone?" he sang. Melanie found herself smiling, but then she burst into tears.

"Oh, Ray, Jesus, this is so hard. How do I say what I need to say?" She dabbed ineffectually at the tears running down her face.

"What? That you don't like *Mission: Impossible?* That's okay. I'll still love you." He grinned.

Melanie took a sip of beer; its coldness made her feel oddly sober.

"Ray, I just don't know, I don't know. It just hit me where we're going, what our life is like, and I realize I can't live like this anymore. No, I don't mean that, I don't," she said as Ray looked at her with a puzzled frown. "I mean . . . oh shit, I mean, things aren't right between us. We were so close after I got out of the hospital; it was so nice . . . This sounds so ungrateful, because you were really there for me during my breakdown, but . . . oh Jesus! What about Lise? Oh, what do I do? What do we do?" Melanie covered her eyes with her hands.

Ray let go of her leg and sat up. "What are you trying to say, Mel?" he said in a quiet voice. He shook out a cigarette and lit it elaborately. "What I think I hear you saying is that you don't want to be with me anymore." Melanie sat hunched up on the mattress with her face covered, wishing she could unsay what she had said, wishing she could disappear. Now that it came to the point, her courage had completely left her.

"Wow! Talk about not having a clue!" Ray continued. "Here I am, contentedly watching the show, enjoying your warm body next to mine, and all the time . . . all the time, *this* is what's been going through your mind. I must have my head in the sand." Ray tugged her hands away from her face and looked at her closely. "You don't love me, Melanie? Is that it? You're not screwing Mike by some remote chance, are you?"

Melanie shook herself free of his touch and wiped her eyes with her sleeve.

"My God! No, it's not anybody else—least of all Mike, although it's been pretty heavy with him coming so often. But I already told you how I felt about that. No," she sighed, "there's no one else. I don't have any plans or even any ideas. I'm just unhappy. It's been eating at me for weeks. I realize to you it's very sudden . . ."

"Maybe this only has to do with you, Melanie, not with us. What's wrong between us?"

"I don't know, Ray. I just feel like I'm slowly being suffocated. I don't know if it's because we have a baby, or if this always happens to people who've been married for a while. When we first got together, even though we were so different, we were pretty comfortable together. And it worked—for a long time, really. But now . . . I feel as if I don't even know who you are. I can't even talk to you. All we ever talk about is Mike and his problems. Jesus, don't you remember, everything was going to be an adventure, a great big adventure? That just seems remote as hell now. We're stuck in a rut; we've come to a dead end! I don't want to spend the rest of my life in the fucking Rosaline Apartments, thank you very much. I might not know what I want, but I know I fucking don't want that!" Melanie gripped Ray's forearm pleadingly, and he frowned. Melanie felt his body stiffen at her touch, felt him imperceptibly withdraw.

"We had Lise, Melanie, in case you're forgetting history. That's made a big difference in our lives," he said quietly. Ray got to his feet and, after taking a beer from the refrigerator, stood drinking it, looking back to where she remained on the mattress. Ray seemed far away, unreachable, and Melanie suddenly felt unbearably selfish. He had been in a good mood, and she had ruined it. Now he was miserable, and saying something hadn't solved anything. It had only put distance between them. Bad timing, bad timing, she scolded herself. Yet how could she take back her words?

"I love Lise as much as you do, but I don't want to be only a mother. I want other things, too," she said despondently.

"But you think it's okay to deprive Lise of a father? You don't care about the effect that might have on her psyche?" Ray snorted. "And has anyone ever, ever told you that you couldn't do other things? I've encouraged you right from the beginning. Why can't we be happy together, all three of us? Why not? I don't see that's there's any problem, Melanie."

Melanie rested her tear-stained cheek against her knees. All her arguments suddenly made no sense. Seeing Ray's pain, all she wanted to do was put her arms around him and make it go away.

"How can we forget all this time we've spent together?" Ray asked. "Don't those years and everything we've done mean anything to you? How can you just throw them away like . . . like that?" He snapped his fingers. "Shit! All these months I thought things were returning to normal, that you were getting better, becoming yourself again, that we were enjoying each other again. I know having Mike around has been a strain, but I told you it won't continue forever." Ray's voice sounded petulant, and Melanie winced.

"It felt like that to me, too," she muttered wearily. "I haven't been phony with you. I love you, Ray; I think I love you anyway. This is not about loving or not loving. It's about wanting to live fully. God damn it! Nothing comes out the way you want it to! I'm just not happy with what we're doing with our lives. I'm not happy with my life! We're not going anywhere. I don't know where I want to go, but I know where we are's not it. In a way it's worse than what Mike has with Dee because it's sneaky; it seems okay on the surface. I can't point to anything in particular, but I can't breathe, Ray. I'm dying! I hate this suffocating apartment. I hate not using my brain, not accomplishing anything. Maybe I wasn't doing much when we met, but I thought I had my whole future ahead of me, and I knew I would do something eventually. I'll never recover that person unless I put up a fight. Don't you understand, Ray? Don't these things get to you, too?" Melanie knocked her knees together hard to keep herself from trembling.

"I don't know. Maybe this sudden dissatisfaction is because of my breakdown. I just see things differently. I had a chance to be alone, and I was getting in touch with myself again. It was the same after I came home, but it's difficult to sustain that kind of energy. I feel so pulled apart . . . I can't concentrate. I show Dr. Huston poems, but what's the point? I'm never going to do anything with them. Eventually, my creativity will be swallowed up. I know you'll take this wrong," Melanie sighed, "but sometimes I feel I'm like Helga, sitting day after day at her goddamn kitchen table. She walks around, she laughs, but she's not alive. She's not going anywhere, doing anything. I know you don't think so, but she's depressed as shit, Ray! I'm not strong enough to shut out the distractions, shut out Mike and all this damn dope smoking that poisons the atmosphere and brings me down. Why should I have to escape to the fire escape for a little peace of mind? Fuck it! I know you're going to take this personally."

"I'm not supposed to take this personally? Oh, that's rich, Melanie!" Ray slammed his hand on the windowsill, and she jumped involuntarily. "This *involves* me, us, Lise. Jesus Christ, how am I not supposed to take it personally?" He scowled. "You know, everything you're saying *sounds* good, Melanie, but I'm not sure you're being straight with me. I think the bottom line is that you've fallen out of love with me, and you won't admit it to yourself. The rest is bullshit." Ray walked over and sat on the end of the mattress. "How can I not take this personally, Melanie, when I love you. We've made it this far; can't we try to work things out? Marie and Pete got past their problems, and now they're really happy. You're my straight man, Mel, and I'm yours. We need to keep each other honest, be there through thick and thin. Don't you remember we promised each other that?" Ray put his arms around her and kissed the top of her head. After a few minutes he stood up, looking distracted and upset.

"Melanie, I've got to split for a few hours. I've got to think about all you said. I need to be alone. Will you be okay, hon?"

Melanie nodded. She did not try to stop him. When she heard the apartment door slam, she felt suddenly terrified and dug her fingers in her hair up to the roots. If she left Ray, where would she go? What would she do? How would she take care of Lise? Was she really blowing everything out of proportion? Did she love Ray? Had she ever loved him? When he told her he loved her, the words had left her feeling strangely cold. Melanie forced herself to breathe deeply, to not panic.

When the clock face read eleven-thirty, and Ray had not returned, Melanie undressed and slid beneath the covers, unable to stay awake any longer. In the past after a fight, they had come back together within a few hours. Yet she felt almost relieved that he was not there, although she ran her fingers nervously back and forth along the edge of the mattress. Was this one of those necessary growing pains she had read about somewhere? Things would hurt for a while; she and he would both hurt for a period of time, but then, afterwards, everything would be for the best. Melanie turned over and over, seeking comfort from the sheets. Finally, hugging Ray's pillow to her chest, she fell into a sleep filled with fitful dreams.

She woke a few hours later, and Ray was not beside her. Melanie sat up abruptly; her face and chest dripped with perspiration. Was Ray trying to punish her, make her realize what she would be missing? She got out of bed, shivering now where she had previously felt hot, and went to the bathroom to splash water on her face. Melanie walked to the window and stared out at the darkness. The pane felt cool and moist against her hand. A few lights shone on the avenue, but there was no noise from the street. It had reached that hour, 4 A. M., when even the latest motorist had gone indoors, when not even a cat or dog was out prowling. Where was he? At Mike's? With Mona? Melanie shook her head, realizing she was making herself crazy for nothing. She didn't think he had seen Mona, or any other woman, in a long time, unless she was deluding herself. Had she hurt him too much? Ray had always seemed so strong, able to take anything. He was the one who helped everybody else—her, Marie and Pete, Norm and Kathleen, Helga, Mike; he never broke down. Melanie wished there was someone she could call and then realized, with a sharp sensation of grief, there was nobody. So here she was, alone after all. And how does that make you feel, smartie? she asked herself angrily. You can't even hold on to what you have, let alone seek what you want. Her heart pounded through the thin fabric of her nightgown.

Was it winter beginning that started thoughts like these going? As in the Tom Rush song "Urge for Going," she always felt the urge for change when winter began to close in. Here it was, another November! Shouldn't she wait to decide anything until spring at least? Where could she go anyway? Melanie sat in the rocker, trying to think of a place. She let the quietness of the night soothe her, watched the sky grow lighter and lighter blue. What finally came into her mind was a house she had imagined as a young girl. While waiting to be retrieved from boarding school, she had daydreamed about a house in the country. The more she had dreamed, the more real it had appeared to her. The house was painted green with black shutters, and the top floor had dormer windows above it that came to a point. Melanie had easily imagined bookcases, a piano, and a fireplace within its warmly lit rooms. Set back from the road, the two-story house was surrounded by oaks (she had had a passion for acorns, had used their cups for king's and queen's chalices). The front yard was covered by thick, emerald-colored grass (to match her eyes); an orange-colored tabby was curled up asleep in the sun; a flat, wooden swing hung on thick ropes from an apple tree. Tulips, daffodils, and violets (the only flowers she was familiar with at the time) were planted along the driveway and in flower boxes jutting from the kitchen window. Neighboring houses were close enough to allow for potential friendships but separate enough to feel private and alone. It was a place that trouble could not enter, a comfortable, comforting home. When she had difficulty falling asleep at night, Melanie imagined tucking herself into bed in this house.

Remembering the daydream house for the first time in ten years, Melanie sighed. The house had never materialized. After four years, she had finally been returned to her parents, only to live in a two-bedroom apartment above a delicatessen, a place as different from her fantasy as it was from her grandmother's apartment. Melanie had hated it and left it soon after graduating from high school.

Drowsy, and unable to contemplate her future or Ray any more, she crawled back under the covers. She lay on her back, gazing at the low ceiling. Tomorrow she could think about what to do. After all, it was a serious step, as Ray had said. He had to come back eventually, and then they would talk, come to terms, make decisions. Maybe. Now she would sleep until Lise woke her, hungry and anxious to be fed. Melanie turned toward the coolest part of the bed. Before she knew it, it was morning.

* * * * *

Upon opening her eyes, she saw Ray sitting in the rocker. His face was drawn and tired. Melanie shut her eyes again, as if by doing so she could wish the vision away and replace it with something more pleasant. Moments passed. She finally reopened her eyes, and she and Ray stared at each other in silence. Melanie heard the crib shake, as Lise pulled herself up with the bars. Her sunny face appeared in the entrance way of the cubby; when she saw her mother, Lise made a movement to climb out, but Melanie rose to get her instead. As she lifted Lise from the sheets, and pressed her face against Lise's soft skin, she felt a sudden pang. What on earth was she thinking? How could she upset this little girl's life? Melanie had once felt they were one, but now they were undeniably two. Reversed as the situation was, her new understanding was filled with painful irony.

After Melanie changed her diaper, Lise crawled to where Ray sat and pulled herself immediately up on his knees, tottering a little as she steadied herself. Ray lifted her against him, and hugged her tightly to his chest, burying his face in her hair.

"Well, I'm already late for work, but I guess I better eat something to fortify myself, as Marie would say," he said after a few minutes. Smiling sadly, he traced Lise's features, and looked into her dark eyes, which so mirrored his own.

Melanie felt as if she were having trouble breathing. She came up behind Ray as he poured coffee grounds into the aluminum percolator. Slipping her arms around his waist, she pressed her body close to his.

"I'm sorry, honey," she murmured, touching her lips to his back. "I know all this came as a shock. I guess because things have been building in me for a while, it seemed more obvious to me. Didn't you suspect that I've been unhappy? I told you I hated seeing so much of Mike."

"If there is a more confusing, contradictory person in the universe than you, Melanie, I haven't met him or her yet. Well, yes, I suppose I realized something was wrong." Ray sighed. "I guess this is all a drag to you—me, Lise, the apartment—the whole trip. I know you'd like something better, that your interests are broader than mine. You read more, you're more cultured. I'm not really satisfied either, you know. It's just that after working all day, when I get home at night I just feel like unwinding."

Melanie drew back and addressed not him but the window. The sun lit up the curtains and table, reminding her of that earlier terrifying morning when the setting had appeared overly bright.

"But isn't that the point, Ray? Neither of our lives should be a drag. Remember our early discussions when we were first together? About trying to be our true selves and living in each moment? That's when we said we'd be each other's straight man. I thought you felt as strongly about those beliefs as I did, that it wasn't just some trite hippie philosophy. I want my life, our lives, to be exciting, meaningful. I don't mean I want to join a commune or follow a guru or something—that's probably as much a cop-out as anything, although it might be neat to learn how to meditate or pray or . . . something. I want to be more disciplined, to not just keep drifting from thing to thing, place to place. Set up real roots somewhere, have real jobs, or careers for that matter, take my poetry seriously, and you your music. Really try to make a go of it, you know? And it might be nice someday to have a pretty home with a yard and flowers . . . maybe that doesn't matter, but maybe it does. I don't see how we can ever have those things if we keep doing what we're doing—me sitting home with Lise all day, and you working at a shit job that you hate. I'm not saying I want to be rich; that's not what this is about . . ."

"I'm not sure you know what you want, Melanie. As I see it, you hardly ever appreciate what you have. It's not what you've got, really, but how you see your situation. Oh, bullshit!" he conceded, laughing. "Talk about cheap philosophy!"

"It's true I've never been an especially happy person. I can't expect you or anybody else to give me what I need—hell, I learned that in a big way a few weeks ago at Group—but I *do* want to be fulfilled. Being in the hospital, though, and talking to Dr. H. made me realize that I'm certainly not going to find it here, that I won't ever be happy here. I mean, Christ, your mother died here, Ray. And I'm not ready to die!"

"Maybe you should just stand still and slug it out," Ray said impatiently. "You always think you're going to find meaning by going somewhere else. You told me once that you just knew California was going to be the answer to your dreams, that once you got here, you'd be happy. Well, we both tend to think like that; it's not just you. The grass is always greener, isn't it? My mother died because she drank too much, Mel. She was dying before she even came to live in these apartments." Ray poured coffee into two mugs and handed her one. "You're so restless, Mellie. I wish I *could* make you happy. I wish just being with me could make you happy . . ."

"Why does everyone think happiness is the answer to everything?" Melanie said after taking a sip. "Was Beethoven happy, or Van Gogh, or anybody who ever tried to do anything worthwhile? Were they?

You make it sound so simple, like if I could just be made happy, then I would no longer want anything. Damn it! Besides, I'm not unhappy all the time. I have plenty of good days—days filled with real joy that can come from the simplest pleasures. Nobody ever mentions those times because I have this screwy face that makes people think I'm miserable even when I'm not. I can't help it.

"All right," she said when Ray glanced at her sharply. "Uncle! Yes, I wouldn't mind being happy, at least sometimes. Is that a crime?" She laughed. "But you know none of this discussion means I've changed my mind. I meant the things I said last night," she cautioned.

"Of course," he mocked. "We can't ever change our minds, can we?" He suddenly gripped her tightly, and Melanie felt her nipples stiffen through her thin nightgown. "Maybe your life will always be hard because you want so much. You won't have an easy time." He clutched her harder. "But no matter what happens, I would certainly miss you, babe," he whispered.

Melanie released herself from his hold and shook granola into the two bowls she had taken from the cupboard. Exhausted, they both ate in silence. Pale early-November light came in through the window, lightening the already shiny white Formica table. Melanie stared at the yellow primroses that now rested on the windowsill.

"That little plant was my salvation once," she finally said. "Its flowers were so perky, they brought me hope. Did I ever tell you about that morning?" She swallowed hard, remembering the white walls and narrow bed in her hospital room. "I guess I am meant to have a difficult course. For years I believed I would be alone all my life, that people would cross my path and fleetingly be friends and lovers, but that my destiny involved being by myself." She chewed a mouthful of cereal. "It's been so long since we've talked like this. If only you didn't have to work at AAMCO. I think that's made all the difference. We don't spend our days together like we used to at the beginning, when we were traveling, and when we were going to Lytton. I mean, if the way you spend your days is tedious and unfulfilling, how can it help but affect your spirit? I don't know, Ray. Should we give this another chance? Make an effort to be closer to each other, support each other more?" Even as the words tumbled out, Melanie could not believe what she was saying. Only hours earlier she had felt so definite. Was she simply afraid to be alone?

Ray lifted his eyebrows.

"Boy, you really are contradictory, aren't you? This is screwing with my mind, Melanie."

"I'm sorry, honey. I'm just so fucking confused. Things are clear, then unclear, then clear again. What's always motivated me to move on before is something inside me. I care about you, Ray, you must know that. As much as I know about love—which is turning out to be next to nothing. Maybe I'm too self-centered to love anybody. The people in that group seem to think so. Am I just a selfish bitch? Is that how you see me? But the bottom line is that I don't want to die inside, Ray."

Melanie put her spoon down and leaned back in her chair. The warm, soothing sun on her face and arms made her remember her water dream in the hospital. How wonderfully cleansing it had felt! After checking to see that Lise was still playing contentedly in the living room, Ray poured them each another cup of coffee, saying he was already so late, five minutes more scarcely mattered.

"You know, when it's pleasant like this—when we're talking honestly—my dissatisfaction seems stupid," Melanie said. "But later, the thoughts return, and then they feel important and real again. Do you really love me and want me to stay? Don't you think there might be someone out there more your type who would be able to give you what you need—someone like that woman you told me you and Mike were both crazy about? Wouldn't you be happier with someone like that, someone less moody, more predictable?" Melanie rose from her chair and encircled Ray's body with her arms. She laid her cheek on his spongy curls and rubbed against them. Ray pressed his face against her breasts.

"When you do tender stuff like that, I want to be with you." He smiled. "You can be so sweet when you want, Mellie. Last night, Mike and I hung out at this bar and matched beer for beer, like in the movies when a guy is trying to get over a broken heart. I must be losing my tolerance, because at one point I thought I was going to pass out. He and I both swore to stay away from women because they only wind up bringing you pain. Now Dee's jealous of some woman in their building Mike's been flirting with, and she's terrified she's going to lose him. Well, truthfully, given Mike's track record, that will probably happen." Ray released her and resumed eating.

"You make me happy for the most part, Melanie, but I'm very aware that we're different, that we have different needs. You're a lot more intense than me. Personally, I don't mind watching television. It relaxes me, like having a beer or smoking a joint does, and I don't think that means I'm selling out. But I know you do." He took a sip of coffee. "Maybe you're meant to be with somebody like the kind of men you used to date—you know, somebody more intellectual, more artistic. Mike and

I discussed that among other things. You and I were raised differently. Nobody in my family emphasized reading, no one listened to classical music or visited art museums. I can't spell worth shit." Ray sighed. "I'm not blaming you, but I think our differences separate us, and maybe with me you'll never have the kind of life you really want, just because of who I am and where I come from."

"Oh, Ray, I can't believe you're saying that. Have I ever criticized you for those things? You know I accept you as you are. All I'm saying is that neither of us has to settle for less. By wanting a different life, I'm not sitting in judgment on you or telling you you're inferior to me."

Ray held her carefully at arms length and then covered her hands with his own.

"Melanie, we *are* different. Maybe we should have seen this coming a long time ago. I've never wanted to go to college or cared about getting a degree or any of that other bullshit success stuff. I enjoy reading and learning new things, but I want to do them on my own terms, in my own time frame. I left New York because it was too much of a hassle, and it was ruining my peace of mind. Maybe we just wanted it to work because we're so great in bed together. That's okay; that happens all the time. It's not a question of blame. But I think neither of us ever really knew the other person, and maybe even our dreams are different."

Melanie freed herself from his grip. She could hardly take in the enormity of his words.

"So . . ." she finally said, "if it was up to you, we'd end things, too? That's comforting to know. Thanks for making me privy to the fact I'm not what you want either."

"Jesus, Mel," Ray said in exasperation, "you're the one who wants more! I could go right along like we've been doing. But you're unhappy. Isn't that what you're telling me? You don't like my father, you don't get along with Helga and Mike. Sure, you're comfortable with some of the people I know, like Marie and Pete and Mel, but they're only a small part of my world. I like all those people, each for different reasons. I accept them, even though I may spend varying amounts of time with them at any given moment. They make me feel at home, like I have family.

"Eventually a person has to just settle down, you know? I mean, my dad always told me that it was good to sow your wild oats, but at some point, you had to knuckle down. *His* words," Ray said wryly. "I mean, maybe I'm finally getting a grip on reality, Melanie, owning up to some responsibility."

"Grip on reality," she protested. "I don't want to get a grip on reality! If this is real, forget it. I'd rather live in fantasy land."

"Look, baby, I don't want us to be on welfare the rest of our lives. At least I have more ambition than that. Sure I'd rather be playing music, but I have to drive across the bridge twice a day, sit behind other cars, breathe in fumes. What would happen if I just got out of the car and started walking along the bridge. Men who have a wife and a baby have an obligation. They don't abandon cars on the Bay Bridge because they feel like it, because they say—oh, fuck it, I've had enough of this shit. I quit."

"That would be interesting to watch, wouldn't it?" Melanie chuckled. "Oh, phooey. Maybe I just don't want to grow up, like that jerk in my group said. I know—I'll be one of the Lost Boys. If Mike can pretend he's Peter Pan, why can't I be a Lost Boy? Oh, well, you better get to work. I'm sorry I made you late."

"Don't worry about it," Ray said. "I don't think they'll fire me yet. They're short-handed right now." He bent over and kissed her on the mouth before rushing into the living room to slip into his mechanic's uniform. Lise, who had been tugging on two snap beads, trying to pull them apart and finally settling on chewing on them instead, pulled up on his calf as he tied his shoes.

"How are *you*, little darling?" he grinned. He picked her up and gave her a resounding kiss. "I forgot. Mike's coming by tonight—to play peacemaker, I think. An unlikely role, huh?" Ray gave her a devilish look.

"Just what we needed to round off this day and night. I'm sure he'll be very successful; his own record is so sterling."

"Look, no matter how this turns out, I love you," Ray said. "I not about to reject you, whatever happens." He tugged her body toward his, and as their lips met, she felt his warm tongue inside her mouth, aggressive and firm. When he pulled away, her legs were trembling.

"Damn you," Melanie whispered, "damn you, damn you, damn you!"

 *Six*

*A*fter Ray left, Melanie paced around the apartment. She stared at the dull green couch, now ripped in places, at their makeshift bed on the floor. Lise was crawling between piles of clothes and books that lay scattered about the room. This was not a place to live, not a way to live, she told herself. To survive, she had to get away; it was stronger than she was. Even when she kept things relatively clean, she did not possess the power to transform it.

"Come on, Lise. Wanna go bye-bye? Bye-bye like Daddy just did?" Melanie asked, sitting on the floor next to her.

She still felt the pressure of Ray's mouth on her own, from another kiss he had snatched before rushing out the door. Watching him from the window as he ran down the walkway toward their car, though, her stomach had turned over. She had felt the same repulsion she had felt when they first met, the intuitive sense that Ray was someone alien to her interests. Why hadn't she trusted her original instincts? But were they right? It was inexplicable—this continuous flip-flop of her emotions, her thoughts. His persistence had brought them together. She didn't want what she had and wanted what seemed impossible to have. What a dilemma! She longed for someone else's life, such as Lynn's, and desired Mel, or another equally unattainable man, such as Mark.

Melanie realized that if the situation only involved Ray and her, she would probably take any available job and leave. Lytton had taught her secretarial skills, and she could always be a theater cashier again as she was in Manhattan, although she hoped her future would include something more interesting and challenging, something more to her liking. After spending three years with Ray, didn't she love him? After all they had been through together? What the hell was love anyway? Melanie thought she had experienced it so often—crushes on boys in school, men she had dated and gone to bed with for months at a time. She remembered how strong her feelings had seemed for Mel. Strong, radiant, transforming. What an amorphous thing, love. Was she incapable of loving anybody in the most genuine, lasting sense? *Was* she meant to be alone?

Slowly, Melanie pushed the stroller up the block—that once fearful block, which now appeared so normal. Children's artwork was pasted on most of the windows; nearly every entranceway sported a wind chime. Some of them were metal, some wooden, but one made of glass produced a completely different sound from the others, akin to the chirping of birds. Melanie was amazed it didn't shatter when the wind blew against it, it seemed so fragile. She reached the co-op and pushed open the door. She took out her grocery list, trying to forget momentarily her concern about how Ray and her breakup would affect Lise.

Tomorrow her first class began, and tonight their "savior" was stopping by to "patch things up." Melanie knew she had to hurry or she would have no time to rest beforehand. How silly, she thought, to have to worry about getting enough sleep. Considerations like those had never been part of her life; now she felt controlled by schedules. She parceled out her energy in small doses, careful not to let herself become fatigued. What kind of person was she turning into? Melanie moved quickly up and down the aisles, buying only what she absolutely needed and could manage to fit into the netted bag hooked onto the back of the stroller. Lise seemed absorbed by her surroundings, and Melanie felt with a pang that as far as children went, she was extraordinarily lucky. Perhaps she could take care of Lise all by herself if Ray helped every once in a while. She wished she could ask Marie's advice.

Marie was helpful during crises—she had certainly proven that—but Melanie was ashamed to burden her again. Besides, she sighed to herself, the four of them saw less and less of each other. It was partly the distance, which in the past had never been a problem, as needing rest had never been; but the real reason was that Ray seemed to loosen up more with his Richmond friends. Everything happened so gradually, Melanie thought. First the pregnancies, then the babies, then Ray's job, then her breakdown. Each change had eroded their original companionable joy.

Although she and Eulalie had never become close friends, had never confided in each other or supported each other as much as she and Deena had, Melanie had felt comforted by her presence. At Eulalie's release, Melanie had hugged her sadly goodbye. However, only a few weeks earlier, she had noticed Eulalie out of the corner of her eye crossing Shattuck Avenue when she was leaving a session with Dr. Huston. Excited, Melanie had run to say hello but stopped as she realized Eulalie was having an argument with someone else on the street. This loud woman, with her face scrunched up in fury, was so different from the Eulalie Melanie remembered that she had remained at a distance. When

Eulalie finally walked away, shaking a cane at the other party, Melanie felt unbelievably depressed. Had the shock treatments completely transformed her? Was it necessary to become this angry, bitter-looking old woman to end a cycle of depression? For Eulalie had appeared older and harder to her—like an entirely different individual. Was that what it took to get well?

Her last contact with Deena had been disappointing also. During their phone conversation, there were weighty silences, which Melanie had tried desperately to fill. Deena had sounded agitated and tense living at her aunt's house; the new situation seemed to be working less well for her even than previous ones. But although Melanie had felt sad hearing about Deena's problems, she had felt disconnected because of the months with little contact. They had said goodbye, promising to keep in touch, but neither had done so. Melanie wondered if she would ever have a close female friend again. If she and Ray broke up, she would not only be leaving a marriage; she would also be friendless.

After she put the groceries away and changed Lise, Melanie poured herself a soda and fell back with relief in the rocker. She wondered if Ray would think she was crazy if that night she told him she wanted to leave again. Did she want to leave? Part of her wanted to stay put forever. Melanie closed her eyes wearily as she rocked slowly back and forth, dimly aware of Lise moving around on the floor. She opened them to see if there was anything Lise could hurt herself with, moved her Pepsi can out of reach. Absently, she remembered that the writing class began at seven o'clock the following evening and that the instructor had told her to bring along something she had written, other than poetry. If she put her mind to it, Melanie thought, she might be able to pull together a character sketch, depending on how late Mike stayed. She drifted into sleep thinking about Mike, about his muscular frame, his dark eyes and hair. She wondered idly what it would be like to be single again, to touch another man, have another man hold her, make love to her, come inside her.

* * * * *

Ten o'clock rolled around with no Mike. She and Ray had finished dinner, and they had laid Lise down in her crib. Melanie sat on the mattress, concentrating sleepily on a description of an elderly man she had seen at the playground. Ray stood staring out the window anxiously.

"I don't understand what's happened to him," Ray said, turning back to look at her. "He said he'd be here by at least eight."

Melanie yawned. "Something probably came up with Dee. I think I'm gonna turn in soon, Ray." She set down the pages she had been working on and rubbed her eyes. "I'm scared about tomorrow. Part of me doesn't even want to go, Ray. I've written five pages, but they sound pretty bad. Do you think the teacher will only want stuff that is already finished?"

"I'm sure anything you do will be fine, Mellie. It's your first class. I'm sure he'll be understanding. I like your writing, don't I?" Ray left the window to get a can of Coors from the refrigerator. "Want one?"

"I'll split one with you. You know what I realized today, Ray? I have no real girlfriends anymore. I've always had at least one close friend, sometimes more than one. Now I have none. There's just you and me, and the people we see together, but that's not the same as personal friends—friends I can talk to and do things with. And I don't even know how to meet someone here either. That's pretty depressing." Melanie took the glass of beer Ray handed her and raised it to her lips. "Mike probably had to do something. I don't know, maybe he decided he couldn't play the great guru after all. I mean, do you seriously think Mike has the answer to our problems, Ray? He'd probably be secretly glad if we split up. Actually, I think it's a relief that he didn't come. Isn't this between us, after all?"

"You don't understand, hon. Mike would have called if he couldn't make it. I tried his number a while ago, but the phone's been disconnected. So, if he were on his way, he would be here by now. I don't know, maybe women think differently than men about these things, but a promise is a promise to a guy."

"Oh, of course women don't know anything about keeping promises! Jesus, Ray! Mike's never struck me as the soul of dependability." Melanie reached for *The Razor's Edge,* which lay next to the writing tablet she had put down. She turned to where her bookmark was. "God, am I glad to finally be able to read again. It was awful in the hospital, not being able to concentrate on anything." She looked back at Ray, who was drumming impatiently on the windowsill. "Listen, sweetie, if Mike's not here soon, I, for one, am going to royally crash."

"I hope he's all right," he said.

"Isn't Mike a little beyond being all right?"

"God damn it, Mel, why don't you shut the fuck up! Why are you being so damned sarcastic and bitchy?" Ray slammed down the can he was holding, and it spun off the sill. Beer spurted onto the floor. "Shit! For being such a supposedly fucking sensitive person, you're as callous as shoe leather. Are you the only one around here who's allowed to have feelings?"

"Touché," Melanie muttered. "I guess I am being a bitch—a bitchy little bitch! Then it's just as well I'm getting out of your life. You'll be a lot happier."

"Oh, brother! Why not just own up to being bitchy and be done with it? Here I am, concerned about my buddy, and all you can do is sit there and snipe. What are you? A fucking princess?"

"I'm not exactly thrilled about Mike thinking he can come along and 'fix' our relationship, if you want to know the truth. And I've never made a secret of how I feel about him."

"You certainly haven't," Ray snorted.

"Why *should* I pretend to like somebody I don't? Do you want me to also be a phony?"

"This has nothing whatsoever to do with being phony or not being phony, although there is such a thing as tact, I believe. You think you're allowed to be honest, Mel, but no one else can be. I tell you what you said was uncalled-for, and you continue like you haven't even heard me. In fact, you become even more sarcastic, as if I've injured *you* in some way. Oh, fuck it, what's the use! You are a baby like the guy in your group said. You don't want to grow up and take responsibility for what you do or say. Grown-ups care about people, care about their friends, their children, their *marriages*, for Christ's sake!"

"Oh, now we're getting down to it. This isn't even about Mike. It's about you and me, and the fact that I want to leave, isn't it?" Melanie picked up her glass and drank the rest of its contents rapidly. Jumping up from the mattress, she went to the refrigerator. She opened another can of beer and poured half of it into her glass. Her hands trembled, as she returned the can to the shelf.

Ray glowered at her. "Well, you can reduce it to that if you want to; you're so good at thinking in black and white terms. People are 'good,' like you, or 'bad' with a capital B, like Mike or Kathleen—or whoever else you choose not to take a fancy to, Miss Priss! Jesus, Melanie, you can be the sweetest woman in the whole world and then turn around and be such a snit, I can't stand being around you! Who needs that shit? My life would certainly be a helluva lot more peaceful without you."

"Right . . . we all love Mellie when she's happy and good, but we completely reject her when she's *bad*—when she says what she feels, or is in a bad mood, or . . . Oh, fuck you, fuck me, fuck Mike, fuck everybody! I was having a peaceful evening before we started talking about all this, let me tell you. I hope Mike never comes. All he does is interfere in our goddamned lives!"

Melanie picked up her book and threw it across the room. She grabbed her hair in both hands and tugged so furiously it made her wince.

"Great, here we go, a tantrum to beat all tantrums! Somebody doesn't agree with us, so we throw a fit. Well, I may love you, Melanie, *unconditionally,* or not, but I'm not going to put up with this shit—not tonight anyway. You're gonna have to have this little party all by yourself."

Melanie leaped from the bed and walked to the collage she had made during her hospital stay. It lay propped against the wall on top of their dresser and was coated with a thin film of dust. Picking it up, she looked at it with disgust and then began to tear it apart, sobbing as she ripped off picture by picture.

"Who am I kidding about making a different life? I'm not a poet, I'm not creative, I'm nothing. I'm a big fucking zero, a goddamn zero! Thinking I had the potential to actually make something! Thinking even now that I can do something meaningful." Melanie turned toward the bed, as if ready to next take the description she had been working on and rip it up, too. Instead, she focused on the collage, yanking at it with all her strength. The cardboard sailed out of her hands, and she collapsed onto the dresser. "You're right, Ray. I am a bitch. I can't do anything right. I'm a crappy wife, mother . . . I'll never make it, never be good at anything. I can't even be a friend when someone needs me to be. Christ, Christ, Christ," she whimpered, clawing at the wood. As her anger dissipated, Melanie felt wave after wave of intense shame. The sensations bent her in half; she felt as if she were being repeatedly punched in the stomach.

Coming up behind her, Ray touched her tentatively, as if fearful she might attack him, as she had other times when she had felt too ashamed to receive his comfort. Now she fell limply into his arms, and he led her to the bed. He laid her down and then searched for a box of Kleenex.

"Shush, Mellie, don't get hysterical. We don't have to see Mike. You're right; he can't fix anything. Even if he does come, I'll send him home. There, there, baby girl."

Between gulps for air, Melanie spluttered, her mouth trembling uncontrollably.

"Oh, Ray, I'm sorry. I'm so sorry. I know I'm awful. Please, please, I didn't intend to be mean. I didn't mean what I said, honestly! It just came out." Ray rocked and rocked her in his arms. She felt weak, spent. Her words felt as if they were being squeezed out of her.

"Poor baby girl. There, there. Wipe your eyes," Ray murmured. "Don't cry. It's okay, I'm here with you. I won't leave you."

"Oh God, I'm such a baby, how can you possibly lo-lo-lo-ve m-m-me?" she stammered. Ray stopped her words with a kiss, and then they were kissing frantically, rolling and tumbling together on the mattress. Between kisses, Melanie muttered, "God, I'm such a mess. You should leave *me*." Scowling at her, Ray covered her mouth with his hand. He traced the lines of her tears, wiping them carefully away with his fingers. "You must love me if you put up with craziness like this," she whispered.

"You're just insecure, Mellie. You'll grow out of it. You could never trust anyone before. Now close your eyes and go to sleep, and everything will appear different in the morning."

"You won't go anywhere?" Melanie pleaded, clinging to his arm. "Even after everything I said?"

"I'm going to lie right beside you until you're fast asleep. I won't even answer the door." Ray smoothed her hair, which lay in snarls around her face. He held her close against his own warm body, and gradually, as drowsiness sifted through her, Melanie cuddled even closer, tucking her arm around his waist. "I love you, sweetie," she murmured. You're so good to me. You're so good . . ."

* * * * *

The next morning when she woke, Ray had already left. Sleepily, Melanie smoothed her arm over his pillow, ran her fingers along the creases his head had made during the night. However, as consciousness returned, her thoughts grew sober, and by the time Lise woke, palpitations were running through her body. She was glad she was seeing Dr. Huston the day after her first class. There was no one else she could talk to so freely, although soon their sessions would be over. Three months. Only three months longer, now when everything was beginning to change. She was still on medication and carried the pills wherever she went. Usually, knowing they were there in her purse was enough; many days she did not feel a need to take them. Sometimes, like Alice biting off pieces of the mushroom, Melanie nibbled at a corner of a ten milligram Valium when she felt anxious. Today, she felt the need for a whole pill.

How could she bear another such evening? It was time to grow up already! Although this outburst had been shorter in length than others, and she had snapped out of it more quickly, she knew it was cruel to subject Ray to such moods, especially since he was so unbelievably patient. If she were alone, no one would need to comfort her in that manner. Despite all her conversations with Dr. Huston about change—and they spoke of it continuously—Melanie did not know if, at bottom, she could act differently. The word change hung tantalizingly between them, like a precipice just out of reach; it had taken on its own shimmering existence. Yes, she would just have to leave; she would take Lise and try to make it on her own. Other women did it; Bea was raising three children by herself. Perhaps such a move would make her finally grow up. She would be the best mother she knew how, even if she would never be as perfect as she wanted to be. Knowing perfection was always out of reach made her want to take a knife to herself at times—to end the unbearable conflict of being flawed, end the reality of never being able to do anything as well as she desired.

With these thoughts rushing through her mind, Melanie did the necessary chores of the day, thinking with trepidation of the night to come. What if the professor said everything she had written was worthless; what if he told her she would never be a writer? Then what would be the point of anything? She would have to settle for the mundanity of an ordinary existence. But did the instructor's opinion matter? What about her own belief in herself? What about her past successes?

Melanie reread the five pages she had written. True, the writing was rough—it was definitely a first draft—but it did not seem *completely terrible*, and after all, she had never written prose before. She had used as much detail as possible and felt she had drawn a pretty clear picture of the man. After she slipped the pages into the spiral writing tablet she had bought for note-taking and cleaned out her purse so it would not appear she was as sloppy as she was, she threw in three pens and one pencil, in case she ran out of ink. The process reminded her of getting ready for school each September. Perhaps she was ready to turn over a new leaf, start with a clean slate—perform all the clichés she could think of, which she had tried carefully to avoid using in her description.

Ray had still not heard from Mike. Melanie prayed fervently that, today of all days, Mike would not show up, would not be there to make her further doubt her ability and drain away her remaining energy. For dinner, she prepared Shake 'n Bake chicken, coating each piece vigorously in a brown paper bag before arranging it in the pan. She sliced carrots and cooked them in butter and brown sugar, recalling a recipe Mel's wife, Joan, had taught her during their brief acquaintance. She wanted to make a special dinner for Ray to repay his kindness, because, although he would have dismissed the idea, she saw his behavior as charitable. Melanie knew from experience he would be as helpful to an animal caught in a trap.

Seven

*L*ater that evening, when Melanie left the Berkeley campus, her mind overflowed with ideas. On the bus ride home, she tried to tie together the myriad strands of what she had absorbed during the three-hour period into a more concrete understanding. The class had been combative in nature, with frequent interruptions and insistent statements, but the intensity had left Melanie feeling charged. Her mind felt clear, electrified in a way it hadn't been since high school.

However, when she thought about sharing the evening's experience with Ray, she realized that although he would appear interested, it would never excite him in the same manner. Perhaps it was true, as he had said that morning: they were seeking different things in life. Maybe it was inevitable that their ways would eventually diverge. So why had they gotten together in the first place? Melanie didn't think everything could be reduced to sex, although it was a powerful element of their relationship. She had never wanted to marry any of the other men she had dated. Yet this night, her mind felt used in a way it was seldom used when with Ray. Melanie sighed as she stared at the dark window pane. Why was knowledge so often painful? Couldn't one grow up naturally without it? Animals came to maturity naturally, didn't they? Then why couldn't she? She was an animal, after all.

Yet while thinking this, Melanie remembered a show she had seen about two cheetah cubs. At a certain point in their development, their mother had left them, abruptly, one day on the plains, where she had been training them to catch prey. The entire day the cubs stood on a rock overlooking the territory, making whimpering sounds. Then slowly, as night fell, they seemed to understand that their mother would not be returning for them, and they resigned themselves to their fate. The cubs searched for a sleeping place, and from that day forth they went on together, motherless. When, accidentally, they met their mother again, some time later, she was with a new family of cubs. Neither she nor they greeted each other. Melanie had been haunted by the cubs' crying; she had wanted to comfort them in their loss. Ray had also seen the episode, but although he had appreciated it, she knew he had not felt the cubs' situation as intensely as she had. He had not been bothered for weeks afterwards. Was it essential to her for someone to feel things as strongly as she did? Could she only love someone who could relate to her on these deepest levels?

Melanie wanted the bus ride to continue forever, wanted to simply drive off into the night to some aimless destination and never go home again, treasuring within her the excitement the class had brought her. But she was also anxious to return to Ray, grateful she *had* someone to return to who could and would listen.

The professor's face flashed before her. How impatient he seemed, how harsh and uncompromising, how demanding he was of the students, how seemingly impossible to please! The other students' work had sounded polished; they were so much farther along than she. He had read two short stories aloud before reading Melanie's description.

"Unfinished?" he had said so loudly that she had jumped. "Well, are you planning to finish it whether we like it or not?" Terrified, Melanie had nodded she would. The woman next to her had smiled sympathetically. Because she was older than Melanie, probably in her thirties, Melanie had felt a bit reassured. But the man's anger had astounded her. What was he angry about? Why was he taking it out on the class? However, when he read her piece, stopping now and again in disgust to point out a grammatical error, he lent importance to her words. The class, too, had responded positively, had treated her piece as if it was legitimate. She had caught something—it wasn't clear what yet, but something. She belonged in that classroom, she realized, even though, without further comment, the professor had swept the pages off his desk in dismissal.

Melanie rose, anxious to be near the front as the bus neared her stop. She reached for the buzzer seconds before she needed to. Saying goodnight to the driver, she clutched her notebook and purse close to her chest with one hand, while with the other she held onto the bar and stepped out into the night.

The apartment was dark. Melanie set her purse down on the dresser and took off her coat. She knew it was silly to feel disappointed that Ray wasn't there on this, her first night trying something new, but she was anyway. She realized he had probably been lonely and had gone to visit someone. Because he had Lise, Melanie reasoned he had gone to Norm and Kathleen's. They were always begging him to bring her by.

Melanie knew Ray preferred to visit his father without her. When they went together, she usually said very little and, hunched over in one of their hardbacked kitchen chairs, looked obviously anxious to leave. When they left, usually after a few hours, Melanie always felt ashamed because she realized Ray wanted to stay longer. However, she seemed incapable of changing her behavior to make the visit go more smoothly. If Ray was there now, it was just as well. Or perhaps he had finally gotten in touch with Mike.

She went to the kitchen and poured herself a glass of lemonade. The cold liquid tasted refreshing after being in the stuffy classroom. It seemed a long time previously that she had felt nauseated by taking a sip of orange juice; those events seemed far in the past, as if they had happened to a different person. Melanie walked into the living room. She kicked off her shoes and, after stretching out on the mattress, closed her eyes, trying to recapture the bubble of excitement she had felt on the bus, the bubble she had tried to retain so Ray could experience some of the pleasure she had received. The darkness in the room was particularly strong, contrasted with the harsh fluorescent lighting of the classroom. Melanie propped her five pages against her knees. Between sips of lemonade, she studied each paragraph and read again the comments she had jotted in the margins. Her words seemed to shrink as she reread them; the longer she read, the more disgust she felt. How clumsily she had expressed that, she thought, although perhaps this phrase wasn't too bad. How did she know? Well, it was what she had observed. It was accurate. But she had barely scratched the surface. Did she have the courage to go from there? Did she want to? Was that what the professor had meant by asking her if she would finish the story, whether they liked it or not? Was that what it meant to be a true writer? To keep writing even if no one likes what you do?

Melanie shivered. Despondently, she tucked the pages back into her notebook. She had enjoyed the class so much, so why did she feel so deflated now? Leaning back against the wall, she lit a cigarette and stared out into the room, listening to the faint ticking of the Baby Ben. Melanie suddenly felt terribly tired, as if she had been walking for blocks. She went to the record player and flipped through the albums, finally selecting *All Things Must Pass* by George Harrison, which they had recently bought. When the music began, she lit another cigarette and settled herself in the rocker. Cool, moist air whistled through a crack at the top of the window, so she retrieved the afghan from the bed and wrapped herself in it.

She half-listened to the easy, slow lyrics, closed her eyes, opening them only to take a drag. Finally, the song came on that she was waiting for, the tune that had leapt out at her when first hearing the album: "All Things Must Pass." Melanie felt the words were significant, that they spoke specifically, directly to her, and she sang along fervently, her being filled with a yearning for resolution, for change, as on that morning now so distant when Rodrigo's guitar concerto had filled her with such hope. When the song ended, she sat thinking: All right, Melanie, this is what it would be like to be by yourself again. You would sit listening to music with no one else in the room. There would be simply music, and then later—silence, darkness. There would be no one to spill the fullness to, no one next to you in bed. It would always feel cold on the other side of the mattress where, yes, you could spread out if you wanted to—but into empty space. Is that what you want, Melanie? Must you be alone to be true to yourself?

Frightened, Melanie strained to see any sign of Ray coming up the walk. She was certain Lise was overtired or asleep somewhere, in some uncomfortable smoke-filled surroundings, under harsh lighting. Maybe they had been in an accident. The pathway beneath the arch was deserted. Everything looked unnaturally still, and she remembered how often she had looked out the window onto this same nighttime scene, in so many different states of mind. Yes, perhaps it was time. It would be lonely, yes, it would be lonely, but it was time, and the loneliness, the moment, this moment, as every other moment, would pass. The song assured her that it would, that she would be all right in the end. She wrapped the afghan around her even more tightly to stop her body from shivering.

As Melanie listened over and over to the album, the sky gradually lightened. At first it was dark blue, then a lighter blue, then rose, then pink. Finally, it turned to the clear white light of morning.

Although raised in New York City, Betty Bernard has lived in the Bay Area at various times of her life. In addition to writing poetry and fiction, she edits educational journals and lives in Silver Spring, MD. Ms. Bernard has three children and a cat named Serge and is working on a second novel about marital cycles.